MW00529678

Forsaking All Others

G. E. Hamlin

Trilogy Christian Publishers
TUSTIN, CA

Trilogy Christian Publishers
A Wholly Owned Subsidiary of Trinity Broadcasting Network
2442 Michelle Drive
Tustin, CA 92780

Manufactured in the United States of America

10 9 8 7 6 5 4 3 2 1

Library of Congress Cataloging-in-Publication Data is available.

ISBN: 978-1-63769-604-0

E-ISBN: 978-1-63769-605-7

This book is dedicated to James and Angel Pennyman.
My life is richer for knowing them.

"Pain removes the veil; it plants the flag of truth within the fortress of a rebel soul."

—C. S. Lewis.

Acknowledgement

First and foremost, thank you, Jesus, for helping me every day and in every way.

On August 17, 2021, my treasured husband, Edward H. Hamlin III, went home to be with his Lord and Savior. I often said to my husband,"I'll love you forever" and he knew I meant it, which is deeply comforting. As a footnote, my husband chose the cover for this novel; he said the colors reminded him of God's refining fire—apropos given the storyline.

I owe a debt of gratitude to our family for their love, support, and encouragement. And to our grandchildren, I say, God has a plan for your life, and when you come into agreement with His plan, the journey becomes joy-filled as you grow in intimacy with your Heavenly Father.

Thank you to my critique partners, Sarah Hamaker, Ruth Reid, and my writing mentor, Gail Sattler.

And for my mother, Billie Jean Johnson, I miss her so.

Chapter One

The computer screen cast the only light in the small home office. A glance at the time revealed midnight had come and gone. Cody James should've called it a night after the eleven o'clock news ended, but once again, he wrestled with temptation in front of his laptop.

"Lord, show me how to give this up once and for all." If only he'd had the guts to share the secret with Kate before their wedding, she might've helped him overcome the addiction that snaked back to his teen years. Too bad time travel was only in the movies. Given the chance, he would've traveled back to himself at age thirteen when he discovered his father's dirty little secret hidden in a rusted toolbox in the family garage.

Cody would have warmed himself not to open the box and not to lift out the glossy magazines. He'd never confided to his father about stumbling upon the private collection of girly photographs—after all, didn't every teenage boy deal with their raging hormones in the same way—in secret?

Amidst the shadowy office, the devotional read earlier lay open and captured his attention. He picked it up, squinting to reread the quote—"Pain," he said barely above a whisper, "removes the veil; it plants the flag of truth within the fortress of a rebel soul."

C. S. Lewis's words spoke to him. Still, he resisted the idea of telling Kate his secret after all these years. "There's got to be another way, Lord. I can't tell her the truth. I'm too ashamed."

He rolled his chair back from the desk, thankful he hadn't succumbed to the lures on the internet so far. "Lord, I'll abstain. This time will be different." With a renewed pledge to God, he closed the browser on his laptop in a few keystrokes, wiped the cache clean, and then deleted the history. He sealed his prayer with a commitment not to visit any site online; he wouldn't ask God to bless, or maybe it was a pep talk.

Leaned back in the office chair, he clasped the back of his neck with both hands and gently kneaded the taut muscles, then rolled his head from side to side. The action helped to release some of the tension in his body—a tension that ached for a release, but he'd take a cold shower over logging back onto the computer.

"Go to bed," he said under his breath. Cody scrubbed one of his hands over his eyes. Being sleep-deprived wasn't a good way to start the workweek.

Thirsty, he lumbered into the kitchen and grabbed a quart of orange juice from the fridge. He held the carton to his forehead for a few seconds before pouring a glass. Leaned back against the countertop, he reviewed the evening's choices and how a lot of things should have been done differently. After he'd finished beating himself up, he tipped the glass to his lips and took a long drink. A software package that blocked computer-porn sites could be helpful. He had read about one yesterday and tried to recall if he'd saved the link. As he rubbed his chin in thought, the bristles on his face reminded him of the need to order razors. "I'll Google filters tomorrow," he mumbled before downing the remaining juice then heading to the master bedroom.

Kate looked so peaceful sleeping he determined to make every effort not to wake her. He brushed his teeth at the bathroom vanity—adjacent to the master bedroom, without turning on any lights, and then eased into bed beside her. Nestled against Kate's warm body, the lingering tension melted, and he gently nuzzled her neck, but his focus ricocheted from her back to the provocative images on the website. This time his body betrayed him with a twinge of excitement.

"Stop it," he said louder than intended into the suffocating stillness.

Kate mumbled in her sleep but didn't wake. Cody scooted closer to focus on her instead of the photographs zinging through his mind. Squeezing his eyes shut, he conjured a memory of Kate on their wedding day—her blonde hair in soft ringlets and her green eyes dancing with the hope of their future together. Then her expression morphed into one of disgust and betrayal as it would when she unearthed more than a decade of virtual infidelity.

Cody rolled onto his back and pressed the heels of his hands against his eyes. Even the possibility of Kate discovering the truth about his secret life prompted a familiar tightening in his chest. He took a guarded deep breath and exhaled slowly.

This will pass.

It always had.

The first time he'd experienced the crushing tension in his chest, he thought heart attack. Although in good physical shape for thirty-nine, heart attacks struck people younger and in even better shape than himself. A flashback of wires running from his body to a beeping monitor with Kate seated beside him in an ER exam room last year sent Cody's pulse racing. Although Hoag hospital had one of the best cardiology centers in Southern California, at this moment, that fact did little to calm his mounting anxiety over a possible misdiagnosis and an untreated heart issue.

He sat up on the edge of the bed. Thankfully, Kate didn't wake. He took a focused breath. Counted to ten, then exhaled slowly. He repeated the relaxation technique. No improvement. His thoughts raced back to the hospital visit.

The emergency room physician and a cardiologist, both of whom assured Cody after they'd run a battery of tests, the tightness was stress-induced. Yet, each time the pressure gripped him subsequently, he could not help but think—heart attack. Kate had accompanied him to his general practitioner's office a few days after the ER visit. His own physician concurred with the emergency room doctors' findings, which Kate reminded him of whenever he became stressed. Part of Cody wished she were awake to speak words of reassurance right now.

His gaze flitted to the clock on the nightstand—almost 1:00 a.m. The alarm would go off at six. He took another focused breath. Counted to ten, then exhaled slowly, and then another breath slightly deeper, which came easier. After repeating the technique several times, he scooted back into bed and gently tugged the covers over his shoulders. He closed his eyes while continuing to concentrate on inhaling and exhaling. Yesterday's conversation with Kate came to mind, and the concentration was broken. There had been no justification for hiding out in the home office all evening, but once again, hindsight came too late, and he was paying the price.

Kate's question replayed in his mind. He could've responded a dozen different ways to her query, but no, he made light of whether she looked fat in a new dress worn for church. The playful pat to her backside and the comment "there was more of her to love" caused the color to drain from her face. Granted, she had laughed off the remark and the gesture, but the wounded look in her eyes remained with him throughout the day. He had tried to backpedal his comment, but that seemed to make things worse, so he'd followed her lead and avoided the topic by hiding out.

Cody's cell phone vibrated on the nightstand. He snatched the buzzing device, glad for a distraction, even if it came in the form of his younger brother, Blake, the only person who would call at this hour.

After verifying it was indeed Blake, Cody answered the call. "What now?" He reeled in his annoyance and lowered his voice in hopes of not disturbing Kate. "If you're in jail—"

"Sheesh. I'm not in jail. Gimme some credit, bro. I'm stuck on the Hollywood freeway. I've got a flat. Yeah, again, but this time I've got a spare."

"So why are you calling me?" Cody kept his voice to a whisper. "Do you even know what time it is?" Kate's warm touch on his bicep startled him. "Hold on." He turned to his wife, "Sorry. I didn't mean to wake you."

"What's going on?" She leaned against him.

"Blake's stranded. He's got a flat tire, again." Cody couldn't make out her expression, but he envisioned concern. Kate attributed Blake's irresponsibility to his youth—twenty-four—and his troubled relationship with God. She viewed Blake as a prodigal whom she could simply love back into the fold. What she failed to see was Blake wanted to pursue what he thought made him happy. Since his choices didn't align with the Bible, he'd thrown in the spiritual towel and blamed God for making it too hard to be a Christian.

"You're going to help him, right?" The subtle encouragement in her question prodded him to accept the inevitability of rescuing Blake. She might as well have handed him the keys to his Jeep as she kissed him goodbye on the cheek.

"Yeah, I'm going to go." Cody tossed back the bedding. He stood beside the nightstand and fumbled in the dark to unplug his phone from the charger. He should have added Blake to their AAA policy after the second time his brother was stranded. As Blake's employer, the annual fee would've been easy to recoup as a payroll deduction.

"Let me guess why you're stuck," Cody huffed. "You have a spare, but your jack is missing?"

"Ladies and gentlemen, we have a winner!" Blake chuckled. "Give the man a stuffed animal from the top row. Actually, it's not missing. I used it a couple of days ago to fix my front brakes. I forgot to put it back."

Cody tensed. For Kate's sake, he fought the urge to ask what was so funny about being held accountable in the moment. Then the verse about removing the plank from your own eye before removing the speck in your brother's pricked his spirit, and the urge to correct Blake vanished. "Where are you? I mean specifically."

"Thanks. I owe you one." This time Blake's attempt to laugh it off came out sounding more like a grunt than a chuckle. "I owe you about a thousand and one, but who's counting?"

"Will you knock off the...." Cody sucked in a deep breath but let it out slowly. In many ways, Blake was like dad—selfish and masking it with corny humor. "What exit are you near? I can only hope you were headed home, so you're southbound, right?"

Kate tapped the touch lamp on her nightstand then scooted out of bed. Dressed in her old University of California Irvine T-shirt that fit snug and pajama shorts, she shooed at Cody, suggesting he stop staring at her. Kate's weight gain had nothing to do with their lackluster love life, but no matter how many times he told her he liked the way she looked—she'd cringe, cover her body, and push him away. Truth be told, the true obstacle was one he couldn't bring himself to broach no matter how many times God convicted him.

Kate walked around to his side of the bed. The oversized terry bathrobe she'd slipped on concealed not only her sleepwear but all traces of her figure. "I'll make you a cup of coffee," she said while twisting her hair into a topknot.

"Thank you."

"No problem." Kate shuffled barefoot down the tiled hallway.

Cody recalled a Saturday afternoon a few years back they had spent home alone. She'd lounged around all day in a silky pajama set he'd purchased as a gift for her. A smile spread into his cheeks but vanished when an image of another blonde in a provocative photograph hijacked the memory.

"Did you hear me?" Blake grumbled.

"Sorry, what was that?"

"I'm close to Silver Lake Boulevard just past Vermont. Are you leaving now?"

"I'll be out the door in ten. It should take me forty minutes." Cody headed to the walk-in closet shared with Kate. "And for the record, I still expect you to be in the pawnshop by eight. In case you hadn't realized, today's Monday."

"Yeah, I know. I'm stranded, not stupid." Blake hung up.

While he picked out his clothes, the aroma of dark roast coffee drifted down the hallway. It would've been just as easy for him to pop a K-cup into the machine and save Kate getting out of bed, but then again, maybe that was her way to show she'd forgiven him for his insensitive comment yesterday. He hoped so.

As he pulled on a pair of jeans, Cody stared at the cockeyed hangers on Kate's side of the closet. Instead of adjusting the jumbled clothes, he retrieved a black T-shirt from one of the built-in shelves then neatly arranged the stack again. On his way out of the closet, he snatched a pair of hiking boots and socks from the armoire. Contemplating what, if anything, to say to Kate about yesterday's blunder, he sat on the chaise lounge near the window to put on his socks and shoes. By the time he had laced his boots, he'd resolved to gauge her mood before bringing up the incident.

He grabbed a jacket on his way to the kitchen. "Thank you for the coffee," he said upon entering the dimly lit space.

"You're welcome," she said without turning to look at him. While her tone wasn't curt, it lacked her usual sweetness. "It's almost ready. I made you two cups."

"Good looking out. I'll need all the caffeine I can get today." He longed to join her at the counter and wrap his arms around her waist but thought better of doing so—it could come across as insensitive in view of yesterday's conversation. After all, he hadn't truly apologized.

"Babe," he cleared his throat to gain her attention, but she didn't respond. "About my comment yesterday, I'm really sorry. What I said wasn't what I meant. It came out all wrong. I think you're beautiful."

He took a step toward her but stopped short as she poured coffee from a cup into a large travel mug. "I know you're sensitive about your weight. I shouldn't have joked with you about it. I'm sorry."

"Apology accepted." She snapped the lid onto the travel mug then faced him. "I'd like for us to talk about what happened, but now isn't the time. If you're home early this evening, we can discuss it then. And Cody, I can handle the truth. I'm a big girl. Pun intended."

The self-deprecating remark caused his heart to hammer with the words—tell her everything.

"Cody, are you listening to me?"

"Yes, I heard you." He averted his gaze. "I don't like it when you take jabs at yourself. I love you, even though I don't do a good job of showing you."

"I love you, too," her voice melancholy. "I've been praying about how I see myself. God's helping me to change my perspective, not as quickly as I'd like, but I'll get there."

"God's working on my perspective as well," he said in a tender voice. Heat inched its way up to the back of his neck and into his face, but he looked her into her eyes despite the shame.

"Good to know." She cracked a smile—the first he'd seen since his thoughtless remark.

She handed him the travel mug. "The Bible says we're two becoming one, but most of the time, I feel like I'm prying when we talk. I hope tonight is different."

He swallowed hard. Dad's choice to keep secrets from Mom had turned out badly. The last thing Cody wanted was to end up in a bitter divorce like his parents. He opened his mouth to speak in spite of his thundering heartbeat.

"Katelyn, there's something I need to tell you."

Chapter Two

Cody drove with one hand on the steering wheel while his other gripped the travel mug filled with coffee. He had rallied the courage to tell Kate about his pornography battle, but her "Hold that thought" response stopped him cold. He appreciated Kate's concern for Blake, yet the diversion left him fearful he'd walk away from a door God had opened. At least she extended an invitation to resume where they left off in the conversation, although his agreement to do so hadn't sounded sincere in his ears, it was heartfelt.

He took a sip of coffee then started an audiobook on spiritual warfare. Pastor Jordan suggested it might help with understanding Blake's rebellion. No better time to glean insight on Blake than while on a drive to bail him out of trouble. A few minutes into the recording, Cody discovered two of the characters were demons, but it still didn't hold his attention. He lacked confidence in how a fictional story, even one by C. S. Lewis, could explain whatever it was Blake was going through. His mind drifted to the impending conversation with Kate. All thoughts nose-dived into scenarios of her reaction after finding out about the pornography.

His chest tightened. He placed the travel mug in the cupholder. "Breathe," he said evenly. "In through your nose and out through your mouth."

He repeated the relaxation technique. Gradually, the narrator's voice replaced his anxiety. As the reader warned of how the devil attacks our thinking through distraction versus arguing with us against God's Word, Cody's concern for Blake collided with thoughts of their mother. Ada had touted Blake as her miracle baby. She'd had two miscarriages after Cody's birth and woefully came to accept there wouldn't be a sibling for her firstborn. Fifteen years later, she joyfully announced God had other plans. Cody no longer held out hope he and Kate might be blessed in a similar way. After several years of trying to conceive, he'd given up on the idea of parenthood. Sometimes he wondered if Kate's refusal to discuss fertility screening or adoption was God's way of protecting her from bringing a child into a marriage destined for failure.

The Vermont exit ramp came into view. He stopped the audiobook, giving full attention to the rescue mission. Cody moved from the fast lane, slowing his Jeep to take the off-ramp, then reentered, heading southbound. Blake had purchased a Jeep this past Christmas, but he'd denied copying his older brother by pointing out a battered '80s white Wrangler hardly compared to a brand new, gunmetal grey, fully loaded Rubicon.

Within a mile, he spotted Blake's vehicle along the shoulder of the freeway. Cody turned on his hazard lights while rolling to a slow stop about thirty feet behind the Wrangler. No traffic on the road allowed him to hop out on the driver's side. He sprinted over to the passenger door of Blake's Jeep then peered through the window. Blake looked as though he'd passed out or fallen asleep. He hoped for the latter. "Hey, open up."

No response. He rapped on the glass with his key ring. "Let me inside."

Blake jolted in the driver's seat, his eyes wild. Once recognition set in, a toothy smile morphed his face.

Cody glared at his younger brother. "Hurry up."

Blake's smile vanished. He reached over and unlocked the door. "Chill out."

"Don't tell me to chill out." Cody climbed inside. "You called me. I get to react how I want at this hour." He sniffed the air. "You haven't been drinking, have you?"

"No," Blake groaned and rested his head against the driver's side glass. "Do you think I'd call you if I was wasted?"

"You better not be drinking and driving." He eyeballed Blake. "It's bad enough you're reckless with your life, but putting others at risk is downright wrong, and it's a felony."

"Downright wrong?" Blake harrumphed. "Watch out, you're sounding like Pops." He righted himself. "You used to party. Do you remember what it was like, or has the memory faded with age?"

"Not funny," Cody recalled a certain club with a proliferation of scantily clad women dancing provocatively. He'd stopped frequenting that business once he and Kate began to date seriously. He shoved open the passenger door and stepped down.

"Your flat isn't going to change itself, and I'm not doing it." Cody shut the door then reopened it. "Turn your hazard lights on. I'll set out some flares. We don't want to become roadkill."

"Yeah, yeah." Blake exited the Jeep.

The cool early morning air smelled like rain. Cody picked up the pace on his walk back to the Rubicon, where he retrieved two flares and a jack. He tucked the jack under his arm while pulling the cap off one of the flares in his hand and used the striker to light it. The sulfur caused him to turn his head to one side as he laid the glowing flare about fifteen feet from the bumper of his vehicle. After he placed the second lit flare on the edge of the road, he rejoined Blake at the rear wheel well of the disabled Wrangler.

"Here," Cody handed him the jack.

"Thanks. I hope Kate's not mad because you're helping me."

"She's never mad when it comes to you." Cody pointed to the tire. "Pay attention. I don't want to be here if it starts raining."

"This won't take me long." Blake set the jack down next to the deflated tire. He walked to the tailgate and grabbed a lug wrench. "I'll be done quicker than you can say—"

"Save it," Cody huffed. "You've said that before. I'm going to get my coffee. How about you make some progress on changing the tire?"

"Aye, aye, Captain."

"Knock it off." Cody shook his head. While ambling toward the Rubicon, he zipped his jacket closed. Good thing he hadn't relied on the seven-day weather forecast, which predicted no rain until the weekend.

"Hey," Blake called. "Kate's a special woman. When you talk to her, thank her for me."

"I know she's special. You don't need to tell me." Cody turned to face him, "And thank her yourself."

"Bro, look out!" Blake pointed toward the freeway.

Cody jerked back around. His jaw dropped at the flash of headlights coming his way—a semi-truck careening toward the shoulder of the freeway. A surge of adrenaline stunned him. Paralyzed in the path of the oncoming big rig, the truck's air horn blasted a warning several times, but Cody couldn't force himself to move.

"Get out of the way," Blake shouted, louder this time.

The second warning unstuck Cody's feet, and he lunged out of its path. He landed in dirt and gravel a few feet from the front bumper of his Rubicon. The wheels of the big rig screeched against the asphalt, obliterating every other sound as the driver tried to gain control of the truck.

Cody closed his eyes tightly. He tensed as he waited for the violent bang of metal against metal. Burning rubber mixed with the acrid fumes from the flares warned impact was seconds away. "Lord, protect me. I don't want to die."

"Bro! Are you okay?" Blake's thunderous voice penetrated the cocoon of prayer. He knelt beside Cody. "Talk about a close call." His words came in a rush that hadn't allowed time for a response.

Cody gripped his brother's lean shoulder, and the two stood. "I'm okay. How about you?"

"I'm good. We're lucky to be alive."

As Cody's heart rate returned to normal, he stepped back to give Blake a visual once over, from his choppy-styled haircut all the way down to his black and white Chuck Taylor's.

"I said I'm fine." Blake leaned in and pointed toward Cody's mouth, "Hey, you're bleeding."

The coppery taste of blood in his mouth led Cody to run his fingertips gingerly against his lips. Instantly, the magnitude of such a close call registered. He spat in the dirt. "I must have bitten my tongue when I landed on the shoulder of the road."

Cody blotted his mouth with the back of his hand. He looked around. "Where's the truck driver? Is he all right?"

Blake nodded to beyond the Wrangler. "He's stopped up the road a few hundred yards. He's an idiot. How could he miss seeing two sets of hazard lights and flares? I bet you a hundred bucks he fell asleep at the wheel."

"Settle down," Cody said. "He may have had some kind of medical emergency. Let's go check on him before you assume anything."

"Medical emergency, my—"

Cody's hand shot up. "That's enough." He took the lead, and Blake followed.

"Well, if he's not dead or having a heart attack," Blake muttered, "I'm going to—"

"Quiet." Cody spotted the driver heading their way and elbowed Blake, who was looking down. He gripped Blake's arm, and the two stopped midway between the Wrangler and the back end of the driver's truck. A heavyset man wearing a black jacket, jeans, and a dark ball cap quickened his steps toward them. Face to face, the man extended his hand to Cody.

"Thank God, you boys aren't hurt. I'm Eugene Polk. I'd say it's nice to meet you, but—"

"What happened, dude?" Blake edged Cody aside. "Did you fall asleep at the wheel?" The pitch of his brother's voice warned things could get heated.

"I'm not going to lie," Polk said sheepishly, "I did doze off, but only for a second." The man redirected his hand to Blake, who shrugged it off.

"I told you!" Blake took a charging step toward the driver, but Cody once again gripped his brother's forearm.

Polk backed away. "I'm awful sorry. I've been driving rigs for over twenty years. I know better than to push myself when I'm tired."

The man removed his ball cap, ran his palm across his bald head then replaced the cap. "What I'm about to tell you boys might sound like an excuse, but it's not. You see, my wife's in the hospital. Emergency gallbladder surgery, and well, I was just trying to get there as quick as I could."

Cody didn't want to make things any more upsetting for the driver. The man's detailed explanation revealed his anxiousness over the near-miss. "I'm sorry to hear about your wife," he said in a calming voice. "Look, we're okay, and you're okay. Let's count our blessings and move on."

"Blessings?" Blake's voice rose. "Are you kidding me? We could've been killed."

Cody shot Blake a look that silenced him—at least for the moment. "Mr. Polk, I'm sure you can understand why my brother's upset. I'm just thankful we're standing here talking about what happened." He turned to Blake, "Right?"

"Whatever," Blake hissed.

"Amen to God's protection," the driver said, recapturing Cody's attention. Polk gazed at the starless sky. "Thank you for keeping us safe, Heavenly Father."

"I'm outta here." Blake broke free from Cody's grip. "You two can stand here all morning praising God, but I'm going to change my tire and get off this freeway before my luck runs out." He headed back to the Wrangler.

Cody waited until Blake was out of earshot. "I take it you're a Christian, too, Mr. Polk."

"Yes, but my walk with God isn't what it used to be." The man's sheepish expression returned, "I suppose we all have our ups and downs with Him."

"I agree." Cody extended his hand, and the driver accepted it with a firm shake. "I'm Cody James, by the way." He gestured over his shoulder with his thumb. "That was Blake, my much younger brother. If you're sure you're all right, I'd like to help him change his tire."

"I'm fine, but I tell you what, I'll not forget this day anytime soon." He smiled, and this time it lingered a bit before disappearing. "I'm humbled by your forgiveness."

"To be honest, Mr. Polk, I'm hoping to receive a little grace myself this evening. Who knows, maybe I'll reap what I've sown."

"Amen. Well, Mr. James, thank you again for being understanding." Polk walked the shoulder of the freeway back to his truck. He climbed into the cab, and after a few seconds, the big rig's engine roared to life as he pulled onto the roadway. The red taillights on the container grew dim as the expanse between them widened. Cody continued to stare down the length of the freeway until the truck was gone from sight.

"Lord, thank you for protecting us." Cody trekked over to the Wrangler with the mindset of powering through the tire change. Afterward, he'd let Kate know the rescue mission had been a success. No need to tell her about the close call with the truck driver—she worried enough about his safety at the pawnshop.

"Are you hungry?" Blake struggled to tighten one of the lug nuts. His lean frame could benefit from regular meals that didn't rely on sugar and energy drinks, but a talk with him about nutrition was the equivalent of a parent lecturing a toddler who refused to eat the "green stuff" on their plate.

Cody stooped alongside his brother at the rear tire well. "Sounds like a roundabout way of getting me to spot you for breakfast. I'll treat, but I choose where we eat. A convenience store cup of coffee and an oversized muffin don't register as nutritious on my radar."

"Wow," Blake snorted. "The putdowns never stop. I don't think you're aware of it most of the time. How is it you can be compassionate to a stranger, but when it comes to me, you're a pain in the—"

"Whoa. Now who needs to chill out?" Cody stood. His posture stiffened, and he folded his arms across his chest. "I bet you only have a few bucks left even though payday was last Friday, so I try to be the nice guy by offering to treat for breakfast, and this is the thanks I get."

"See. You did it again." Blake looked up at him. "Just because you sign my paychecks doesn't give you a say in how I spend my money." He resumed working the lug nut putting extra force in his thrust. "For your information, I was going to treat you to breakfast."

Cody's shoulders slumped. As much as he tried to distance himself from his dad's critical thinking and sharp tongue, God rest his soul, the trait often wormed its way into him. "Hey, I'm sorry. I don't want to treat you the same way Dad treated me, yet here I am repeating it with you. I'm not proud to have to admit this to you, but it's easier for me to see the faults of others than my own."

"You have faults? Nah." Blake cocked his head in Cody's direction and grinned. "Seriously, though. Thanks for the apology."

Cody returned the grin. "So, don't keep me in suspense. Where were you going to take me for breakfast?"

"Who said anything about taking you anywhere? I was going to share my stash with you." Blake laughed. "Pop-Tarts."

"You're kidding, right?" Cody joined in his laughter.

"If I'm lying, I'm dying." Blake pointed to the front of his vehicle." Check my glove box, but don't ask how long they've been there."

"Why? Because the artificial preservatives will keep them fresh until—"

"The second coming," Blake snickered.

"Okay, let's not go there." Cody pointed to the tire. "Finish the tire change so we can get going. I'll be waiting in my Jeep."

On the walk back to his Rubicon, Cody pulled his cell phone from his back pocket to call Kate. He checked the time on his phone. It was only quarter to five, but if he didn't touch base with her soon, she'd call him. Kate had confided she didn't take pleasure in checking on him, but given his long work hours and defensiveness whenever they talked, she had a hard time making the distinction between his father's unfaithfulness and him.

Cody suspected even though Kate overheard the phone call with Blake, she'd question whether or not he had actually gone to help his brother. The conversation with her this evening couldn't come soon enough. Unlike dad, Cody would come clean about everything, and he hoped the outcome wouldn't end like his parent's failed marriage, with the truth coming too late to save it.

Chapter Three

A few bars of The Eagle's song "Peaceful, Easy Feeling" played, pulling Kate out of sleep. Alerted to Cody's call, she patted the nightstand in search of her cell phone as the singer warbled on. At last, Kate's fingers located the phone, and she swiped the screen to answer the call. "Where are you?" She rolled over to Cody's side of the bed and snuggled his pillow.

He chuckled. "I'm with Blake, silly. Have you forgotten?"

Kate yawned. She had forgotten, but before she could say so, he spoke again.

"Babe, you sound groggy. Sorry for waking you. Should I call back?"

"No. I'm glad you called." She checked the time on his bedside alarm clock. If he got home soon, they would have almost an hour together before they needed to get ready for work. Breathing in a sigh, she braced herself for the excuse she knew would come but asked him the question anyway.

"Are you on your way back here? I'll get breakfast started."

"Well, I uh, didn't plan on coming home."

"Oh." She'd learned to play it cool when faced with these types of situations.

"Rather than come all the way back home, I figured I'd grab something to eat with Blake and start my day early," he paused. "That is, unless you need me to come back for something."

"Something? Gee, thanks. How about someone?" Kate hadn't intended to reveal her disappointment through sarcasm. She closed her eyes and pursed her lips. Fabulous, she sounded like a shrew.

"Now you're mad," Cody spoke after a few seconds of silence. "Babe, I didn't get the chance to tell you, but I was also calling to make plans with you for dinner. I want us to finish our talk from earlier and—"

"Who said I was mad?" Of course he was right. She sighed again. Maybe they should hang up and start the call over, but instead, she pressed forward with truth. "I was mad, but now I'm feeling disappointed we can't have a conversation without arguing."

"I'm sorry," Cody exhaled loudly. "This is my fault again. I could've told you I wasn't coming home differently. I've misspoken a lot lately."

Verbal apologies from Cody were rare. He tended to apologize through gifts of jewelry from the pawnshop, and while she appreciated those gestures, Kate couldn't help but feel as if he thought he could buy forgiveness.

She hesitated, not wanting to stir the I-only-want-to-be-helpful pot, but did so anyway. "Have you listened to the audiobook on spiritual warfare Pastor Jordan gave us? I know he said it might offer insight into what your brother is going through, but I think we could benefit from it, too."

"As a matter of fact, yes, I started it on the way to get Blake. I've got a lot on my mind right now, so I wasn't paying it as much attention as I should have."

Kate released Cody's pillow, rolled onto her back, and stared into the darkness. She needn't remind him how seeking God first was missing from their lives. She had said it enough times; it should have sunk in by now. Besides, he'd likely view it as finger-pointing. Sometimes, though, words did slip out before she could stop them, yet Kate wasn't sure she shouldn't speak the truth because it made him uncomfortable.

The temptation to correct Cody's thinking won out. "Do you understand putting God first is going to make all the difference in our—"

"Lives?" He groaned. "Sorry for interrupting, but I don't like it when you micromanage my relationship with God. You don't like it when I assume how you're feeling about something instead of asking, right?"

"Point made." Kate resisted the urge to say she'd only wanted to help. Over the past ten years, she'd tried numerous ways to get Cody to do things God's way. The laundry list of efforts included: arguing, pleading, ignoring, avoiding, confronting, debating, and the silent treatment, all of which were outlined in the latest book she'd begun reading, *The Power of a Praying Wife.*

"Katelyn, I said I'd listen to the audiobook later, and I will."

He hadn't said he'd listen to it later because if he had, she wouldn't have persisted. As of late, whatever she said, Cody tended to disagree with it, if for no other reason than to underscore he didn't want her telling him what to think.

"Blake's signaling he's done. I need to get going."

His sentence oozed impatience, and she stifled the urge to comment.

"Babe..." Cody remained quiet.

"Yes?" She pressed the phone to her ear. Perhaps the call had been disconnected. Kate sat up in bed and was about to speak when he resumed his thought.

"About tonight, I want to...never mind," he finally said.

Better not to press him. In the continued silence, she tamped down her enthusiasm at finding out. Kate leaned back against the headboard. She ushered up an unspoken prayer he'd choose to put her first instead of another night of working late. "If you think you will be home early tonight, I'd like for us to have dinner on the patio."

"Sounds good, but I have a guy coming in at six who wants to sell two guns. I might be able to buy them for a good price. Maybe we could set a time to talk for later in the evening."

"I guess." Once again, Kate wrestled with letting him off the hook.

Cody blew out a breath. "The whole point of obtaining my federal firearms license for the pawnshop was to improve our income. Guns sell. I need to increase the inventory at the shop."

"I know." The frustration wasn't hidden. Yet try as she might, an additional response didn't follow. Her work was important too, but she didn't allow it to come before him. Based on Cody's impatient tone, the call had gone south—again.

"Katelyn, are you there?"

"Yes. I'm here." She stifled another sigh. "It's okay about dinner tonight. We can talk whenever you get home."

"I'll try to wrap up early. I'll text you when I'm on my way home. It may not sound like it, but I do want things to be different between us. If I'm going to be later than seven-thirty, I'll let you know. Love you."

"I love you, too." She laid the phone on the mattress. Cody's hollow-sounding "Love you" dredged up recurring fidelity concerns. At six-foot-two, he frequently attracted attention from the opposite sex with his lean but muscular build, thick chestnut brown hair, and babyface. His shy nature around women often resulted in them misconstruing his actions as flirtatious, but he never hesitated to politely set a woman straight about being a married man—at least in her presence.

Kate slid down in bed and hugged his pillow to her cheek. The bold scent of tea tree oil from his shampoo last night lingered on the cotton, and she breathed deeply.

The niggling thoughts about fidelity returned. She retrieved her phone and opened the photo album section. Scrolling through a collection of pictures as a couple, anyone would think they were happily married, which is the way Cody wanted it, even if it wasn't wholly genuine.

Gradually, the negative feelings subsided, but then she landed on a picture she'd seen as a screensaver on Cody's laptop computer a few days ago. The plan was to take a photograph of the barely dressed woman and ask him about it. As the days passed without opportunity to mention it, Kate reasoned he must have a legitimate explanation for using the image and gave up on the idea of questioning him—even though the buxom blonde holding the military-style rifle looked like she'd be more at home on an adult magazine cover.

###

Kate stared at her reflection in the mirror above the bathroom basin. She leaned forward to study her face. Tilting her head to one side, then the other, a faint smile surfaced at the thought of Cody's scent on his pillow only moments ago. But the early morning sunlight highlighted her crow's feet, and the thought dried up. If only she had to worry about crow's feet—it was the rest of her that was lumpy and bumpy these days.

She stepped back, turned sideways, and sucked in her budding waistline. The snug-fitting T-shirt emphasized the thirty-pound weight gain during the past year, yet this look was still much better than parading around in one of those skimpy pajama sets Cody occasionally purchased as a gift.

Kate relaxed her stomach. The fast-food runs were a poor substitute for healthy meals on evenings when he worked late; add to those empty calories the frequent trips to a gourmet candy store and voilà, a thirty-pound weight gain. In seven months, she'd turn forty-one. Changes were needed between now and then. A determined smile surfaced. By October seventh, a thirty-pound weight loss could be achieved. Even a meager three to five pounds a month meant the goal could be achieved with pounds to spare. Today was a good day as any to begin to do things differently. The disappointment over another meal without Cody threatened her motivation. She squared her shoulders while continuing to stare into the mirror. "Don't make excuses," she ground out.

Her gaze shifted to the hodgepodge of department store cosmetics collecting dust on the vanity. Since Cody rarely commented one way or the other when she wore makeup, she'd all but stopped using it. Many of the products were unopened.

A red lip liner caught her attention. She grabbed it, removed the protective seal, and then leaned over the basin to write on the mirror, "I can do all things through Christ who strengthens me" (Philippians 4:13).

She stepped back, and a smile surfaced. Kate tossed the lip lining pencil onto the vanity then marched to the clothes closet. She needed an outfit to support the new mindset. On one side of the shared space were Cody's pants and shirts, which he hung in seasonal order of cool weather articles to warm weather items, with the cooler attire currently at the front of the closet. Cody also grouped his clothes by color—the dominant shade in his wardrobe being black.

She crinkled her nose over his fastidiousness then turned her attention to the jumble of clothes hung on her side of the closet. The shimmery sleeve of a red blouse jutting out from a hanger ignited a thought. She'd planned to wear the blouse with a white eyelet skirt this Saturday for Valentine's Day but now envisioned coupling it with black slacks for work. Besides, it was unlikely Cody would be home on a Saturday—Valentine's Day or not.

Her focus shifted to the cloth-covered jewelry box on a shelf at the rear of the closet. She gingerly rummaged through the assorted trinkets, locating a delicate pair of white earrings with hand-painted roses. Cody had purchased them last year on a day they had spent together at the beach in Santa Monica. While walking on the boardwalk, hand in hand, he had spotted a little shop and insisted on buying something as a keepsake. The day flashed before her eyes. It had started out good. A petty conversation over something she couldn't even recall now had ensued during lunch and washed away any hope of a romantic evening. Maybe a better memory would be created this evening.

Most of their disagreements were unremarkable, yet her insistence in ferreting out the underlying problem generally resulted in it turning into something that lasted hours. Cody ended lengthier discussions by saying he didn't appreciate having a topic belabored as if he were a child, despite his toddler-like obstinance when it came to conflict resolution in the marriage.

Kate laid the red blouse across the unmade bed and placed the white skirt below it. She set the earrings near the collar of the blouse and surveyed the outfit. Today she'd wear her hair down instead of in a ponytail, and she'd spritz on a little of one of the many perfumes Cody had given her over the years. If he got home too late tonight, and he missed seeing her in the outfit, it was a safe bet the residents at Brighton Assisted Living would acknowledge her new look.

Today, a van outing to a local farmer's market was scheduled for the Brighton residents. She would get to show off the more flattering attire while having fun with those she had come to love. In addition to numerous food vendors at the farmer's market, there would also be several craft booths. Perhaps she'd find a Valentine's Day gift for Cody.

A touch of sadness blanketed Kate's thoughts as she recalled her favorite resident, Grace Fisher, who had always enjoyed the van outings. The ninety-eight-year-old woman would often sing show tunes to and from their destinations. Today's outing wouldn't be the same without her.

Kate stepped back from the bed and admired the simple triumph of choosing something other than a pair of loose jeans and a baggy T-shirt for work, even though Cody's preferred attire was similar. To be fair, while he often wore jeans, they fit well, and his T-shirts with interesting logos embraced his muscular chest and abs as if they'd been painted on.

She sat beside the clothes on the bed, bowed her head, and closed her eyes. "God, please help me to make healthy food choices today. No fast food and no chocolate," Kate winced. "Yes, I'll get rid of the twenty percent off a pound box of chocolates coupon stashed in my wallet."

She firmed her lips, hesitant to voice one final concern. "While I'm working on getting in better shape, please help me to stop doubting my husband when he says I'm beautiful. I want to believe what he says."

The unsavory image from Cody's laptop screensaver flashed before her eyes.

She collapsed backward onto the mattress. "Shut up, Devil. Cody isn't cheating. Sure, we have communication issues, but what married couple doesn't at times?"

Kate tipped her chin up and waited for a retort. "Like I thought, you got nothing." She stuck out her tongue but retracted it, not wanting to taunt the devil any further.

The familiar bars from "Peaceful, Easy Feeling" played again. Kate rolled onto her side and fumbled for several seconds to locate her phone tangled in the bedding. "Hello," she finally answered.

"Please don't say anything," Cody began. He exhaled loudly. "I've been insensitive. I want to make it up to you—especially for the long hours over the past few months."

Kate opened her mouth to say how much the call meant, but it was as if Cody saw and silenced her by resuming.

"I should be able to wrap up this gun deal by six-thirty—if there's no haggling. So, if you're game, I'd like to have dinner with you, but out, not at home. How about we go to that Chinese restaurant you like? We haven't been there in months."

"I'd love to." She fingered the rose-painted earrings as she spoke. "Cody, if you were involved in something bad for us—as husband and wife, and you didn't feel as though you could come to me about it... you'd ask God for help, right?"

Silence followed.

Kate could hear him breathing, but other than that, the lull in the conversation continued. She began to dread what he might say. *What if the issue was infidelity? What if he didn't have the courage to confess it?* She swallowed hard. If he didn't say something, and soon, she would break the silence by asking again, but this time she'd assure him they could—what—work it out? That wasn't something she could promise.

Dread escalated to fear. "Cody?"

"Katelyn, if you have something you want to say, just say it." He exhaled another long breath, but this time it was filled with annoyance, not regret.

She sat up in bed. "Please, let's not argue." Kate plastered on a smile, hoping he'd hear it in her tone. "You phoned to invite me out to dinner, which we haven't done in a long time, and I accepted. Let's leave it at—"

"Why do you always have to press me on things?" He huffed. "Maybe I want to be the one to open up and in my own. Your way creates angst between us."

Kate's shoulders drooped under the weight of the conflict. Once again, she struggled with how to make peace with him without compromising the need to speak openly.

"Sweetheart," she began. The genuine endearment might diffuse things. He'd always be her sweetheart. Whatever bridges they crossed in life, they would cross them together. With one exception, but it wasn't as if she hadn't been vocal on the subject of infidelity.

Kate closed her eyes to refocus her thoughts on the conversation. "You know that movie, the one with Bill Murray where he repeats the same day over and over?"

"Groundhog Day," he mumbled.

"Yes," she opened her eyes. "Can we start over with my accepting your invitation to dinner?"

"Sounds like a good idea." After a moment, Cody spoke again. "I'll make it a point to wrap things up by seven. Meet me at Ling's at seven-thirty. And babe, I have a little surprise for you. It's a little something I picked up a few days ago."

"I can hardly wait." Kate glanced at the earrings. "I have a little surprise for you, too."

Chapter Four

The bell for access into the pawnshop rang. Cody glanced at his watch. Quarter to six. He hoped the elderly man on the other side of the metal security door would be Mr. Kennedy, a little early for his appointment to show and possibly sell two of his guns.

He peered through the screen. "May I help you?"

"Good evening, sir. I'm Martin Kennedy, and I am supposed to meet Cody James at six."

"I'm Cody James. Let me buzz you in." He'd talked to the potential seller once over the phone, but the man standing on the other side of the secured entry looked nothing like what he expected. Based on the man's baritone voice, Cody envisioned a much younger, barrel-chested, ex-military guy. Instead, this gentleman with smiling eyes reminded him of someone's grandpa.

Cody reached for the lock release button to the right of the door handle, but behind him, Blake cleared his throat and drew Cody's attention. He half-turned to look at his brother.

"Bro, I meant to call the service guy today, but I forgot." Blake smiled sheepishly from behind the counter.

Withdrawing his hand, Cody glared at Blake, then turned back to Mr. Kennedy, "Just a moment, please."

Cody pushed past Blake as he moved to the showcase that displayed a dozen handguns. He pressed a hidden lock release button under the counter, and the magnetic catch on the security door buzzed loudly, allowing the older man entry into the shop.

"Good to meet you, Mr. Kennedy." Cody extended his right hand as the gentleman drew nearer to him.

"Likewise, sir." The smile in the man's eyes brightened as it reached his lips. He gently placed the metal case he'd carried on the glass countertop, then shook Cody's hand with gnarled, arthritic fingers that led Cody to relax his grasp.

Blake sidled up alongside Cody. "Let's see what you have for us."

"I've got this covered." Cody deliberately put steel behind his words, which prompted Blake to walk away with a shrug. Once Blake had taken a seat at the opposite end of the counter, Cody resumed his conversation.

"Kid brothers," Cody winked. "You can't live with them, and you can't live without them."

Mr. Kennedy's thick brows crinkled. He moved the case closer to himself. "Maybe this isn't a good time to discuss business."

"It's a perfect time. In fact, I appreciate your early arrival." The last thing he wanted was for the old man to change his mind.

Cody straightened his shoulders and used his most professional tone, "I apologize for the distraction. I'm the owner and federal firearms licensee, so may I take a look?"

The man hesitated a moment before his gnarled fingers fumbled with the numeric lock on the case. Once the latch clicked open, he turned the case toward Cody.

The gentleman's three pistols were nestled in a red velvet-lined interior. One glance at the patina of the barrels, and he put their provenance in the Civil War era. Cody tried not to gawk at the collector pieces—Remington and Colt revolvers—clearly kept in pristine condition. No sense tipping his hand to how much he wanted to buy these firearms, so he swallowed his excitement. "May I ask why you want to part with the guns?"

Mr. Kennedy placed his hand with an obvious quiver atop the pearl-handled Colt Navy revolver. "First, I have a question for you."

Cody drew back his head. The man's tone suggested the sale might hinge on his answer. "Shoot." He chuckled at his unintentional word pun. "Not literally, of course."

Mr. Kennedy chuckled, too, softening his tense expression. "It's been sixteen years since my beloved wife, Beatrice, passed away. I miss her as much today as the day she went home to be with our Lord and Savior."

Cody nodded his understanding, not sure why the man had changed the topic from the guns to discussing his wife, but he often heard extraordinary tales before making a sale. If Mr. Kennedy wanted to reminisce about his wife for a few minutes, he would happily listen. He'd wait for the question and hoped to have the right answer. Those guns would be worth his time.

"Mr. James, plenty of good folks don't mean any harm when they say things like 'She's in a better place' and 'God must have needed another angel,' but what those people don't realize is when someone you love dies, hearing 'God picks His best flowers first' isn't as comforting as they think it will be. What gets me through each day without my wife, even after all these years, is sound theology. One day, I'm going to be reunited with my Beatrice. The Bible tells me so."

"Mr. Kennedy, would you like to have a seat in my office?"

"Thank you. I'd like that."

Cody walked around to the other side of the counter and rested his hand on the man's frail shoulder. When the gentleman looked at him, tears welled in the older man's eyes. For a split-second, Cody feared the man might reveal he wanted to get rid of the guns because he'd considered using one of them to join his wife. Then he remembered Mr. Kennedy said he had a question to ask, not a confession to make.

Seated in the small office with the door closed, Cody apologized for the cramped quarters, even though Mr. Kennedy hadn't said anything about the two large gun safes against the back wall used for overnight storage. Four smaller safes lined the wall on the opposite side of the room, making the crowded space even tighter. He thought about getting back up and opening the door to create the illusion of more room but decided the older man might value the privacy, so he remained seated.

The poster of a bikini-clad model holding a Springfield XDM pistol hanging behind Mr. Kennedy caused Cody to tap his foot in place. Had the older man not shared about his wife and

God, the poster would've been inconsequential. He hoped Mr. Kennedy hadn't noticed the racy picture but instead spotted the framed reproduction of the constitution alongside a mounted and framed watercolor painting of the Ten Commandments that hung behind his desk.

To restart the conversation, Cody offered a sympathetic smile. "I'm sorry about your wife. It sounds like you two shared something very special."

"Please, call me Marty." He returned the smile. The man rested his folded hands atop the case in his lap, and it seemed to steady the tremor in his voice. "When you love someone like I loved Beatrice, you wake each morning with a longing to be near the person, and it doesn't let up."

At a loss for words, Cody eyed his own wedding band, but then his focus shifted to the scantily clad model on the poster. Talk about guilt. After nearly two decades of widowhood, this endearing man continued to profess love for his deceased wife, yet Cody rarely made it home in time to eat dinner with Kate.

"I believe I already have the answer to my question," Marty said.

"Really?" Cody kept his expression neutral, but alarm beat in his chest. He could only hope the older man hadn't seen the poster and been offended by it.

"You're a Christian, aren't you?" Marty pointed one of his knotted index fingers behind Cody, who swiveled his chair to see the Ten Commandments wall hanging.

"Yes. My wife and I are both Christians." His cheeks warmed. Great, he'd volunteered he was married, and there was no way to escort the old guy out of the office without him seeing the bikini model poster—if he hadn't already seen it.

Cody turned back to him, hoping his face wasn't noticeably flushed. "That's your question?"

"In part." Marty leaned forward. "I also—"

Two loud raps on the office door broke into their conversation. Before Cody could react, the door slammed open against the gun-safe bedside Mr. Kennedy's chair.

Blake hung onto the door handle. "We got a problem!"

Cody's gaze traveled from the wide-eyed seller to Blake. "What's up?" He hoped his nonchalant response conveyed to his younger brother that he needed to dial down his emotions.

"She's back." Blake used a more controlled tone. He nodded over his shoulder. "She says she will only talk to you."

###

"Stay focused," Cody muttered as he approached Chelsea, an achingly beautiful brunette at the display counter. The undeniable chemistry between them both scared and exhilarated him.

He'd hoped she wouldn't return. Two months ago, she had brought in a Blu-ray player without the remote and asked for a loan against it. At best, he should've offered her half of what she asked for, but she'd pleaded her case for gas money to get to and from work through the end of the week. He'd heard all kinds of stories over the years, but the gas money plea was the most repeated. Like other customers who hocked non-essentials, Chelsea assured she would be back to retrieve her merchandise in a couple of weeks. Blake had offered to process her loan, but Cody rejected the idea. In retrospect, Blake had probably read his impure thoughts and attempted to intervene. Instead, Cody ate up Chelsea's flattery. He'd given Chelsea a business card with his cell phone number scribbled on the back—in case she needed to reach him after hours regarding her loan. At least that's the lie he told himself. Why he'd done something so reckless nagged him for days. When she didn't call or return to the shop, he chalked it up to horrible judgment on his part, never to be repeated.

The shapely brunette with her back to him leaned over the display counter. She appeared to be eyeing jewelry in the case, but his instinct warned otherwise. He swiped perspiration from his forehead and swallowed hard as he approached her. The black dress she wore embraced her hips and inched up her thighs when she leaned further over the counter. He should have insisted Blake handled this transaction. Another bad decision, but it was too late now. All he could do was close out the loan quickly, get back to Mr. Kennedy, make a deal on the guns, and then meet Kate at the restaurant. They'd have a wonderful evening. He would make sure of it.

That dress is sexy. Such an awful thought had no place in his head. Cody blinked several times in rapid succession to refocus. He cleared his throat, and Chelsea turned slowly to face him.

"Well, hello, stranger," she grinned. The color of her eyes reminded him of Kate's green eyes, except this woman's gaze was flirty and playful—something his wife hadn't exhibited for a long time.

Chelsea eyed him up and down. "Sorry I didn't make it in as promised. You said I had ninety days. Some unexpected expenses hit me. I'm sure you can't relate—being a successful business owner."

He fought the temptation to stare at her cleavage as his thoughts unraveled. "Do you see something you like?" His face warmed as the innocuous question romped about like an elephant in the room. "That came out wrong."

Chelsea arched a brow and parted her full lips but said nothing.

"Are you here to pick up your VCR?" He tugged at the neckline of his T-shirt.

Her face contorted then she burst into laughter.

"Did I say VCR?" He shook his head. "I meant Blu-ray player. Boy, I'm dating myself." He wished Blake would burst into this room, but he'd taken Cody at his word about keeping the old man company.

"Yes, you totally said VCR," her laughter resumed. "I know what they are; I just never owned one. Not unless you count the fact my mom and dad had one when I was a kid. I used to watch recorded episodes of a kid's show called *Punky Brewster*."

She winked, "You don't know the show, do you?"

"I can't say I've heard of it." Cody moved behind the display case. He needed to create distance. "Forgive me, I don't mean to be abrupt, but I have a customer waiting for me in my office. Do you have your loan ticket, Chelsea?"

"Awww," she bent at the waist, placed both elbows on the glass top, cradled her face, and looked up at him. "You remembered my name. You're so sweet."

He averted his eyes from the deep V neckline of her dress to the rings and bracelets on either side of her in the case.

"Your name is easy to remember. It's lovely." As the words spilled out of his mouth, if he could've sucker-punched himself in the back of the head, he would have.

She grinned. "Would you like to see my ticket?"

"Yes, please." He swallowed hard.

Chelsea straightened seductively, or maybe his imagination had gotten the better of him. She set her purse on the counter, pulled out her wallet, and rifled through it. "Here you go."

The rumpled ticket carried the scent of her perfume. Chelsea's fragrance was light but sensual. He breathed deeply. Kate no longer wore perfume, even though he'd given her several expensive scents over the years. To add insult to injury, she'd joked about having re-gifted them to friends.

"Roses?" He stopped at the sound of his voice betraying his private thoughts.

"Yes." She locked eyes with him. "It must be close to quitting time. How about you help me refresh it—at my place?"

Chapter Five

Kate used her menu to discreetly watch a younger woman in a hot-pink dress cross the restaurant dining room. One of Ling's waiters seated the blonde with long legs, who embodied the stereotypical California girl. Kate slumped as she placed her menu on the table. She glanced down at her own appearance. The shimmery red blouse paired with the white skirt now seemed frumpy in comparison to the woman's outfit across the room.

Early in their marriage, Cody worked out with her. That changed after he purchased the pawnshop. He moved their exercise routine from mornings to evenings; getting motivated after 7 p.m. proved too much, and she made excuses until he no longer asked her to join him. Once she'd gained weight, dressing stylishly fell by the wayside. Although Cody still complimented her figure, the words didn't penetrate the negative self-image she carried in her mind. As a result, his compliments typically triggered an argument.

Recalling the oath to make healthier choices, she straightened her posture. Today was a new day. This morning breakfast of steel-cut oatmeal, half a grapefruit, and black coffee had been followed by a chicken salad for lunch, an apple, and a bottle of sparkling water, instead of the usual pastrami dip sandwich, fries, and a milkshake from one of her favorite Farmers Market vendors. Already, her body felt cleaner from the nutritious choices. She'd continue the pattern by ordering wisely for dinner. Maybe tonight, if Cody suggested something flirty, she'd be receptive, as long as he didn't keep her waiting much longer.

A male voice overrode Kate's thoughts. She looked up at the waiter, who moments ago had seated the California girl.

"I'm sorry." An awkward smile tugged at the corners of her lips. "I missed what you said."

He bowed. "May I get you another iced tea with lemon?"

"Yes, please." Kate followed the waiter's gaze to Cody's glass of tea, now diluted with melted ice.

"I'll bring a fresh glass for your husband, too," the man volunteered. "Would you like an appetizer while you're waiting?"

"No, thank you." Her cheeks warmed, and to cover her embarrassment, she prattled about Cody's tardiness. "I tried calling him, but he didn't answer. He said he'd meet me here at seven-thirty. Then again, he's a workaholic. I imagine he's just running a little late. His shop is fifteen minutes from here, so I expect him anytime."

Cody hated it when she divulged personal details. His rule of thumb—less is more. He'd asked her numerous times not to be so forthcoming, especially with strangers. Kate smiled and apologized for her chattiness.

"I'm sure he will arrive shortly." The waiter stepped back from the table and bowed. "I'll be right back with your iced teas."

"Thank you." Her attention returned to the young woman, seated alone at a table set for two. The last thing Kate wanted was a sexy blonde and one of her gorgeous friends a few feet away. Granted, Cody would do a mediocre job of pretending not to notice them, but gazes don't lie, and she'd seen his attention drift more than he would admit when a beautiful woman was in the room.

Kate picked her cell phone up from the table and double-checked to make sure the ringer wasn't off, or she hadn't inadvertently set it to do not disturb. It wouldn't be the first time. She was about to redial Cody's number when her phone played the I Love Lucy theme song.

"Sandie, thank goodness it's you." Kate sighed into her best friend's ear. "As usual, your timing is perfect." Kate had nicknamed Sandie "Lucy" for the shenanigans Sandie had dragged her into over the years. Sandie dubbed Kate "Ethel"—hence, the I Love Lucy ringtone.

"I'm worried about Cody." Kate kept her tone hushed. "We were supposed to meet at seven-thirty at Ling's. It's now eight—no Cody and no phone call."

"He's fine, Ethel. He always is. Did you try calling the shop? He's probably tied up with a customer."

"Hold on a second." Kate smiled at the waiter as he set down two iced teas. "Thank you." Once he walked away, she resumed the conversation. "Okay, I'm back. Yes, I tried the shop, and no answer there either."

"Have you tried calling Blake?"

"No. Great idea, I'll try Blake. Talk to you later. Wait." Kate shook her head to dislodge the tunnel vision regarding Cody's whereabouts and not taking a moment to find out why Sandie had called. "Is everything okay with you?"

"I'm fine. I just wanted to gab. We can talk another time. Call Blake and put your mind at ease. I'll say a prayer for Cody. Give me a jingle tomorrow, and we'll play catch-up. Unless—"

"Unless what? Something's happened to him?" Kate choked on the words. This wasn't like Cody. He knew how much she hated being kept in the dark when it came to his whereabouts, and especially since he'd started buying and selling guns. "He's fine, right?"

"Of course he is. Now hang up, then call Blake. PS I don't expect to hear from you until tomorrow because you're going to discover time just got away from him—as usual. You two will laugh about this later. I love you, Ethel."

Kate cracked a smile. "Love you, too, Lucy." She toggled her phone to favorites and chose Blake's number. As the call connected, she ushered up a silent prayer her brother-in-law would answer and have information about Cody.

"Yo-ho-ho and a bottle of rum, sorry I missed your call. Leave a message. I'll get back to you. Unless you're a bill collector, then it's a walk on the plank for you. Arrr."

"Blake, it's me, Kate. When you get this message, give me a call back right away. I'm concerned about your brother." She hit pound to stop the message, then followed the prompt to erase and rerecord her message.

"Hey, Blake, it's Kate. Do me a favor; whenever you get this message gimmie a call. Okay, thanks. And by the way, your new greeting is pretty funny. I like the pirate lingo." She chuckled before ending the recording in hopes it would remove any hint of urgency. Cody was probably okay, and she didn't need Blake sensing otherwise then ribbing Cody about it later.

Kate set the phone back on the table. She exhaled a breath she hadn't realized she'd been holding, then looked casually around the restaurant. The blonde across the way stood and smiled before crossing the room—headed in Kate's direction.

The woman's smile deepened. Kate turned to look at the table behind her, surely she was smiling at someone else, but the other diners were engrossed in conversation—oblivious to the woman, closing the gap between them.

"Hello," the stranger practically purred. She gestured to the chair opposite Kate. "May I?"

Kate suddenly recalled the episode of *I Love Lucy* in which Barbara Eden portrayed a blonde vixen and had the men tripping all over themselves to gain her attention. Kate half-hoped Cody wouldn't show up right now.

"I should introduce myself before asking to join you." She extended her hand. "My name is Grace."

Kate accepted the handshake. "It's nice to meet you. I'm Katelynn."

Grace released her grip, and Kate spotted the large diamond ring and wedding band on her ring finger. At least she was a married woman, a young and very attractive married woman, but no less a married woman. Maybe her husband was running late, too.

"Please, have a seat, Grace." Kate nodded at the chair directly across from her. Once the woman was seated, Kate leaned forward. "Forgive me for being direct, but have we met before?"

"Not exactly..." Grace's eyes welled, but she blinked back the tears. "If I had known I was going to have this reaction, I may have decided against approaching you."

Kate sat back. "Take your time." She struggled to be patient while waiting for the young woman to reveal her intentions, but concern for Cody once again claimed Kate's thoughts, and she tapped her foot under the table.

"This is God's timing," Grace's voice cracked, "meeting tonight. I'm leaving the area tomorrow. If we hadn't met tonight, well, we may have never had the opportunity."

"You said we haven't *exactly* met before...what do you mean?" Kate rested her hands on the table and interlaced her fingers, her foot still keeping beat to anxious thoughts about Cody.

"You knew my grandmother, also named Grace," she cleared her throat. "Granny Grace was a resident at Brighton Assisted Living. In her letters to me over the years, she'd sometimes include photographs of the outings you took her and the other residents on."

The woman's smiled returned. "Granny referred to you as her bonus-daughter. In most of the photographs, she would draw a heart around your face." Grace's smile remained. "She told me the facility provided the disposable cameras."

Kate returned her smile. She chose not to reveal the act wasn't as generous as it appeared. The facility did buy the disposable cameras but billed the residents, who also had to pay for their own film development.

"I recognized you from the photographs Granny sent me. I could hardly believe my eyes when I spotted you. I know this is God-ordained."

"Your grandmother was Grace Fisher?"

The young woman nodded, tears brimming.

"I'm sorry for your loss." Kate handed her one of the white cloth napkins from the table.

"Thank you." Grace dabbed her eyes. "I'd planned to come see her this past Christmas, but I couldn't get away."

"Your grandmother spoke about you quite a bit. She bragged about you being a big-time model and living in New York. Are you headed back there?"

Grace nodded again.

Kate recalled the elder woman's smiling face days before her death. The funeral had been a week ago. She'd wanted to attend the service, but the facility's administrator gently pointed out it wasn't possible given the assistant activities director was on her honeymoon. Kate at least had the opportunity to go to the viewing and say her goodbyes. She'd signed the guest book and left behind a bouquet of wildflowers with a card attached that read, "To my huckleberry friend, Love Kate."

Even now, the encrypted message caused Kate to sniffle back her emotions, which drew a response from Grace.

"I'm sure my grandmother meant a lot to you, too." Grace hung her head for several seconds before looking up. "I should've made more of an effort to meet you. I've been pretty self-absorbed the past few years."

"No explanation is needed." Kate could relate to the young woman's missteps. Most of her own good intentions had a high degree of failure.

A faint smile surfaced on Grace's lips and blossomed in her eyes. "Granny Grace told me she'd sing on the van rides to and from the outings. She said you'd often cheer 'Encore. Encore.' Granny sure liked those old movies. Her favorite movie was—"

"*Breakfast at Tiffany's*," Kate chimed in.

Grace's eyes sparkled. "I'm not surprised you knew that."

Kate considered mentioning the flowers and the card she had left at the mortuary, only because she wanted to convey how much the elder Grace meant to her. But the young woman seemed to have her emotions under control again, and she didn't want to upset her.

As Grace spoke, Kate half-listened to an explanation about her husband being tied up on an overseas business call, and she'd likely dine alone. The woman may have elaborated further, but Kate couldn't be certain.

"Well," Grace said, glancing at her watch. "I don't want to take any more of your time. I see you're waiting for someone."

Instantly, thoughts of Cody invaded Kate's mind, and a surge of adrenalin raced through her. Something had to be wrong. She was seconds away from revealing this to Grace when the familiar bars of "Peaceful Easy Feeling" played on her phone.

"Excuse me for a moment, Grace." Kate grabbed her phone from the table then stood. "I've been waiting for this call." Walking briskly toward the women's room, she answered en route.

"Cody, give me a second." Holding the phone to her chest, Kate stepped inside the women's room and peered under the stalls, which were, thankfully, unoccupied. If he was okay, boy-oh-boy, was she going to give him a thorough tongue-lashing.

Returning the phone to her ear, Kate tried to still her pounding heart. "Are you all right?" Silence greeted her question. She paced back and forth in front of the basins, catching haphazard glimpses of the worried expression etched across her face as she passed each of the gold-framed mirrors hung above the sinks.

Puzzled by no response, she asked more urgently. "Cody, talk to me."

A faint noise snagged her attention. Stopping in front of the far sink, Kate pressed the phone to her ear and covered her other ear with her free hand. Her strategy worked because now she could hear more from the other end of the phone. A moan, followed by a woman's voice repeating the same thing over and over, "Don't stop, Cody."

The words washed over her like a tsunami, and she slumped against the wall. Powerless to end the call, tears streamed down Kate's cheeks. Her stomach clenched. The emotions see-sawed between nausea at having her worst fear confirmed and thankfulness she would no longer be one of those wives who hadn't a clue about their husband's fidelity. She loosely cradled the phone to her ear and listened to a vile exchange no wife should ever have to hear involving her husband. Visions of Cody in the throes of passion with a faceless woman plagued her mind. The woman must have gripped Cody in such a way as to trigger the lethal pocket dial. In the past, Cody had apologized for the occasional pocket-dials. They'd even laughed about her overhearing fatherly lectures to Blake on alcohol and partying, but at the same time, she'd cautioned Cody to be more vigilant and suggested he keep his phone in his shirt pocket.

All at once, the lights dimmed, and the room spun. The phone fell from Kate's limp hand to the floor, shattering the screen against the hard tile. She slid down the lavatory wall in slow motion, wilting against its surface. The outer door to the restroom opened. Someone walked in, but she couldn't make out the person.

"Katelyn, are you hurt?" Grace knelt beside her. "What can I do for you?"

Kate fought to stay conscious as the darkness pulled at her. "God sent you. He knew I'd need help," she said as the room spun into darkness.

Chapter Six

Cody lay motionless on his back in the full-sized bed; his head turned to one side. The Blu-ray player on a dresser a few feet away caught his attention, and he blinked back burning tears. Disgust tightened his throat as Chelsea slept with her head on his bare chest. The scent of her rose perfume infused the small room. What initially stirred desire now assaulted his nostrils with a repugnant smell. Ending up here had been a colossal mistake—one he'd pay for with his marriage if Kate found out.

He closed his eyes in hopes of refocusing his thoughts, but an image of Kate in her wedding dress crippled the effort. Unable to form the beginning of a prayer, tears trailed down the sides of his face in a fiery blaze. *Kate can never find out about this—never.*

Cody gently eased Chelsea's head from his chest onto her pillow. He inched over to the edge of the bed then slowly sat up. She muttered something. As if tugged by an invisible chain, he glanced over his shoulder to see if she was talking in her sleep. Her open eyes snagged his. He didn't ask her to repeat her words because there wasn't a reply to give; nothing said would make their time together right. Perhaps she already knew this, as her eyes darkened with an emotion he couldn't label.

The longer he looked at her, the more he identified with her. He wanted to turn away, but the truth continued to unfold—a "do whatever makes you happy because you only live once." The motto now sickened him. She rolled away with her back to him. After several seconds, he stood, thankful she had faced away from him. In the quiet, maybe she'd fallen back to sleep. Better to avoid saying goodbye and inflicting more damage.

Once dressed, Cody stood beside the bed. The honorable thing to do on her behalf would be to own up to the truth—Chelsea hadn't forced anything. Cody took a step back. If he dared to confess he'd wanted to be alone with her, she might toss aside the sheet and invite him back into bed. As shameful as it was to admit, the temptation would be difficult to resist. The visible curve of her hip lured him into taking a step forward, but he stopped himself. The longer he stood there, the more his body would betray him.

Leave. Do it now.

Cody grabbed his phone off the bedside table and dashed out of Chelsea's apartment. The battery had died on his cell. His watch revealed nearly eleven. He'd charge the phone on his way home and touch base with Blake before trying to reach Kate—if she'd accept his call.

She undoubtedly tried to get a hold of him when he hadn't shown up at the restaurant. Once she couldn't reach him, she would've likely called Blake. Then again, Kate might have assumed the gun deal took longer than expected and gone home angry.

Outside Chelsea's apartment building, Cody paused on the top step of the landing. The parking lot glistened with the remnants of an unexpected rain shower. He drew in a deep breath of crisp air, zippered his lightweight jacket then sprinted in the mist toward his Jeep.

Several small puddles dotted the asphalt, and he sidestepped each, thinking if only he'd avoided Chelsea. Standing next to the driver's door, Cody depressed the alarm to unlock it but didn't immediately open the door. Instead, he craned his neck toward the night sky. "This is the worst thing I've ever done in my life. How do I recover from this one, God? How?"

His heartbeat in anticipation, perhaps tonight of all nights, God's love and mercy, would envelop him. In its place, a crushing wave of guilt washed over him. "Lord, you say you will never leave us or forsake us. Where were you tonight? As a matter of fact, where were you all those nights leading up to this?"

He shook his head, disgusted by his actions—and for expecting something different from God. He snatched the Jeep door open, climbed inside, and started the engine. As the motor idled, he plugged in his cell phone to charge. Unable to face going home, he sat staring out across the parking lot.

"Lord, if Kate finds out about this, it will crush her heart, and it will be the end of my marriage." He clenched his fist then slammed it against the steering wheel repeatedly. "Yes, I did it. Me. Me. Me. Is that what you're waiting to hear? I don't deserve to be married, and I certainly don't deserve a wife like Kate." He sobbed. "My brother is right, Kate's special. She's too good for me."

He collapsed forward onto the wheel and wept. "I can't keep this from her." Each time he tried to speak, garbled words came out, followed by a deeper ache. Finally, he melted back into his seat and stared at the roof. "God, please help me tell her everything."

###

"Yo-ho-ho and a bottle of rum, sorry I missed your call. Leave a message. I'll get back to you." Cody tapped his fingers against his thigh while listening to the remainder of Blake's phone greeting. How he wished he were at home in bed with Kate, instead of seated behind the steering wheel of his Jeep not knowing where to go or what to do.

After the beep, Cody spoke, "Call me." He ended the message and clasped the back of his neck with both hands. He massaged the tight muscles, working his way down to his shoulders.

When his cell phone lit up on the dash, he looked at the screen before answering. His body relaxed, viewing the caller ID. Thankfully, it was Blake.

Cody answered the call using the speaker function. "Are you at home?"

"Well, hello to you, too."

"Did you hear me? I said, are you at home?"

"I heard you. Where else would I be this time of the night?" Blake chuckled. "Don't answer. Yeah, I'm at home. Why?"

"Good." Cody put the Jeep into reverse as he spoke. "Are you alone?" He caught one last glimpse of Chelsea's apartment building as he exited the parking lot, and his stomach clenched.

"Kind of..."

"What's that mean?" Cody gripped the steering wheel. "Is Kate there?"

"Kate! What would she be doing here at almost midnight?"

"So, Kate's not with you?" He relaxed his grip on the wheel.

"No, she's not with me. Where are you? What's going on?"

Cody blew out a long breath. His banter at the pawnshop with Chelsea came back in a rush and jumbled his thinking. If only he hadn't mentioned her perfume and jokingly agreed to help freshen it back at her place. "It's complicated. I—"

"Bro, say it ain't so." Blake exhaled heavily into the phone. "You didn't hook up with Black Dress. Did you?"

"I'm on the way to your place. I need to get my head together before I talk with Kate."

"Wait! You haven't talked to Kate?" Blake groaned. "I had a feeling something might go south between you and Chelsea. I don't blame you for enjoying a little attention from a hot girl, but I didn't think you'd play backseat bingo with her."

"Now, who's sounding like dad?" Cody shoved thoughts of his father aside. He'd sworn he wouldn't follow in the man's footsteps, yet the choice tonight could mirror what happened between his folks—divorce.

"Hold on! Did you say you're coming here? You can't come here."

"Why?" Cody slowed the Jeep for a red light. "I'm less than ten minutes away. What do you mean I can't come over? You're my brother. I need you. Think of all the times I've been there for you!"

"I'm not alone. I'm watching a friend's kid so she can work tonight."

"You're babysitting? Heaven help the child." Cody thumped the steering wheel. "That came out wrong."

"It didn't come out wrong. You meant what you said. There's a Bible verse about what's in the heart comes out of the mouth. I'm sure you know it better than your heathen brother."

Blake snickered. "Then again, speaking of heathen, I'm not the married man stepping out on his wife. Look, my suggestion is you go home. Best bet, cross your fingers Kate has written this off as another one of your no-shows. She might even be asleep, and if she is, don't wake her to spill your guts and ease your conscience."

The light turned green, and Cody punched the gas. "As many times as I've rescued you, you're going to bail on me now. Fine. Who needs you? You are just like dad. You do what you want when you want, and blame God for the fallout."

"Bro, news flash, we're both more like Dad than either one of us wants to admit."

"Thanks for nothing." Cody hung up. "And you're like dad, not me!" He spotted a police cruiser parked along the side of the road and eased off the gas pedal. He'd only had one glass of wine, which was hours ago, but the way things were going, he'd be pulled over and fail a sobriety test.

As he turned onto his street, the memory of Kate making coffee this morning caused a lump to settle in his throat. "Lord, I'm asking this for Kate more than I am for myself. Help me. Protect my marriage. I'll change. I'll be and do anything you want. Just please, please don't let my marriage end."

Chapter Seven

Cody pressed the remote for the garage door to open on their single-story home. While he waited for it to ascend, potential scenarios of what to expect when he walked into the house past midnight flitted through his mind—Kate, asleep in bed and thus spared the heartache of betrayal until morning or Kate awake and worried about his safety. Although she'd called him more than once, she had surprisingly only left one message a little past seven-thirty to ask about his eta to the restaurant.

The garage door rose, but in place of Kate's car sat two suitcases. He drew his head back in bewilderment. Seeing the luggage, spotlighted by his headlights, was odd enough, but then his attention shifted to other parts of the garage.

He squinted at his shirts exploding out of two large trash bags, with more clothes spilling onto the concrete floor. He swallowed hard. Did Blake rat him out?

Cody didn't pull into the garage but killed the engine with the Jeep partway into the space. He stared at his belongings, staggered by the extent of Kate's anger. This was about more than him coming home late. She knew. She's not even home. Why bother going inside? Still, he had to make sure.

He climbed out of the Jeep and entered the house through the utility door. Inside, the kitchen was dark, but rather than turn on any lights, he navigated through the living spaces and headed for the hallway leading to the master bedroom. Cody's booming heartbeat reverberated in his ears as he spotted a light shining from underneath the closed door onto the tiled hallway. On the short walk toward their bedroom, images of Kate, wild-eyed, throwing things and demanding a divorce, riddled his thoughts. He reached for the doorknob but quickly withdrew his hand as his wife's voice filtered through the door. Unable to make out more than his name, Cody pressed his ear against the wood. It was no use. Kate spoke in a hushed tone. Maybe she knew he had come home and didn't want him walking in on her telephone conversation. More than likely, it was her best friend, Sandie, she'd confided in. He took a deep breath, gripped the door handle, and with an exhale that burst from his lungs, eased open the door and entered.

Of all the possibilities he'd entertained on the drive home, he hadn't imagined this one. His wife struggling to get one corner of a fitted sheet over their mattress as an unfamiliar woman tugged on the other side. Cody's gaze darted from Kate to the stranger, then back to Kate.

"It's about time you showed up." Kate finished her task. "I was beginning to think you weren't coming home." She walked close enough to poke him in the chest with her index finger. "Where have you been?"

He glanced over Kate's shoulder at the blonde, who had made her way from the bed to the chaise lounge by the window and took a seat. Surely, Kate didn't expect an explanation in front of a total stranger.

"Kate, since your husband is home now, I think I should leave." The woman grabbed a pair of high heels beside the chaise. She slipped her feet into them while keeping her face turned down.

Cody studied the much younger woman in hopes of recalling how they knew one another, but there was zero recognition, so he turned his attention back to Kate. "Who is—"

"Allow me to introduce you, Cody." Kate faced the window. "Grace, this is my cheating husband, Cody James."

Despite his best intentions, anger rose. "Now wait a minute—"

"No. You wait a minute." Kate whirled and locked eyes with him. "I never understood why you didn't want me talking about any aspect of our lives with others. Now I know. It's because you wanted to keep people at arm's length so they wouldn't discover the lie we're living."

"Katelyn, please let's not have this conversation now." He tried to rest his hand on her shoulder, but she smacked it off and stomped over to the woman on the chaise.

"Grace, you don't have to leave. I don't know what I would've done had you not been at the restaurant." Kate glared over her shoulder at him, "You're the one leaving, Cody. Not her." She arched her brows. "Your stuff is in the garage."

The woman stood. Her face flushed. "Cody," visibly uncomfortable, she averted her eyes while speaking to him, "maybe it would be best if you gave your wife some time to sort through things."

He cocked his head to one side and narrowed his eyes, not caring if his impatience was evident. "Excuse me, but who are you again?"

"I met your wife this evening at Ling's. She cared for my grandmother and—"

"Grace doesn't need to explain anything to you." Kate pointed to the door with a shaking finger. "I want you to leave, Cody. Now!"

"Okay, okay. I'll leave, but can I have five minutes alone with you first?" He modulated his tone. "Please."

Kate held his gaze. Tears brimmed in her eyes, but he didn't dare make a move to console her. Not that he could. She tipped her chin toward the door, suggesting they step outside of the bedroom.

"Thank you." He turned and walked out of the room, half-expecting Kate to slam the door and lock it behind him. When she joined him in the hallway, he took the lead toward the living room. Normally Kate wasn't a violent person but judging by the way she'd slung his clothes together and dumped them outside, he couldn't help feeling vulnerable.

###

Kate snatched a throw pillow off the end of the couch and plopped onto the middle sofa cushion. She hugged the pillow to her chest as a makeshift shield in hopes of warding off any affectionate apology Cody might try to make. "Say what you're going to say, then get out." She tapped her foot on the floor.

"May I," he hesitated, "sit next to you?"

"No." Kate stared into the darkness. She couldn't be sure if his voice was intentionally pitiful or if he was genuinely ashamed. It didn't matter. She could never trust him again. "And don't bother turning on a light. You like living your life in the dark."

As expected, he had nothing to say. She harrumphed. "Why so quiet now? You weren't quiet earlier when we should've been having dinner together. In case you're wondering—yes—I know what you've been up to—I heard you having sex with another woman, thanks to a pocket dial from your phone. You're disgusting."

Cody's deep inhale and protracted exhale claimed the silence in the room. "I deserve any and everything you say to me."

When he took a seat on the coffee table, facing her, she considered making a snide remark about his coming home but reasoned he might misunderstand the sarcasm and instead view it as gratitude.

"I don't get it," she said snappishly. "If you were so miserable in the marriage, why didn't you tell me? How long has this been going on? Are you..." Kate's voice broke "...in love with her?"

"No. I'm not in love with her." He leaned forward, rested his forearms on his thighs, and clasped his hands. "I made the biggest mistake of my life tonight."

"At least you didn't start off with 'I'm sorry."

The woman's lust-filled words echoed in Kate's head, piquing an unpleasant curiosity—what had attracted Cody to this other woman, big boobs and a flat stomach? She closed her eyes and tried to focus on the Bible verse written on the bathroom mirror, but the image of Cody with another woman persisted—it was as if Kate had been involuntarily transported to the room with her husband and the interloper.

Bile rose in the back of her throat. "I can't do this right now," she tossed the pillow aside and stood. "Go back to whoever she is, or stay at a hotel. I don't care. I want you gone."

Kate's stomach roiled, and she clutched her abdomen.

"Are you okay?" Cody stood, too, blocking her exit.

"You can't be serious," she lowered her voice. "Of course I'm not okay. My husband had sex with another woman and has come home like all is normal. I'll never be okay again!"

She took a step to get around him. "I… I don't feel so good." The queasiness rose quickly from her abdomen to her throat, leaving no time to cup her hands over her mouth or dash out of the room. In a flash, she heaved the contents of her stomach onto Cody's shoes. Nausea gripped her in another wave. Despite his confusion, Cody helped to steady her as she swayed back and forth. "I think I'm going to be sick again."

Kate broke free. This time she covered her mouth as she darted out of the room and down the hallway. Cody followed her into the bathroom. He stood at a distance as she leaned over the commode, dry-heaving.

"I'm sorry," he said in a raised voice. "If you want me to help in any way, just say so."

"Stop talking to me." After a few more gut-wrenching spasms, Kate righted herself and turned to him. Her eyes fixed on his. "I hate you for doing this to us."

A distant memory from their first year of marriage flickered through her mind: an early morning in bed during a chilly winter, snuggling under blankets while playing the game rock-paper-scissors, to see who would be the one to get out of bed to make coffee. Another memory from their life together coalesced in her mind's eyes: a summer evening listening to The Eagles, sipping wine, and kissing him with her eyes open because she loved seeing his handsome face.

A tear rolled down her cheek. Cody's brows creased, and emotion welled in his eyes, too. Had he read her thoughts?

He took a step toward her, reached for her waist, but she stepped back. "Do you feel any better?" The absurdity of his question was like a potent whiff of smelling salts that cleared her head of sweeter times.

Kate looked down at his hiking boots, splattered with her lunch. "You need to clean your shoes and then leave."

"I don't care about my shoes," Cody hung his head.

"Hello?" Grace called out from the other side of the partially closed bathroom door. "I'm going to head out now."

"Would you give me just a moment, Grace?" Kate locked eyes with Cody.

"Sure." Grace moved down the hallway, her high heels clacking on the tile floor.

Cody's eyes brimmed with tears again. "Let's talk privately. Okay?" His question was like a tidal wave that threatened to capsize their future. He turned his face away and sniffled hard. When he faced her again, the sorrow in his eyes had been replaced with a look of strength, but she knew better. She'd seen him respond with the same artificial strength over the death of his father.

"There's nothing to talk about." Kate moved around him and out of the bathroom. She leaned against the wall and steeled her emotions. The sour stench in the air threatened to make her sick again. "Cody, I'm going to say goodbye to Grace. I'd like you to clean up then go."

After thanking Grace and seeing her off, Kate retreated to the kitchen for a glass of cold water. She opened a cabinet near the sink to get a glass and paused. The magnitude of Cody not being here later in the morning hit. She spotted the coffee maker on the counter and fought back the tears. Such an incidental thing like handing him a cup of coffee and telling him "Have a good day" may never happen again. For the first time since the revelation of the other woman, the idea he could end up with this interloper surfaced and triggered the obvious question. *Does Cody love this person?*

Kate called out to him as she made her way back to the bathroom. Maybe she had been rash in her decision to have him leave. She hadn't even prayed about it. Since she'd gotten home with Grace, all she'd done was vent. Well, that and strip the bed—the last thing she wanted to do in his absence was breathe in the scent of his tea tree oil shampoo.

"Cody?" She stepped into the bathroom. Kate's shoulders wilted at the sight of the empty room. He hadn't even bothered to say goodbye, let alone fight for her. He had fled the conflict by escaping out the front door instead of going through the kitchen.

No mistaking it, he chose to avoid her.

Chapter Eight

Cody knocked on the front door of his brother's second-story apartment. No answer. He leaned in and listened for any sounds on the other side of the door. Quiet. He knocked again, this time a little harder. No response. Either Blake was sound asleep, or he chose to ignore him.

Light rain covered Cody's face as he sprinted back to his Jeep. He chirped the alarm, climbed inside, and locked the doors. Reclined in the seat, the turn of events that landed him in this mess replayed in his mind.

His chest tightened. He took a guarded breath and tried to dismiss the likelihood of an anxiety attack. Cody eased the driver's seat up halfway, but the tightness in his chest persisted. He closed his eyes focused on the breathing technique to help settle the mounting anxiety, but the image of a boa constrictor devouring him caused him to gasp. His controlled breaths turned shallow. In a haste to get out of the small space, he shoved open the driver's side door and set off the Jeep's alarm. The horn blared, and the lights flashed. A rush of adrenaline surged through his body as he fumbled for the keys in the console. At last, his fingers closed over the keys, and he pushed the button to disarm the system.

Cody got out of the Jeep and leaned against the vehicle. He sucked in a cleansing breath. Had it not been for the constant light rain, he'd have opted for a few more minutes of fresh air. Instead, he reluctantly got back inside the Jeep. At least the anxiety attack had resolved itself in the few chaotic seconds of dealing with the alarm. He slumped in the driver's seat and hung his head. He'd made a mess of everything and not just tonight. When he finally looked up, someone stood a few feet away from the hood of the Jeep. Cody leaned into the steering wheel and peered through rain droplets on the windshield as his brother came into view.

Blake motioned for Cody to follow him then headed back toward the two-story building. Cody trailed his brother up the stairs and into the one-bedroom apartment.

"A word of caution," Blake said in a hushed voice, "we need to keep it down. The kid's in my bedroom. He only fell asleep an hour ago. Trust me. You don't want to wake him if you get my drift."

Cody gently shut the front door behind him. "The kid?"

"I told you I was watching a friend's kid, so she could work tonight."

"I forgot." He followed Blake to the small kitchen with its black paint and no windows but stopped short of entering to avoid feeling claustrophobic.

Blake cast a sideways glance at him as he filled a small pot with tap water. "And before you say anything, I'm not helping her with her kid so I can get her into bed. She's a nice girl. She just doesn't have anyone to give her a hand."

"I wasn't going to say anything." Cody rested his shoulder against the doorjamb. "I'm in no position to judge you or anyone else."

Blake placed the pot on the stove. "I hate to burst your bubble," he turned on the flame for a back burner, "but you've never been in a position to judge anyone."

"Here we go," Cody righted himself. He stepped into the kitchen but maintained enough space between Blake and himself so as not to feel boxed in. "Your understanding of judging isn't biblical. Christians are called to recognize ungodly choices, but we're not to condemn people for their ungodly choices."

Cody eyeballed the kitchen walls. "Look around you. Ever since you walked away from your faith, you've been dabbling in spiritual death."

"Ha—" Blake faced him and scowled. "You're going to talk to me about ungodly choices when you cheated on Kate." He took a step toward Cody. "I suggest you examine your own actions before you start throwing stones my way, big brother."

"Oh, yeah?" Cody narrowed the gap between them, his adrenaline spiking as his body tensed. "Or else what?"

"You don't want to find out." Blake's jaw clenched, and his lean chest heaved.

"Go ahead," Cody grunted. "You wanna take a swing at me? Do it? I figure Kate wants to slug me for being with another woman, so you'd be doing her a favor."

"Wait." Blake's posture relaxed. "Let me get this straight." He reclined against the counter and rested his palms on either side of him. "She knows?"

"Yes, she knows. At first, I thought you said something but she—"

"Me? Why would you think I told her? I'm the one who said keep it to yourself, for her sake as well as yours."

"She found out the worst way possible." Cody rubbed his bristled chin. "Kate heard me with Chelsea thanks to a pocket dial from my phone. I mean, she heard everything." He pointed to the pot on the stove, "Your boiling water is going to evaporate."

Blake turned off the flame under the pot. "Wow. I was going to offer you coffee, but I think you could use something stronger."

"It wouldn't solve anything. Besides, you're babysitting."

Blake opened a cabinet and grabbed two cups. He added a heaping spoonful of instant coffee to each one then poured hot water from the pot into the first cup. "No sugar, right?"

"Hasn't changed," Cody said, regretting his tone.

Blake set the empty pot back on the stove. He pointed to Cody, "Let's go into the living room."

Cody led the few steps into the living room. The black paint made him feel as though he was being buried alive for his indiscretion. He took a seat at the far end of a zebra print futon. Blake turned on a light before joining him on the opposite end of the makeshift sofa. The instant coffee reminded Cody of vending machine brews, but he took a sip anyway. It tasted as horrible as he recalled. His face puckered. What he wouldn't give to be at home, in his own bed, waking next to Kate in the morning and sharing a cup of dark roast coffee.

He would be the most thankful husband on earth.

Cody set his cup on the end table. "Why do you subject yourself and your guests to this barbaric drink?"

"Did you come here to rag on me?" Blake shot him an exasperated look. "I'm assuming Kate tossed your sorry butt out, or you wouldn't be here. If you want my advice—"

"Advice!" Cody laughed, "From you?"

"Shhh, you're going to wake the kid."

"Don't shush me." Cody turned sharply to face Blake. "Who do you think you're talking to?" His voice rose even higher. "I'm not one of your party-buddies."

The wounded look in Blake's eyes was deflating Cody as quickly as the anger had puffed him up. He ached to take back his words. Blake no more deserved his outrage than Kate. "I'm sorry—"

"Save it." The hurt in Blake's eyes flashed to anger. He set his cup on the coffee table hard, spilling the liquid.

"Bro, I'm sick of your high and mighty attitude." Blake walked over to the door and held it open. He made a sweeping gesture. "Just because you're my older brother doesn't give you the right to speak to me any way you want. Get out!"

###

Kate stared at the clock on Cody's side of the bed. Nearly 3:00 a.m. Grace had been so sweet to offer to stay the night, but there was no way she would keep her new friend from her husband a moment longer.

Husband, reality landed another blow. Cody had discarded his wedding vows. She rolled onto her back and broke down sobbing, which turned to wailing. Kate muffled the sound with his pillow.

Several minutes later, she uncovered her face. "God, why did he do this to me?"

She swiped at her tears with a corner of the sheet. His unfaithfulness played in her mind like a nightmare. Surely, any moment she'd wake, shuffle down to the home office, rap on the closed door, and voilà, he would appear.

But he wasn't down the hall in the office—she'd kicked him out of their home.

Kate rolled onto her side. She drew her legs into a fetal potion and closed her eyes. In the midst of the pain, a Bible verse landed in her thoughts: "Be still and know that I am God" (Psalm 46:10).

Hope washed over her helping to soothe her battered soul. More tears fell, but this time with a quiet acceptance. Cody's betrayal hadn't been a surprise to God, which helped to cement God, had a plan.

As she continued to lay there, several different responsibilities clamored for attention, but the one that gripped her thoughts was calling out for work. Besides being emotionally unable to meet the needs of her seniors today, she didn't have a car to get to work. Compiling a mental to-do list might help to take her mind off Cody—at least temporarily.

Task number two: Call Sandie. She'd share about discovering Cody's unfaithfulness last night. About meeting Grace and how the woman drove her home and stayed with her until Cody arrived.

Task number three: Coordinate a time with Sandie to pick up her vehicle from Ling's. The owner hadn't questioned Kate's tears or why another customer assisted her out of the ladies' room. He had even volunteered to follow them to the parking lot and held their purses. He assured Kate her car would not be towed and she could pick it up the following day. How foolish she must have looked being led like a distraught child out of the restaurant. Even now, her cheeks burned with embarrassment. She tried to think of something else to distance herself from the mental picture.

A box of gourmet chocolates flashed in her minds-eye. Kate sat up in bed. She would not give in. Once that temptation had been rejected, another reared its head. Cody's absence in bed tugged at her thoughts. After a few victorious seconds of resisting the urge to look over at the empty space and feel sorry for herself, she succumbed and touched his pillow. Kate traced an outline of the place his head should rest with her fingertips as she nibbled her bottom lip.

If only she'd suggested meeting him at the pawnshop instead of the restaurant, maybe all this heartache could've been avoided. He had asked her several times to come by the shop to see the improvements made to accommodate firearms, but guns interested her as much as boxes of chocolates interested him. Clearly, they had grown apart. Pinning down when it happened was ambiguous.

She couldn't recall the last time they had sat and talked about their day at work without it turning into a competition over whose job had been more challenging. As for lovemaking, sexual intimacy was practically non-existent. When sex did happen, the absence of passion had reduced it to a physical release. Church attendance for Cody had also become sporadic due to his wanting at least one day to sleep in. Lately, she'd fallen victim to justifying her absence based on his non-attendance.

Still seated upright, she drew her knees to her chest and wrapped her arms around them. Most divorces were a result of couples growing apart, with one or both of the spouses citing they had fallen out of love. Part of the breakdown in their marriage had to be her fault. Didn't it?

Kate flung Cody's pillow across the room. No one put a gun to his head and made him sleep with another woman. If he was unhappy, he could've said so. It's not like she hadn't tried time and time again to get him to share his feelings with her. She stomped over to the vanity area of the bathroom. Even in the dark, the Bible verse written on the mirror remained illuminated in her mind's eye.

"I can do all things through Christ who strengthens me," she said softly. Kate flipped on the light switch and repeated the words. At first, she recited the verse in the same soft voice, yet each time she repeated the passage, her voice became stronger and louder. "I can do all things through Christ who strengthens me!"

Kate walked over and snatched her purse from the doorknob to the walk-in closet. She removed her wallet and opened the credit card section, then inched the candy coupon free from between two credit cards. She tore the coupon into pieces then dropped them into the toilet. One flush and the temptation disappeared in a swirl and gurgle as the water drained. Kate returned to the vanity area and locked eyes with herself in the mirror.

"I hate what he's done, God." She studied her reflection in spite of the ache in her throat, red-rimmed eyes, and messy hair.

Thoughts banded together into one certainty. *I don't want to be married anymore.*

Chapter Nine

Cody sprayed glass cleaner on the gun display case and rubbed at smudges with a paper towel rather than look at his brother. Trying to sleep in an office chair had put a crick in Cody's perspective as well as his neck.

"I'm sorry about kicking you out of my apartment," Blake sidled alongside Cody and picked up the roll of paper towels. "I can finish this for you."

Cody pointedly glanced at the wall clock then snorted. "You're supposed to be here at eight."

Blake shifted his feet in place. "It's eight-fifteen. I'm only a few minutes late."

The lame excuse was all Cody needed to release his pent-up anger. "You're late almost every day." He clenched his jaw. "Am I supposed to ignore it because it's only fifteen minutes?"

"This isn't about me being late. We both know it." Blake drummed his fingers on the counter. "You've helped me out more times than I can count. I should've been there for you."

"Should've, would've..." Cody bit back the rest of his response. Blake was right. The anger wasn't about Blake refusing to help or even Kate throwing him out, but rather the stupid choice made to get involved with Chelsea.

"About being late, you're right. And oversleeping is no excuse." Blake's bloodshot eyes caught Cody's attention for the first time.

Cody merely grunted and sprayed more cleaner on the glass counter. He wasn't ready to let on he'd already forgiven him and not just for being late.

"How about I make my big bro some coffee? You look like you could use it. I know I could." He cracked a smile. "I won't be so quick to babysit again."

"Thanks, but I've already had three cups." He continued to hold Blake's gaze. "Just a heads-up, I'm going to call Mom and ask about staying with her for a while. It's not like she doesn't have the room and I—"

"Mom?" Blake snatched the spray bottle from Cody's hand and held it protectively against his chest. "You've been breathing too much cleaner."

Cody furrowed his brows. He didn't have the patience for jokes today.

"Bro, seriously, please tell me you're kidding."

"Why would I be kidding? Mom's going to find out what's happened anyway. Better she hears it from me first." He held out his hand for the bottle. "Give it back. I've got work to do."

"Calling her is a bad idea." Blake set the bottle of glass cleaner on the counter out of Cody's reach then pushed Cody to a stool at the far end of the display case.

"Sit. Mom's going to go ballistic if you tell her you cheated on Kate. In case you haven't taken notice, our mother is not only a Jesus-freak, she's president of the Almighty's fan club."

"Better not let her hear you—not if you want to remain in the will." Cody gave his brother a playful shove as he rose from the stool. "After all these years, your twisted sense of humor has finally rubbed off on me."

Blake leaned back against the counter. "Are you going to listen or not?"

"Sure, go ahead." Cody folded his arms across his chest. "Make it quick."

Blake righted himself. "If I was you, I wouldn't tell Mom what's going on right now in your marriage. And if Kate was my wife, I'd ask her to keep things between me and her."

"Even if I didn't tell mom, do you really think Kate would agree to not say anything? I'd be surprised if Kate hasn't already called her. I know Mom better than you, and it's going to be a lot easier to digest if I feed her the news bite by bite versus Kate shoveling the whole enchilada down her throat at once."

Cody started to walk away, not wanting to continue the discussion, but Blake placed his hands on Cody's shoulders and guided him back onto the stool. "Bro, you need to trust me on this one. Given Mom's history with Dad and his cheating, she's going to side with Kate. Women stick together when it comes to stuff like this. If you don't want to end up divorced, keep her out of it."

Blake removed his hands from Cody's shoulders, "I'm done."

"You make some good points, but I don't believe Mom wants a repeat of what happened in her life for her son. Parents want better for their kids, and whatever you think about Mom and, more specifically, her faith—I trust she will have my back."

Blake rolled his eyes. "Take off your rose-colored glasses."

Cody chuckled. "You not only sound like dad, but you're sounding like mom, too. Rose-colored glasses—really?"

"Okay," Blake shook his head. "You've been warned."

"Duly noted, and I appreciate it." Cody stood, sidestepping Blake, "I'll be in my office. I'm going to talk to Mom before any more time passes. About that coffee, I've changed my mind. I'm going to make a pot, so if you want a cup, help yourself."

"You'll regret telling mom," Blake called after him.

Cody turned to his brother, who made a praying hands gesture and flicked a comical gaze upward. He often traced Blake's stunted maturity to the time of Mom and Dad's divorce. A child needs a father, and a boy, who lacks a positive male role model during his early developmental stages, is likely to challenge adult males later in life. Hence, Blake's near-constant friction with Cody. Although he'd tried to step into a fatherly role, Blake wouldn't have it. He was too angry with the adults in his life. Besides, the fifteen-year age difference between them translated into Cody being viewed as another grownup who couldn't be trusted.

Blake chuckled, "You'll be sorrrrry."

"I'll risk it," Cody paused, knowing he should do more to mend the growing rift between them. "Hey, for the record, I really do appreciate your looking out for me. I'm sorry about last night, too. I said some things out of anger I shouldn't have."

"Don't worry about it." Blake waved him off.

"Thanks." He might as well offer another olive branch. "I'm going to invite Mom to meet me for lunch this afternoon to tell her what's going on." He paused a few seconds to reevaluate, including Blake, and recognized he could use the emotional support. "Do you want to join us?"

"Sure," Blake grinned.

"What's with the look?" Cody braced himself for a wacky comeback.

"After Mom is done thumping your head with her Bible, you're going to need me to take you to the hospital."

"You're twisted." Cody cracked a smile. "You know that, right?" He'd allowed himself to relax for the first time this morning

Blake pointed at Cody, then himself, "It takes a twisted person to know a twisted person."

"Yeah, yeah. So you're coming?"

Blake nodded. "I wouldn't pass up an invitation to tell you 'I told you so' for nothing."

Cody walked away, second-guessing his decision to call his mother. Sometimes Blake could be spot on in his observations. He'd mull it over a bit longer.

In his office, he unlocked the gun safe nearest his desk and retrieved the metal case with the three pistols he'd purchased from Mr. Kennedy. Seated at his desk, he opened the gun case, enjoying the industrial smell of cleaning lubricant that attested to well-kept weapons. He studied engraving on the frame and cylinder of the Navy Colt. He'd list the guns for a nice profit and dedicate all of the proceeds toward conventional firearms for the shop's inventory.

As he replaced the Colt, he noticed a sliver of white paper wedged between the velvet lining and metal box. Cody tugged gently on the paper, but it didn't come free. Using his pocket knife, he carefully pushed the lining away from the side of the case.

His curiosity piqued as he extracted the folded slip of paper. Faint handwriting scrawled across the front of a small square of folded notepaper. Not a receipt. He squinted as he attempted to make out the words. Love, Beatrice.

Cody held the paper up to the light but couldn't decipher lines of script on the inside. Only opening it would satisfy his curiosity, but he couldn't bring himself to read something so personal.

He retrieved his cell phone from the corner of his desk. He'd call Mr. Kennedy to let him know about the note, and then he'd call Ada. Cody located the saved number and pressed dial.

Curiosity as to the message bore down on him as he waited for the call to connect, but he resisted.

"Hello, this is Marty."

"Good morning, Mr. Kennedy." Cody sat tall in the chair. "This is Cody James from the pawnshop."

"Good morning, Mr. James. What can I do for you?"

"Well, sir, I was just admiring the pistols and—"

Blake approached the open office door with his coffee cup. Cody motioned with his free hand for him to enter.

"Who are you talking to?" Blake mouthed as he pointed to the phone.

"Mr. James, you still there?" the old man said.

"Yes, I'm here," Cody stammered. "Forgive me, could you hold for a moment?"

Cody muted the call. "I'm talking to the seller from yesterday. Get your coffee and go. I'd like some privacy." He motioned to the door. Thankfully Blake got his coffee then left.

"I'm sorry, Mr. Kennedy. I discovered a note tucked between the lining and the gun case. On the front, it reads, 'Love, Beatrice.' I believe that's your wife's name, right?"

"You're correct. A note you say? Did you read it?"

"No." His face warmed at having been tempted. "Would you like to pick it up?"

"I would indeed. May I come now?" The man's enthusiasm pricked Cody's heart. The passion in Mr. Kennedy's voice stirred regret in how easily he'd neglected Kate.

"Sure. You can come by now."

"Good. I should be there in about twenty minutes."

Cody thought perhaps the old man had hung up, but Mr. Kennedy added, "I'm surprised Beatrice would tuck something inside the case. You see, my wife wanted nothing to do with any guns."

###

Kate pushed her half-eaten lunch entrée of chicken chow mein aside. "Sandie, thank you again for taking your lunch break to drive me here." She leaned across the table. "Do you think the staff knows what happened last night?"

"I seriously doubt they know anything about the incident." She smiled. "When we came inside, the young man who seated us complimented you on how pretty you look today, but you were busy rummaging in your purse. I don't think you even heard him."

"He did?" Kate had thrown herself together this morning and found it hard to believe anyone would find her appearance worthy of a compliment. "What did he say?"

"He said you have a beautiful smile."

"I'm glad he couldn't tell it was forced." Kate reached for the cloth napkin in her lap and dabbed her eyes as tears welled once more. "Here I go again."

"Why are you crying?" Sandie's brows furrowed. "Consider that stupid question number one—I'm allowed ten for the day, remember?"

Kate sniffled. "I remember." She blotted her nose. "I came up with the rule during our freshman year of college."

"Yes, you did." Sandie reached across the table and rested her hand on Kate's forearm, her own eyes glistening. "I'm sorry Cody did this to you."

Kate looked around the room, thankful only a few other customers occupied the restaurant. "I've had a feeling he was up to something for years. I kept talking myself out of it."

"Really?" Sandie's eyes widened. "What made you think so?"

Kate sat back. "Little things, like all the time he spends on the computer at home and how he logs off whenever I enter the room." Allowing her suspicions to spill out was freeing, so she continued in hopes of further release from the self-doubt that plagued her for years.

"Those racy women's posters at the pawnshop, another red flag. I understand they're supposedly modeling the guns, but c'mon, Cody is a Christian, yet he sees nothing wrong with having pictures of nearly naked women at his place of business. The posters are a big part of the reason I rarely go to the shop. I don't like them, but if I say anything negative, we'll get into an argument."

"Kate. I'm certainly not going to defend Cody, but—"

"There's more." Once Kate had started to piece together the puzzle, although unsettling, she couldn't stop. "Cody's dad cheated on his mom from the beginning of their marriage. I only know this from talking with his mom. She said her husband was addicted to pornography. She also said she suspected it long before his affair, which ended their marriage."

Sandie shook her head. "Why haven't you told me about any of this before today?"

"Cody doesn't like me talking about our marriage with anyone, and especially you."

"I'm not surprised. He knows I'm not a fan." Sandie shook her head. "Sorry, but I've always thought you got taken in by his good looks and gave him too many free passes when it comes to how he treats you."

Kate's guardedness throughout the marriage now pushed to the background; she refused to let fear stop her from asking Sandie for help. "How would you feel about putting your college computer hacking skills to a test? I want to know what Cody's been up to online. I can't help but think it's connected to this woman and maybe others."

Sandie frowned, "No way am I getting involved."

"Why?" The need to know if Cody had cheated before last night became the driving force behind her pursuit of truth.

"For one, Cody already dislikes me—"

"Sandie, I have to find out how far back this goes. I can't do it by myself. It's not like I haven't asked him about fidelity in our marriage in the past. I can't trust what he says nowadays, so I want you to help me find out."

Sandie's posture stiffened. "You're asking me to spy on your husband." She shook her head. "Let's say I agree, and we don't discover anything, then you two work it out and get back together."

"I've already decided I don't want to work on the marriage." As much as Kate had hoped for things to be like they were at the beginning of the relationship, truth had uncovered problems that ran deep—deeper than the computer images of other women and his long hours at the shop. Cody appeared to be mirroring his father, which scared Kate into facing the truth—the marriage was over.

Sandie stared across the room. "I think this is a bad idea."

Their waiter appeared at the table and smiled at Kate, then bowed. "Would you like a take-home container?"

"Yes, please." She returned his smile. "Thank you."

He faced Sandie. "Would you like to order anything else?"

"No, thank you. Could you please bring the check?'

"Actually, I'd like some coffee." Kate shot Sandie a glance then turned her focus back to the waiter. "Make it two coffees, please—one black for my friend and one with cream for me."

Sandie raised her eyebrows. "Coffee?"

Kate nudged her under the table with her foot. "Yes, coffee, we have time." She read the name tag pinned to his white dress shirt. "Thank you, Chao."

The waiter smiled and bowed again. "I will be right back."

Sandie glared at Kate. "I won't do it. I don't think you're ready to deal with what I might find."

"I disagree. If I'm wrong and it proves to be too much to handle, then God and you will help me process whatever information is uncovered."

Chao returned to the table. He set the cups of coffee before them along with a bamboo basket that held containers of cream and sugar. He placed a take-home container next to Kate's uneaten entrée and laid the bill on the table between them.

Kate waited until he'd gone before resuming the conversation. "I know this isn't the best way to get to the truth, but it's obvious after last night Cody won't come clean."

"Probably not," Sandie cringed. "If I were married, and this happened to me, I know you'd be there in any way you could."

"So, you'll help me?" Kate's kept her expression as neutral as possible even though her heart pounded.

"Yes, I'll help you." Her shoulders sagged." I feel like I'm going to regret this, but like I said, I know you'd be there for me."

"Thank you. Thank you." Kate took a deep breath and exhaled audibly. "So, how will you do it? He keeps his laptop with him practically twenty-four seven."

"Chances are he's got a backup of passwords on your home computer."

Kate saw a sparkle of interest in Sandie's eyes as she outlined how to infiltrate Cody's online world. "What if you can't find them?"

"I'll find them as long as the file isn't protected. It will take a little more work if I don't have access to his laptop, but even if his files are protected, most people use a combination of loved one's names and special dates to secure their information."

Kate's conscience pricked by this backdoor method triggered a gut reaction to withdraw the request. Yet the idea of unearthing the truth about Cody's activities in the home office all those late nights muzzled her conscience. "I have confidence in you."

Sandie pushed her untouched coffee cup aside. "My lunch break is over in fifteen minutes. Can we get going?"

"Yes." Kate rested her hand atop Sandie's and gave it a light squeeze. "Thank you again. I know this isn't an ethical way to get to the bottom of things, but he isn't behaving ethically."

Sandie eyed her for several seconds. "I hope you know what you're doing."

"I believe I do." Kate insisted on paying the check. In the parking lot, she set her boxed entrée on the roof of Sandie's car, leaned in, and gave her a hug. Kate broke from the embrace first.

"I'll call you after I get home from work," Sandie said. "We'll set a time for me to come over this Saturday. Wait. Valentine's Day is Saturday"

"Unless that's a problem for you," Kate said, "I'd like to go ahead with the plans for this weekend."

Sandie sighed, "Unfortunately, my social calendar is wide open."

"Then let's keep things as they are for now." Kate dipped her chin but willed her head back up and locked eyes with Sandie. "Thank you for thinking of me, but the irony of doing the search on Valentine's Day is fitting."

"If you change your mind, I'll understand."

"I'm not going to change my mind." Kate retrieved her container of food and stepped back.

Sandie got into her car and rolled down the window. She wriggled her fingers at Kate. "I'm doing this because I love you and because you made a good point about Cody not coming clean on his own."

Choked with emotion, Kate nodded her understanding.

"Call me if you need anything between now and Saturday—any time of the day or night. I mean it, I don't care if it's three in the morning. I love you, Ethel."

"I love you, Lucy." Kate waved goodbye, then climbed into her own vehicle. On the drive home, the muffled bars of "Peaceful Easy Feeling" sent a shockwave through her. Cody had taken his sweet time, waiting until after two to phone. Maybe she should ignore the call, but curiosity got the better of her. She'd hear what her lying, cheating husband had to say; then, with Sandie's help, Kate would discover what had really been going on during all these years of marriage.

Chapter Ten

"I'm surprised you answered." Cody took his cell phone off speaker and pressed it to his ear. Short, shallow sounds of Kate's breathing were his only reply. At least she hadn't hung up. His heart hammered. He tried to think of how to reveal the mistakes made and his commitment to do whatever it took to save their marriage.

He'd wait as long as it took for her to respond.

Cody covered his eyes with his free hand. God needed to help if there was any hope of saving their marriage. The thought crossed his mind to ask if it would be all right to pray, but feelings of unworthiness prevented him from doing so.

"I'm surprised I answered, too," she finally said.

Cody uncovered his eyes. "We need to talk." Place no demands on Kate; he reminded himself. "I mean—can we talk?"

Everything he'd planned to say to her on voicemail dissolved when she'd answered the call.

She sniffled. "Give me a second."

"Are you crying?" His shoulders clenched. He'd never known how to respond to Kate's tears. Her crying, whether over something he'd done or completely unrelated cut to the core of a husband knowing how to console his wife, yet he'd failed countless times.

"Gee, what makes you think I'd be crying?" Kate cleared her throat. "Hold on. I'm driving. I need to pull over."

Her sharp tone was deserved. Truth be told, he'd rather face her anger than her tears any day. He stared through the Jeep windshield as Blake and Mom embraced near the trunk of her Cadillac.

After Mom drove off, Blake approached the Jeep. Cody signaled with his index finger he needed a moment of privacy. Thankfully, Blake nodded and walked back toward the restaurant they'd had lunch at only moments ago.

"Kate," Cody broke the silence. "I want you to know I slept at the shop." He hoped to clear any assumption she might have right out of the gate. He didn't want her thinking he'd returned to the arms of the woman he had cheated on her with.

"I didn't actually sleep," he continued, "but my office is where I stayed—in case you wondered. I'm trying to do things differently by telling you what's going on without you having to ask."

His mind raced in the silence that followed. The only truly important thing was them setting a time to talk face-to-face without interruptions. He needed to explain what happened as best as he could, but not over the phone. Looking into Kate's eyes would reveal whether or not there was any hope for them staying together.

"What's next?" Her question pierced his thoughts. "Are you going to tell me all the sordid details of the past twenty-four hours? Why couldn't you have opened up to me before this happened?"

He closed his eyes and scrambled to organize his thoughts. If only the call had gone to voicemail like he had anticipated. He'd practiced what he hoped would convince Kate to agree to a face-to-face conversation. "Kate..." he blew out an exasperated breath. Who was he kidding? Anything he said was likely to come across as insincere.

"Babe, I know you're angry." He shook his head. "I meant to say. I know you're hurt, and you need time to—"

"You have no idea what I need, which is a problem," she huffed. "I wasn't going to call you, but since you called me, there is one thing I'd like to know. And I need you to be honest for once in your life."

Cody slumped forward and laid his head against the steering wheel. He'd answer as truthfully as possible, even if it shot down any hope for reconciliation with his wife. "Ask away."

###

Kate pulled into the parking lot of an appliance store and turned off the car. "I'm not an angry person. You've made me an angry person!" She lowered her voice, not wanting to give him a reason to end the call. "Did you cheat on me because you don't love me anymore?"

He would probably say he'd changed over the years, or she'd changed, or some other stupid cliché excuse for being with another woman. He might add in a rush he didn't want the marriage to end. That everything could be worked out, and she was the only woman he'd ever love. After all, that's what husbands often said when caught with another woman, but Kate had a prepared response.

Instead, Cody's silence was deafening. The answer she'd expected to hear from him didn't come. Even if he had professed his love, would it be enough to alleviate all doubts? Not likely.

"I'd like for us to talk in person," he said.

He'd skirted the question. Kate's heart dropped to her stomach, and she blinked back tears.

"I know I said you could ask me anything, and I'd be honest," Cody cleared his throat, "but there's so much I want to say and..."

She clamped her mouth closed to keep from trying to pry the words out of him. He was the one who called to talk, yet she couldn't get a coherent sentence out of him. She glanced at the dashboard clock. He had one minute to speak.

"Babe—"

"Stop calling me babe." Kate sat tall and squared her shoulders, a sense of empowerment building her resolve. "As much as I've always been the forgiving Christian, I'm not right now, so don't assume you can talk sweetly, and all is forgiven."

"Babe, I mean, Kate, you've suggested counseling for us in the past, what if we—"

"What if we go to counseling?" She cut across the words, not wanting to hear him dangle a carrot she would've jumped at this time last year. Her body tensed as past resentments gripped her thoughts. "I think it's best you see a counselor on your own. You did this to us, so you go find out why."

Cody's refusal to share his innermost thoughts had gutted their marriage, and a counselor may have helped them to do things differently a year ago, but now it was too late. Sometimes the truth hurt. But love without truth isn't love—it's fear. She'd spent far too many years walking on eggshells.

He remained quiet. Maybe he was annoyed, but she couldn't care less. She glanced at the clock. He'd better say something, and he'd better say it soon. Kate mentally ticked down what time he had left to make his point. *Five. Four. Three. Two.*

"You're right," he said. "Maybe seeing a professional will help me get to the bottom of why I made this stupid mistake. I'll do whatever it takes to save our marriage."

"Do it for you—not to save our marriage." She sucked in a deep breath and, feeling empowered, continued. "Our marriage has been in trouble for a while, but neither of us wanted to face it."

"You're right, but it takes two to make a marriage work, and it takes two when it fails."

Kate firmed her lips. He had no right to try to pin this on her. "Our marriage failed because of you. You're the one who cheated. And for the record, marriage takes three: God, husband, and wife."

"Babe, I agree, but your constant checking on me hasn't helped our relationship. I've always felt like I couldn't talk about things I was dealing with because you saw me as guilty before I—"

"Actually did anything?" Again she interrupted. Her indignation at his trying to paint her as guilty in his affair rising with each word he uttered. "You may want to rethink what you're about to say."

She rolled her head from side to side, which did little to relieve the tension that had wormed its way down her neck, and knotted the muscles between her shoulder blades. "Another thing, I've asked you not to call me babe during this conversation."

"I'm sorry," he mumbled.

Sitting tall in the seat, she caught a glimpse of her narrowed eyes in the rearview mirror. "I think we should end this conversation before either of us says something we might regret."

"All right, but..."

"But what?"

"Kate, you're entitled to be angry, and I wouldn't think of arguing the point, but I need to know—"

"Stop it, Cody. Just stop it. I'm tired of hearing what you need. Listen to yourself. I mean, really. The world doesn't revolve around you. I don't think you really understand—"

"This call was a bad idea," he interjected. "I should have given you more time before I called. I just needed...scratch that." He blew out a long breath. "No matter what I say, it won't be the right thing."

She had no desire to pray for God to help calm her emotions and every desire to continue to lash out at the man who had promised love and faithfulness. "I don't want to talk anymore."

Kate closed her eyelids tightly, the feelings of the past twenty-four hours rolling over her. Anger at Cody for his betrayal and annoyance at how much she longed for him to say he loved her fought for the upper hand in her heart. The frustration spilled over, and she muted the phone, sobbing freely.

"Kate, I love you," he said in a tone she hadn't heard since their wedding day.

She'd hoped hearing him declare his love would somehow mend what had been broken between them, but instead it spotlighted everything wrong in the marriage.

Chapter Eleven

A marriage and family counseling office was the last place Cody would've pictured himself this morning. After the conversation with Kate yesterday had gone so poorly, Cody reached out to their pastor, who suggested Dr. Samantha Novak.

Thankful to be the last patient before lunch, the empty waiting room didn't seem as intimidating as he'd expected. He turned another page in the magazine. Unable to focus on an article about hybrid cars, he placed the magazine back on the table in front of him. Apparently, this doctor had helped other couples who were a signature away from divorce. While the pastor didn't reveal specifics about the other couples, he did share that pornography had played a role in some of the marriages. Even now, shame warmed the back of Cody's neck and made his palms sweaty over having told the pastor everything. He ran his hands down his pant legs as he checked the time by a clock on the wall behind the receptionist's desk—ten minutes until his appointment time at eleven.

The receptionist, a mature woman, who reminded him of his mother, caught his eye and smiled. Cody returned the smile but looked away quickly. Did she know his appointment was related to porn and adultery? Probably not. He shot a prayer Heavenward the doctor didn't also resemble Ada. There was no way he could fully open up to a woman who looked like his mother.

Pastor Jordan must have picked up Cody's reservations about seeing a female counselor because he alleviated most of the concerns by pointing to Dr. Novak's relationship with the Lord and the pastor made it clear this was the person he felt most confident in recommending. He also shared her impressive credentials as well as her years of involvement with the church.

Cody admired the artwork on the walls from his seat. The abstract paintings most likely helped to guide patients toward introspection even before they stretched out on her couch. Then again, he might be overthinking things. He tapped his foot then caught himself. Cody checked the time on his watch to avoid another forced smile with the receptionist.

Five minutes and counting.

"Mr. James," the receptionist called.

"Yes." He rose.

"I didn't return your driver's license and insurance card." She extended another motherly smile.

"Thanks." Cody stuck the cards into his wallet and headed back to his seat.

"Excuse me, Mr. James," she called out again.

"Let me guess," he turned to face her. "You forgot to make copies."

"I made copies." The receptionist chuckled. "Dr. Novak is ready to see you now."

"Oh, okay," he stammered. The door to his right swung open. A petite woman in her late fifties to early sixties held out her hand. Thankfully, she looked nothing like Ada.

"Good morning, Mr. James. I'm Dr. Samantha Novak."

"Good morning." Cody shook her hand firmly, but not too firmly. He followed her down the short hallway into a room—surprisingly welcoming. One large window was covered in a fabric that afforded privacy but allowed natural light to illuminate the space. He suspected the window covering was a solar shade based on the reading material in her lobby. A large wall-mounted shelf displayed a collection of conch seashells, driftwood, and cream-colored ceramic plaques with various Bible verses. Her orderly office without clutter or messy stacks of papers stirred respect for the doctor.

"I like your office," he volunteered.

"Thank you." She pointed to one of two oversized sand-colored chairs opposite the desk. "Please. Have a seat."

Cody sank into the comfort of the chair and rested his forearms on the armrests. "This place is really peaceful." He chuckled. Mindful, the nervous laughter probably conveyed insecurity.

"Is there something amusing?" Dr. Novak kept her tone neutral, but her eyes already seemed to be searching his for unspoken truths.

"To be honest," he straightened in the chair, "I expected a nondescript room with a desk, a chair, and a couch." He chuckled again. "You know, for patients' to stretch out on while they share all of their problems."

She smiled. Cody waited for her to say something, but when she remained quiet, longer than was comfortable, he spoke again to fill the silence. "I hope I didn't offend you. I was trying to make a little light conversation. You know, to lessen the tension in the room."

"Do you feel tense?" Dr. Novak angled her head to one side.

"Well, to be honest, yes—a little." Actually—a lot, and she had to know this. Clearly, she wanted him to acknowledge his feelings. He swallowed hard. "I'm glad there isn't a sofa for me to lie on while we talk. Makes being here seem less hopeless."

"Would you care to expound, Mr. James?"

"Please, call me, Cody." He understood her goal was to get inside his head. He tugged at the collar of his shirt and instantly regretted having done so. The doctor would be cataloging each action, no matter how subtle or unintentional. A part of him wanted to bolt, but all it would accomplish would be clearing the path for Kate to proceed with a divorce.

"And please feel free to call me Dr. Sam, short for Samantha." She retrieved a notebook from the desk and jotted something down, then looked up at him. "Before we begin the session, I want to cover this time in prayer. For me, inner healing is connected to biblical philosophies. As such, I like to invite our Heavenly Father into the healing process. Is that all right with you?"

"Sure." He bowed his head.

"Lord," she said softly, "You know our shortcomings, and yet your heart is full of compassion for us. Thank you for your healing balm poured out on us when we seek you. We ask, Father, that any condemnation Cody is under be lifted from him. We ask that you quiet the inner storm in him and that he trust you to have his best interests in mind. We invite you to guide us with your love and wisdom. In Jesus' name. Amen."

"Amen. Thank you for your prayer." His voice broke. He blinked back tears before looking up. The doctor's compassionate smile, which also rested in her eyes, revealed she understood the prayer had deeply impacted him.

"Cody, would you like to take a few minutes before we begin?"

"No, I just…." The emotion heavy in his voice, he took a deep breath and blew it out slowly. "You really got me with your prayer."

"That's the Holy Spirit ministering to you." She remained observant but in a concerned way, like a sympathetic friend. After a moment, she posed her pen over the page of the notebook. "Getting back to your comment about hopelessness a few moments ago, would you say you feel hopeless in regard to your counseling expectations?"

He shifted his weight in the chair. "I've seen quite a few counseling sessions in movies, and the therapy always involves people, who spend week after week, month after month, year after year, on a counselor's couch, spilling their guts, but they never make any headway toward getting better."

"Are you fearful you will invest a lot of time and energy into a process, and it will fail you?"

Cody shrugged. "I wouldn't call it fear, but sure, I'm concerned this could all be for naught."

"I appreciate your honesty." She leaned forward. "And you might like to know while I don't have a sofa in my office, those two chairs," she pointed to the one Cody was seated in and the one beside it, "are recliners."

He chuckled, and this time, it was sincere. "May I ask you something?" He'd given Pastor Jordan free reign in sharing with the doctor about the porn struggle and Chelsea in hopes of fast-forwarding toward resolutions. Dr. Sam also came across as a cut-to-the-chase type, so he hoped she'd answer a direct question without trying to analyze why he was asking.

"I have one caveat." She sat back in her chair and clasped her hands in her lap. "After I've answered your question, I want you to answer a few questions in return. Fair enough?"

Cody nodded, then plunged directly in. "Do you know why I'm here?"

"I believe I have a good idea. Based on my conversation with Pastor Jordan yesterday, I know you're struggling to overcome pornography addiction, and you were unfaithful to your wife, but I'd like you to tell me why you've chosen to get help."

He glanced at his watch. He had fifty minutes to share about what led up to Hurricane Chelsea and the damage his marriage suffered from the winds of lust. Cody's stomach grumbled, distracting his thoughts to lunch.

"What are you thinking right now?"

The question brought to mind Kate. She'd asked the same question hundreds of times over the course of their marriage. Sometimes, she'd asked the question while lying beside him in bed with her head on his chest. She probably just wanted to hear how much he loved her, and he did, so why hadn't he said so instead of becoming annoyed with her probing? Maybe the doctor could help get to the bottom of that, too, but first things first, he needed to speak what was on his mind, whether it made him look good or not.

"If you want the truth, my thoughts are all over the place." He shook his head. "Of course you want the truth."

She smiled, "It would be helpful."

"Something just dawned on me," he volunteered. "Do you mind if I share it with you?" The question was rhetorical because the doctor's objective was to get him to open up.

"Please do." She seemed genuinely interested.

His heart pounded as he tried to put his thoughts into words. "You mentioned a storm in your prayer, and well, I consider the mistake I made with the other woman as a hurricane. Before you say anything, I know it's not her fault. But she did know I was married."

He tapped his chest. "And *she pursued me.*"

"Wait." Gone was the doctor's encouraging tone, replaced with a sternness that made him squirm. He opened his mouth to speak, but she held up her hand, silencing him.

She sat forward. "Do you think you're taking full responsibility for your actions?"

While he appreciated her direct approach, Cody was disappointed to have been misunderstood so early in the session. Now he'd have to spend the remaining minutes clearing up any misunderstanding about shifting the blame.

"Cody, the choice you made to bring another woman into your marriage bed is yours and yours alone. While it's human nature to deny our weaknesses, it's not what God desires of us."

Dr. Sam closed her journal and laid the pen she held on top of it. "Are you familiar with the passage in second Corinthians about God's grace?"

"I'm not sure." He tried to pull the verse to mind, but it was overshadowed by a need to defend his position.

She retrieved a large black Bible out from one of the desk drawers. "Here. Please read out loud 2 Corinthians 12:9-11 (NIV)."

Cody opened the Bible and ran his finger down the page until he reached the referenced Scripture. "But he said to me, 'My grace is sufficient for you, for my power is made perfect in weakness.'"

"Reread it, and this time, insert your name in the place of 'me' and 'you' in the verse."

He looked down at the page. "But He said to Cody, 'My grace is sufficient for Cody, for My power is made perfect in weakness.'"

The need to defend his earlier point lessened. He set the Bible on his lap. "I know this in my head," he said while still looking at the verse. "But there's a disconnect between my heart and my brain."

"You're not alone. Many Christians, even mature Christians, have experienced the same disconnect. It's been said, 'The longest journey you will ever take is the eighteen inches from your head to your heart.' I find this to be profoundly true when it comes to letting God take control."

His eyes burned with tears. He dare not look up. The words on the page were no longer discernible, and he blinked several times to clear his vision. While trying to reel in his conflicted emotions, a tear dropped onto the page. He swallowed hard but couldn't bring himself to lift his head.

"Cody, what are you feeling at the moment?"

"I can't." He closed the Bible but kept it on his lap. The doctor's name was engraved across the bottom right corner. *Mrs. Samantha Novak*. He'd have commented on it, but she would have known he was trying to change the subject.

"What's preventing you from telling me?"

He sat the Bible on her desk then looked her in the eyes. "If I tell you everything going on inside of me from childhood to present day, I'll break down crying, and I'll never stop."

"Crying wouldn't be as catastrophic as you fear, Cody. You've been protecting yourself from the very thing that can set you free."

"Yeah, what's that?" Adrenaline coursed through his body; he wanted to leave.

"You protect yourself from your feelings," she said. "Many adults go through life telling themselves their childhood traumas don't matter; they just need to get a grip and get on with their lives. They pretend to be grownups, but in reality, most, if not all, are emotionally stuck at the age the trauma occurred. They're making decisions as adults based out of injures."

"So what you're telling me is my addiction to porn was birthed out my father's addiction to porn?" Cody couldn't stop the blunt words from pouring out of his mouth.

"The short answer would be yes." She glanced at her journal but instead gestured to the Bible on his lap. "May I have my Bible? I'd like to read the rest of the verse to you."

He picked it up but then set it back down. "What's the long answer to my porn addiction?"

"The question is not why the addiction, Cody. The question is, why the emotional pain? Porn is one of the ways many hurting people self-medicate, but there are a number of ways: Alcohol, drugs, overeating, promiscuity, becoming workaholics, fitness fanatics, overspending. The list goes on and on."

He rested one of his elbows on the arm of the chair and cupped his chin. "I have a lot to think about." His mind traveled simultaneously down two trains of thought. One, he could easily become like those patients in the movies where therapy is never-ending, or the shame could be so consuming he'd throw in the towel like Blake.

Neither track was one he wanted.

"I agree, it is a lot to think about, but the Lord is able to help you." She stood, retrieved the Bible then retook her seat. "Close your eyes as I read the rest of this passage to you."

Cody didn't even try to resist. The energy to challenge her had drained from his body. He closed his eyes and exhaled a slow breath, releasing more control.

"Listen," she said in the same encouraging tone from earlier. "You read part of verse nine, here's the rest of verse nine, ten and eleven.

Therefore I will boast all the more gladly about my weaknesses, so that Christ's power may rest on me. That is why, for Christ's sake, I delight in weaknesses, in insults, in hardships, in persecutions, in difficulties. For when I am weak, then I am strong."

He cleared his throat and sat taller in the chair. "I have a confession to make."

Chapter Twelve

Kate took an early break to avoid the lunchroom rush. The staff at Brighton Assisted Living was friendly, but one particular young woman, the dietician, monopolized the noontime conversations with nutrition and fitness tips. The microwave pinged. Kate removed her chicken chow mein from yesterday's lunch with Sandie. Seated at one of several round tables, she said a blessing over the food, which included no mention of Cody. The sadness in her belly left little room for food, but she stabbed a piece of chicken with her fork and consumed it anyway.

In three days, it would be Valentine's Day. While she still wanted Sandie to unearth the truth about Cody's online life, Kate had second thoughts about involving her best friend. If Cody had owned his actions during their call yesterday, she could've asked him for answers to all the questions keeping her awake at night. Instead, he chose his typical response to conflict—shifting the blame anywhere other than himself.

She'd minimized Cody's deflecting early on in the marriage, believing she could lovingly have him take a closer look at his shortcomings then submit those weaknesses to God. Granted, she hadn't been a good example of applying the same approach to her weight insecurities, but at least she didn't make Cody responsible for her shortcomings. He, on the other hand, always pointed a passive-aggressive finger at his father, his mother, Blake, and even God.

Kate took another bite of the chicken chow mein. The noodles were dry, so she uncapped the bottle of lemon water and took a long swig. An image of Cody and the other woman flashed before her eyes, and it took everything in her not to overturn the small table. The rage had to be dealt with, and one way was to put even more distance between Cody and herself. Tonight she'd pack the rest of his belongings. He could come and get them tomorrow before she got home to avoid another face-to-face confrontation.

She'd let him know the plan now and ask him also leave his house key and garage remote on the kitchen table. Kate pulled out her cell phone and located Cody's number under favorites—another change to be made. The call went to voicemail. She clenched her jaw while listening to his upbeat greeting.

"Cody, it's me. I need you to get the rest of your things tomorrow—before six." She shoved the Styrofoam container of chicken chow mein aside as her anger erupted. "I understand coming before six means you'll have to tear yourself away from the shop, but so be it. The silver lining is, after tomorrow, you'll be free to spend your time with whomever you choose whenever you choose."

Tears burned her eyes. Nothing she'd said was a lie, but it was meant to hurt him more than it hurt her. A part of her wanted to take care of Cody even in these hellish circumstances.

###

"I'm sorry," Cody said to Dr. Novak. "I need to take this call. It's my wife." He walked over to the two windows on his right for a little more privacy and pressed the answer button, but the call had already gone to voicemail.

Staring through the taupe-colored window coverings into the courtyard, he gripped the phone. Her message couldn't be good. She'd made it abundantly clear she wanted distance, and even if he saw a counselor, she didn't need to hear about it. The only reason he could think of for her to call was she'd contacted an attorney.

Dr. Novak cleared her throat. "Is everything all right?"

Cody faced the mounted shelves. He zeroed in on the display of ceramic plaques with the various Bible verses. His gaze landed on a larger piece with the verse he'd read—Second Corinthians 12:9.

He shoved his phone into his pocket. "She left a message. I don't know if I'm ready to listen to it. I don't expect her to ever forget what I've done or to even forgive me. I just can't bear the thought of her hating me."

"Let's continue talking." Dr. Novak asked him to retake his seat. "I'd like to get back to the conversation we were having before your wife called. I presume the two are related."

"The confession I was about to make is connected." He sank into the chair. "No one else knows about this. If my wife finds out, well, any hope of saving our marriage is gone. Before I tell you, I need to know what I say will stay here. The whole patient confidentiality thing means you're bound to protect my privacy, right?"

"Cody, there are limited exceptions to the clinician-patient privilege—the legal term for 'medical confidentiality,' which I believe is what you're referring to. Am I correct?"

"Yes." He sat forward and clasped his hands. "What are the exceptions?"

"Information may be disclosed if there is evidence of physical, sexual, serious emotional abuse, or neglect. And of course, if suicide is threatened or attempted or evidence of serious self-harm and that includes drug or alcohol misuse that could be life-threatening."

"Do you have to memorize those lines when you become a doctor? It sounds textbook." Cody smiled, his nerves making him jittery inside.

Dr. Novak didn't crack even the slightest of a smile. "There comes a time, Cody, when suppressing the truth doesn't work for a person and what's served as a defense mechanism no longer protects the individual. Typically, it's at that point the person will begin to make worse choices driven by fear of discovery which is what I wanted to share with you a few minutes ago."

His heart beat wildly. Cody's nerves screamed run, run, run, but his mind held fast. He needed help. He needed to confess.

"Chelsea, the woman I was with," Cody began, faltered but pressed on, "she wasn't the first." He braced for her disgusted reaction. *Scumbag* wasn't a strong enough word for what he'd become.

After a long moment of silence, Dr. Novak pointed to the Bible on her desk. "Jesus is the place where healing and transformation begins, Cody. He provides unconditional love to the undeserving, and we are all undeserving.

While he didn't feel free from the consequences of his actions, he didn't feel condemned. "I haven't had physical contact with another woman, but I've done things online beyond looking at pictures. I imagine in this line of work; you know what I'm talking about."

"I've got a pretty good idea, and I don't need the details unless there's something specific you want to share. Is there?"

Cody shook his head. It had become difficult to maintain eye contact with the doctor, but he resisted the urge to turn away.

She rested her elbows on the arms of the chair and clasped her hands. "Now, I'd like to ask you a few questions, okay?"

He nodded. Within the past few minutes, he'd gone from a thirty-nine-year-old man to a sixteen-year-old boy awkwardly nodding and shaking his head to answer her questions. A part of him still wanted to bolt from the session. Thankfully, another part of him longed to sit it out and discover where this would take him.

"Cody, how did you come to faith in Jesus Christ?" Dr. Sam picked up her pen and opened the journal.

"I think I was about ten or eleven." He waited for her to write down the response, and when she didn't, he pressed for more information. "Why do you ask?"

"I didn't say when Cody; I said how? What led you to make a decision to follow Jesus?"

"Sorry." Warmth crept up to the back of his neck. "I misheard the question."

"No apology needed." A smile appeared on her lips but faded. "Do you remember what prompted you to invite Christ into your life?"

"Sure I do, my mother. She's a good Christian woman—a little zealous at times but well-meaning. After my dad ditched us, she worked hard to raise my brother and me."

The desire to end the session returned. He glanced at his watch, then back to her. Dr. Novak's eyes searched his, and he succumbed to turning away.

"Would you like to leave, Cody?"

He shook his head and instantly resented the action.

"Good. I'm glad you're staying the course. It shows me you're willing, at least for now, to discuss uncomfortable topics."

"Thanks. I guess."

"The reason I asked about how you came to your faith is that many people claim to have a relationship with Jesus, but they only know of Him, versus knowing Him personally."

"Hold on." He stood, crossed his arms over his chest, and narrowed his eyes. "Are you saying you doubt my faith?"

"No. I'd like to establish what your relationship with Jesus is, for the reason that knowing will shed light on how I can best help you."

Cody studied the doctor, but her expression was unreadable, and his frustration mounted. "Look, doc, it's almost noon, so let's wrap things up."

"We have fifteen minutes left in your session. Please, sit." She gestured to the chair he'd been parked in for the past forty-five minutes and waited until he retook his seat.

"Are you offended by my questions?"

Cody stood again. This was exactly why he had avoided counseling. "I get it. The next session is where I stretch out and revisit my childhood traumas. I tell you about how badly my dad treated my mother. I enlighten you to the fact he never once said he loved me or he was proud of me. I come clean about resenting having to take care of my kid brother when no one took care of me. Thanks, but no thanks."

Chapter Thirteen

Cody stuck his key in the ignition of the Jeep, but he couldn't bring himself to start the motor. His family's ugly history had triggered a kneejerk response of avoidance. He adjusted the rearview mirror to better see Dr. Novak's office but also caught sight of himself.

"This isn't about just you." He scowled at his reflection. "Go back inside, apologize, and make another appointment."

The pep talk hadn't been enough to move him from the driver's seat. He reached over and slapped the rearview mirror, so he could no longer see the office or himself. A story from the Gospels about the invalid man beside the pool flashed in his mind. In many ways, he identified with the cripple. When Jesus asked the man if he wanted to be healed, rather than voice a resounding "Yes!" the man prattled on about healing being beyond his reach. Like the invalid, Cody's hopes of change had been bled dry by years of disappointment. Even now, the temptation to do nothing tugged at him. In defiant opposition, he snatched the keys out of the ignition to prevent a hasty decision.

"Lord, I know I've asked you for help in the past, but if you walk alongside me one more time, I promise to keep pace with you as best as I can. I need to know you haven't given up on me."

Cody took a deep breath. "Will you help me?" He closed his eyes. "I'll wait for you to give me a sign. Just don't let me miss it." In the stillness, Cody rejected a grim possibility God had finally given him over to his lustful desires, and his future was sealed. Tension squeezed his chest. He opened his eyes as an image from one of the porn sites exploded into his thoughts.

"I need you. Please, help me, Lord." He took another breath, which came a little easier. The tightness in his chest still present, but to a lesser degree, he took a deeper breath and exhaled slowly. "I know there have been many times when you tried to steer me away from bad choices, but I wanted what I wanted, so I tuned you out. I'm sorry."

He swallowed hard. "I'm ashamed to say I've pushed you away. But right now, I feel like you are coming after me—to help me change—even though I don't deserve it. Am I right?"

Tears filled his eyes as he stared out the windshield, hoping to see something, anything to confirm God was indeed extending His grace and mercy.

As a new believer, when he'd sought God's will on a matter, he would randomly open the Bible to a passage and be amazed when it spoke to the circumstance. After several more minutes had passed without a spiritual tap on the shoulder, he turned on the radio. Maybe a worship song playing on his favorite Christian station would lend itself to the sign he craved. There was a new song he'd heard recently, and it spoke about brokenness and having faith in God to rebuild what's been shattered. If only God made a way for that song to play, all doubt would be removed. He looked at the time—almost twelve-thirty. Hard to believe he'd been sitting here dithering for fifteen minutes.

Cody's enthusiasm dipped as two announcers on the radio discussed the station's annual pledge drive, yet he wouldn't give up so easily. Leaning into the steering wheel, he waited.

Maybe a call to the station was what God wanted. He'd donate money, and the person he spoke to might ask if he needed prayer, then he'd confided he had been waiting on a sign—Cody shook his head. Now he was really grasping at spiritual straws. He glanced at the dash clock; the office had probably closed for lunch by now. When he'd booked the appointment late yesterday, the receptionist mentioned they were fitting him in before lunch.

He checked the rearview mirror—no activity in the courtyard outside Dr. Novak's office. The office must be closed. Then again, there was one way to find out.

Cody climbed out of the Jeep and crossed the parking lot at a brisk pace. "If this is your will, then someone will be there." He tugged on the door handle to the doctor's office. It opened. "Lord. I trust this open door is a sign from you."

###

Kate didn't recognize the number of the incoming call on her cell phone. Her initial reaction was to decline the call, sending it to voicemail. As she stared at the screen, curiosity won out, and she answered despite being at work. "Kate speaking, who's calling please?"

"Hello, Kate, this is Grace, from—"

"Oh my goodness, I'm so glad it's you." Kate cut across her new friend's voice in her hurry to explain why she hadn't called yesterday. "I'm so sorry I didn't phone you before you returned to New York. You are back in New York, right?"

"No apology needed. And yes, I arrived in the wee hours yesterday. I had a photo shoot for a magazine cover at sunrise. My flight was a redeye, but thankfully with makeup gurus and photoshopping, no one will be the wiser."

"Grace, I want you to know I feel terrible you were caught in the middle of everything between Cody and me." Kate motioned to the assistant activities director to take over in helping one last resident to the dining room for dinner. After the woman had taken control of the client's wheelchair, Kate exited through a side door and headed to the back patio.

"Stop apologizing," Grace said sweetly." You handled things better than I would have."

Kate squeezed her eyes shut as a rush of embarrassment warmed her cheeks. "Thank you for saying so. I still feel terrible you had to witness it."

"Enough already, I'm calling for two reasons, Kate, and neither is to receive an apology. First, I want to know how you're doing. Have you and your husband talked?"

"Not really." The thought of throwing up all over his shoes seared into her memory. "I don't have the stomach for it. Thank you for not mentioning the mess in the living room. I'm still mortified."

"If you don't stop with the apologies and being embarrassed, I may have to fly out there and paddle your tush—as grandma Grace used to say." The younger woman chuckled. "To be honest, I wish I had seen your husband's face."

Kate joined in the laughter. Grace had been so contrary to Kate's initial perception she couldn't help but be as genuine. "If the circumstances had been different, I would have enjoyed spending more time with you. It's clear why your grandmother always spoke so highly of you."

Kate debated whether to continue in the vein of transparency with someone she barely knew. "I want to confess when I first spotted you in the restaurant, I felt threatened by your looks. You're stunning. The last thing I wanted was Cody ogling a gorgeous woman during our romantic dinner."

"Well, thank you for the compliment, but I think you're beautiful, so I don't know why you would feel intimidated by me or any other woman."

Again, Kate's cheeks warmed. "You don't have to say that because I said it." Grace was just as lovely on the inside as she was on the outside.

"I'm not just saying it. You have a lot to learn about me. One of the things grandmother and I shared besides our first name is we say what we mean, and we mean what we say. You really are a beautiful woman."

Kate swiped at tears that caught her off guard. "Thank you."

"You're welcome."

"I agree your grandmother didn't hesitate in speaking her mind." Kate breathed in the cool evening air, relaxed for the first time since Monday night.

"I remember one time your grandmother firmly instructed a new aide not to disturb her during Canasta. However, she did make one exception to that rule—if the actor Dick Van Dyke ever became a resident, she would give up Canasta altogether to help care for him."

"I know who is. He's from the movie Mary Poppins." The younger woman laughed, and Kate joined in.

"Your grandmother was, without doubt, a special woman, and the apple didn't fall far from the tree."

"Sounds like something grandma would say. She was my touchstone. Everyone needs someone who holds them accountable when others are too afraid to speak their mind. Do you have anyone like that in your life, Kate?"

"I thought Cody was, but I was wrong." A wave of disappointment washed over her.

"I'm so sorry, Kate, what a stupid question to ask. Now look who's apologizing. Will you please forgive me?"

"My best friend and I have a quota for stupid questions. We're each allowed ten stupid questions per day. Consider yourself a member of our exclusive club. You now have nine stupid questions left for the day." Kate snickered to convey the comment was intended lightheartedly.

"I'm honored to be a part of such an exclusive club," she gushed. "I'll try not to use any more questions up today."

Grace cleared her throat. "Now onto the other reason I called. I want to invite you to New York this weekend."

"What?" Kate's jaw dropped. "New York? I couldn't. This weekend I have to—"

"I know it's short notice, but the idea of you being alone for Valentine's Day makes me sad. And yes, I know you have a close friend there, but I think a change of scenery is needed. In fact, you can bring her along. I'd have called sooner, but this is the first chance I've had with work and the time difference."

"Wow. New York. I've never been." Just moments ago, she was looking forward to going home, crawling into bed with jammies on, and watching reruns of I Love Lucy. Grace's zeal had stirred excitement in her. Maybe this was God providing an out from wallowing in self-pity.

"Kate? Are you still there?"

"Yes. I'm thinking."

"You already told me you're off work this weekend because you had made plans to surprise Cody with a drive up the coast. That sounded incredibly romantic, but things have changed."

Chapter Fourteen

The conversation with Grace was lasting longer than she'd anticipated, so Kate walked over to one of the cement patio tables on the Brighton Garden grounds and sat. She'd be off work in a few minutes anyway, so there was no hurry to get back inside. The sun hung low in the sky. A gentle breeze rustled her hair, along with the palm fronds of the recently planted young trees.

"Why not?" Kate brushed loose strands of hair away from her face with her free hand and held them in place. "I'll do it."

The moment the words left her mouth, she gave thanks to God for Grace's generous invitation. A weekend away couldn't have come at a better time.

"You will?" Grace let out a sigh. "To be honest, I was prepared for a battle."

"I'm a little surprised myself." Kate chuckled. "But you're right; things have changed, and driving along the coastline with Cody isn't a trip down Memory Lane I want to experience."

"I'm so excited you're coming. You don't have to do a thing," Grace said. "I'll have my assistant book the flights and arrange to have a car pick you and your friend up, provided she's free to come, too."

How wonderful Grace had thought of everything. Usually, Kate had to oversee the details relating to a trip. A peace flooded her and underscored sneaking behind Cody's back to ferret out secrets on his computer wasn't a godly way to handle things.

"Thank you for inviting me. I have another confession. I had plans for Saturday, but they felt wrong. This feels right."

"I'm glad you changed your mind." Grace's enthusiasm spilled over the phone line. "Can you leave first thing Saturday morning?"

Kate mentally reviewed her schedule. "Yes. In fact, I could leave Friday evening after I get off work. I'll need to check with my friend Sandie about whether she'd like to come. I will say, knowing Sandie, she's going to jump at the opportunity. May I confirm later this evening?"

"Absolutely. I know this is a difficult time for you, but I think getting away is going to do you good." Grace's tone turned serious. "I'm not just referring to the fun we'll have sight-seeing and dining out. It's much more. I believe God is behind it."

"I feel the same way." A lump formed in Kate's throat, but she swallowed hard and pressed on with what she wanted to say. "I'm excited to see what God's going to do with our time together."

After a few more pleasantries, Kate ended the conversation. She stared at the raspberry-colored sunset and breathed deeply. "Thank you, Lord." Her phone sang out the Eagle's song "Peaceful, Easy Feeling," and a shudder racked her body.

Kate nibbled her bottom lip, staring down at the phone in her hand as the song continued to play. No matter what he wanted to say, it couldn't change anything. She considered ignoring the call, but impulsively, she swiped the respond option—"Hello?"

"I hope I didn't call at a bad time." Cody's voice held a tentative note. He ought to be unsure of how she'd receive his call. "I waited until I thought you'd be off work," Cody rushed on. "If you're driving and you would rather not talk right now, I understand."

"You answered, so I guess you're okay with talking," he groaned. "I'm nervous. Can you tell?"

She could but didn't want to give him the satisfaction of noticing. "Cody, if you're calling to—"

"I'm not calling to talk you out of whatever you've decided. I just wanted to let you know I'll get the rest of my things. I missed your call earlier because I was with a counselor. We were in the middle of my session."

If this was his way of encouraging her to ask about the session, she wasn't taking the bait. "I'd like you to get your belongings while I'm not home."

"Um." He cleared his throat. "Would it be all right if I came this weekend? I have something I want to give you." He couldn't be less insensitive if he tried.

Kate closed her eyes tightly. "Is it for Valentine's Day?"

"No. It's something I picked up last week."

Eyes still closed, she said, "I'd prefer you come tomorrow while I'm at work. And please, don't leave anything for me other than your house key."

Kate opened her eyes then stood to head back inside. The call was over as far as she was concerned. "Anything else you want to say?" She stopped short of entering the facility.

"No. That's it."

"Are you sure?" The question betrayed her objective to end the call. A part of her wanted to hear about the session with the counselor, but she overruled her emotions. "What I mean is, are you sure you'll be there and gone before I get home tomorrow?"

"You won't have to see me, Kate. I promise."

She firmed her lips and her resolve and ended the call. Cody had made the choice to abandon the marriage vows—not her. He was the one who discarded the promise to forsake all others.

###

Cody pulled out one of four chairs from his mother's dinette table. "I shouldn't have invited Blake to join us for lunch this afternoon. He's a goofball."

"Your brother's young." Ada turned on the flame under the kettle for her usual cup of chamomile tea before bed. She faced Cody. "In many ways, Blake reminds me of your father; God rest his soul."

She slipped her hands into the patch pockets of her bathrobe and shuffled toward him in slippers. Seated across from Cody at the table, she smiled. "You boys each remind me of your father but for different reasons."

"How so?" He tensed. "If Blake's the lighter side of dad, are you saying I'm the darker side?"

"Your father not only had a silly side to him, but he also had a serious side. That's the side I see in you." She placed her hands on his forearms then gave them a little squeeze. "If I had something more to say, you know I'd say it."

"Yes, I do, which is why I'm surprised you haven't voiced your opinions about my and Kate's separation."

He'd braced himself for interrogation during the lunch this afternoon, but she'd steered the talk to lighter topics.

"I figured with you staying here, we'd get around to what's brought about the separation when you were ready."

Cody leaned forward. "I—" If he told her everything, she'd discover how awful a man and a husband he'd become. He averted his eyes to the clock on the stove—8:45. If he tried to end the conversation based on the lateness of the hour, she would likely see through it. He turned his attention back to her. "I don't know where to start."

"Take as long as you need." Tears welled in her eyes, contrasting the smile lingering on her lips. Time had been gracious to her. Even at age sixty-five, fine lines around her eyes and mouth were the only telltale signs of the struggles she'd faced as a single parent raising two headstrong boys. In his youth, she had lectured on choosing the narrow path God spoke of in the Bible. Ada explained the narrow path meant not doing anything you couldn't ask God to bless.

The C. S. Lewis quote, 'Pain removes the veil; it plants the flag of truth within the fortress of a rebel soul,' dropped into his thoughts. In spite of the shame and a desire to run away from this conversation, he forced himself to stay put. He nodded toward the whistling kettle. "Mom, go ahead and fix your tea, then we can talk."

After she'd prepared the cup of tea, she rejoined him at the table. "I prayed for you while my chamomile was steeping," she said tenderly. "When I look back on the faithfulness of

God in my life, it gives me confidence and hope in His future faithfulness. God wants to do the same for you and Blake. You boys don't know it, but one of my daily prayers is you two will come to trust God. Your Heavenly Father is not like your dad."

He shrugged, "I know."

"Do you?" She firmed her lips. "I don't think you do."

Again, the quote by C. S. Lewis claimed his thoughts. Kate deserved a husband who was all-in, unlike his father, who bailed on his wife, so if all-in meant sitting through emotionally hard conversations with a counselor, his mother, his brother, or anyone else, then so be it.

The resolve strengthened him. He met Ada's gaze as he launched into the fray. "I always hear you talking about God's faithfulness, but how has God rewarded your faithfulness—with dad's abandonment?" Cody winced, then added quickly, "That's not an attack on you."

A mothers' knowingness danced in her eyes. "Sounds to me you're attacking God's faithfulness."

She took a sip of the tea, but her concentration remained on him. He recalled her watchful eyes and gentle touches over the years, soothing everything from scraped knees to teenage heartbreak, as well as the sadness, confusion, and anger over his father's abandonment. She often said more than he'd wanted to hear about God and the Bible during those difficult times. Still, he watched her, and what she'd espoused was backed with action—she never disappointed.

"I guess I am questioning God's faithfulness," he blurted.

She moved the cup of tea aside and folded her hands on the table. "Define faithfulness."

"You've got to be kidding." Before he could explain his sarcasm, she shushed him with her right hand in the air.

"Cody Michael, you're thinking in terms of yourself. You've already admitted you are questioning God's faithfulness, so I'll ask you again, define faithfulness."

Cody sat back in his chair. He thought about what she'd said moments ago about God the Father being different than the father who'd abandoned them. "God's faithfulness is supposed to be unwavering, which means it should be consistent."

"Should be?" Ada's eyes widened. "The root of the problem is you haven't learned to trust God's faithfulness. Trusting His faithfulness comes through getting to know Him, not by proxy. You must experience your own personal relationship with Him."

Cody harrumphed. "My pastor referred me to a marriage and family counselor. The first appointment was today. She asked me about my faith, too."

"God loves you, son, and while you may not understand what's going on in your life right now—He does."

"Christianese bugs me." He stood and crossed his arms over his chest. "I'd rather you just say I'm getting what I deserve for stupid choices."

"Cody, sit." She pointed to his empty chair. Ada narrowed her eyes until he'd retaken his seat.

"This is the second time today I've been told to—"

"Button it." Had her stern tone not been accompanied with a lighthearted gesture of buttoning her own lips, he might have walked out of the kitchen. Besides, she'd earned the right to reprimand him. The longer he sat quietly waiting for her to speak, the more he became amused by the charm she'd used to shush him.

"I have another question." Ada paused, clearly testing his resolve to remain quiet. After a few seconds had passed without interjection on his part, she spoke. "Would you loan your brand new Jeep to anyone who asked?" Her serious expression warned he should answer accordingly.

"No. It would have to be someone I know and someone I know well."

"What if the person promised to be careful, and if anything happened to it, they'd take full responsibility?"

"No, mom." He blew out an exasperated breath, struggling to keep his voice even. "I wouldn't loan my Jeep out to a stranger just because someone promised me something. I'm trying to be patient, but you're certainly taking the long way around the barn to make a point."

"I wouldn't disagree." She smiled. "Sometimes, the long way around the barn gives the traveler a chance to take everything in. Son, trust isn't extended blindly. God understands until we know Him—personally—we're going to be afraid to trust Him."

"So, how do I get to know God?" He cringed over sounding like a new believer rather than someone who had grown up with the Lord in his life. Maybe she was right—he'd ridden the coattails of her faith instead of getting to know Jesus for himself.

Cody's phone buzzed in the pocket of his pajama bottoms, but it wouldn't be Kate. He'd already talked with her, and the conversation hadn't gone well enough that she'd be calling.

"Are you going to answer your phone?" His mother tipped her chin in the direction of the buzzing sound emanating from beneath the table.

"It's probably Blake. He can leave a message." Cody pointed to her cup. "Are you going to drink your tea?"

"Are you saying you'd like to continue our talk?" A twinkle danced in her eyes.

"I guess it is?" He smiled.

"Then yes, I'm going to drink my tea, but first I'm going to make a trip to the bathroom. Getting older isn't for sissies."

He glanced at the milk separating from the tea in her cup. "I'll make some fresh for you." Cody checked to make sure there was enough water in the kettle then turned the heat on under it. As the water was warming, he rinsed out the cup. His cell phone vibrated again, alerting of either a missed call or a new message. On the outside chance it might be Kate, he retrieved his phone and stared at the missed call log.

Chelsea Monroe.

Chapter Fifteen

Cody leaned back against the kitchen counter. Chelsea had left a message, and though he had yet to listen to it, it couldn't be good. His mother reentered the room. "Your tea is steeping. Would you like me to bring it over to you?"

"Well, I can't drink it from here." Ada smiled and retook her seat at the dinette table. "Are you okay?"

He smiled to appear nonchalant, "Why do you ask?"

"You have a strange look on your face—like you're trying to hide something. Was it Blake calling?"

"No." Cody slid his phone back into the pocket of his pajama pants. He crossed the room and placed the cup of tea on the table in front of his mother before taking his seat. "Be careful. It's hot."

"You don't say." She narrowed her eyes. "Are you sure you're okay?"

He hung his head. "I've got a problem."

"Whatever is going on, you can talk to me." She cleared her throat. "I need you to look at me."

He lifted his gaze to meet hers. The concern in her eyes made him sick to his stomach—so many years of lying to those he loved with Kate at the top of the list. "Mom, it was more than an argument with Kate. I had an affair."

Saying the words out loud made him wince and turn away.

"I had a feeling it might be something along those lines," his mother sighed. "I hoped I was wrong, but my motherly intuition warned me to prepare for the worst."

"You saw what your dad and I went through—all the years of pain and suffering and how it affected you and Blake." Her voice stayed soft, but her words hit hard. "Why on earth would you choose this path for yourself?"

"I didn't choose it." He would never have chosen something so destructive. Cody clasped the back of his neck with both hands. "It just happened."

"Stop it!"

The words crackled across the kitchen, jolting his body.

"Nonsense," Ada exhaled loudly. "It's not true for you or anyone else who makes the choice to cheat on their spouse. It doesn't just happen. You're not taking responsibility."

"Thanks." He stood, locking eyes with her for the first time since his admission. "Blake said you would side with Kate, and he was right. You haven't even heard the whole story, and you're already angry with me."

She pointed a steady finger at him, her eyes compassionate but stern. "I didn't raise you to shirk responsibility. I doubt there was a gun to your head. I love you, but I'm going to speak the truth."

"You're right. I'm sorry." Cody ached to have his mother wrap her arms around him, but she remained seated. He blinked back tears. "I've let everyone down."

He pressed on despite fresh tears spilling from his eyes. "The counselor I saw is right. Everything in my life has been a stepping stone to this destination. I've made choices all along the way, and they've landed me where I am in this pathetic moment."

"Son—"

"Let me finish." Now he'd started to speak; the words tumbled out. "When I was a kid, I found dad's stash of girlie magazines in the garage. I knew I shouldn't, but I took one of the magazines. My bad choices started back then."

Cody sat at the table but stared at the floor as he spoke. "I felt like God was telling me to put the magazine back, but I didn't listen. It's become the story of my life—not listening to God. Every time God tells me to do one thing, I do the other. What's wrong with me?"

"You're not alone," she said in a softer tone. "Your dad and I had conversations about this very subject. I reminded your father, the apostles were men who followed Jesus, and yet they still stumbled."

"Not like me," he croaked. "I understand the apostles were imperfect men, and there's only one perfect person, Jesus." He looked over at her and forced a smile. "See, I was listening during Sunday school."

"Cody, you're missing the point. Jesus knew they were imperfect, and they would stumble, but He still chose them. He wasn't surprised when Judas betrayed Him any more than He was surprised when Peter denounced Him."

What she said made sense, but the disciples hadn't cheated on their wives. He shook his head. "You don't get it." Granted, his mother could be overbearing about her faith, but then there were times like now when the love of Christ shone through her like a beacon directing the way to godly choices.

"I don't get what, son?"

Cody pulled the phone out of the pocket of his pajama bottoms and set it on the table. "I should delete the message I just received. It's from the woman I was with a few nights ago. But part of me wants to know why she's calling. I'm torn between doing what I believe God wants me to do and what I want to do—even though I know what I want to do is wrong."

She picked up the cell phone. From his peripheral vision, he watched as she tightened and released her grip on the phone. He half-expected her to ask for his passcode, so she could delete the message for him. The coward's way out, of course. No. He needed to be the one to delete the message, but only after he responded and told Chelsea he'd made a mistake and could never see her again.

As if reading his thoughts, Ada set the phone on the table. "The apostle Paul wrote about the struggles you're talking about." She didn't wait for a response. "Paul wrestled with doing the things God wanted him to do versus doing the things God didn't want him doing. Don't you think God knows what you're going through? Paul understood the only one who could save him was Jesus."

Cody let the truth sink in. He'd read the passage in Romans several times but somehow never managed to see himself in Paul. After all, he was Paul the apostle, who had done great things for the kingdom of God. Not someone like him, who couldn't stop watching pornography.

"I keep making poor choices," he blurted out. "You'd think at some point the spiritual light bulb would come on, and I'd see things differently. But it hasn't." He drummed his fingers on the table. "I'm stuck in this endless cycle of wanting to do the right thing and always picking the wrong thing."

"It's not too late." She handed the phone to him. "You can do it differently right now. The choice is yours to do the right thing."

###

"Are you sure you can't come?" Kate kept the cell phone pressed to her ear as she fell backward on the mattress. It was one thing to fly to New York for the first time with a trusted friend, but the prospect of flying almost three thousand miles alone to meet up with Grace, a woman she barely knew, prompted second guesses about the trip.

"I wish I could," Sandie said.

"What if you—"

"I can't," Sandie interjected. "I already promised to watch my niece and nephew, so my brother and his wife could get away for the Valentine's Day weekend. They had wanted to leave Saturday morning. I told them I wasn't free until late afternoon but that I could stay until Sunday evening."

Kate stared at the ceiling. "Drats, it won't be the same without you."

"To be honest," Sandie said. "I'm relieved you accepted Grace's offer. I didn't have a good feeling about snooping on Cody's computer."

"I realized it's a bad plan, too." Kate rolled onto her stomach. "I want Cody to tell me the truth, not learn it by snooping. The idea seemed like a logical way to get information, but prayer changed my perspective. I shouldn't sneak behind Cody's back—even though he did it to me and for who knows how long."

"I'm thankful to hear you say so. When were you going to tell me?"

"Tonight, and I'll have you know I came to the conclusion before Grace's invitation."

"Even better to hear, but no more of talk of Cody, okay? I want you to think about yourself for a change. Got it?"

"I got it."

"So what time is your flight?"

"I'm not sure." Kate's gaze darted to the digital clock on the bedside table. "I need to touch base with her. I'll let her know you're not going to make it then she'll book my flight. I wanted to wait to talk to you before confirming anything with her. It's after ten now, and there's the three-hour time difference, so I'll call first thing in the morning."

"Are you excited?"

"Yes and no." She grabbed her pillow from the head of the bed and tucked it under her chin. "I hardly know Grace. What if she turns out to be weird?"

"From everything you've told me about her, she's not going to be weird. I bet she's going to line up some wonderful things for you two to do while you're there. Trust me; if it was anyone other than my workaholic brother, I'd renege on babysitting and join you on the flight."

"I know you would but hearing you say it means a lot."

"My brother is a great guy, but he's materialistic and puts his career before his wife. I'm glad to help my sister-in-law wrangle sometime alone with him. I'm a little concerned about their marriage."

"I'm sorry to hear about your brother and his wife. Have you talked to him about your concerns?"

"Not really. It's hard to talk to him without his getting defensive. And he doesn't want to hear about God, which makes conversation with him more of a challenge."

Kate closed her eyes tightly. This hit close to home. "I must look like a hypocrite. Here I am, a Bible-believing Christian, and where's my faith? I've told God I don't have what it takes to stay in my marriage. A part of me wonders if I'm running away versus facing things by taking off to New York."

"I thought you agreed to no more talk about Cody? The choices he made are his and his alone. While you might be struggling with your faith, at least you're being honest with yourself and God."

Kate opened her eyes. "I can do all things through Christ who strengthens me."

"That's my girl," Sandie beamed.

"Thanks for the vote of confidence." Sandie's enthusiasm helped to clear Kate's mind of the lies fighting for her attention. "Can I ask a favor?"

"Anything," Sandie replied.

"Could we pray for Cody?"

Silence emanated from the other end of the line.

"If you think I'm foolish for wanting to pray for him after what he's done—"

"Foolish?" Sandie sniffled. "I'm sorry for getting all weepy, but I think you're amazing."

"I don't feel amazing." Tears filled Kate's eyes. "Now we're both crying."

"Trust me, you're amazing. Do you want to pray for Cody right now?"

Kate's head swirled with thoughts about his poor choices and the consequences, but as she began to pray for her wayward husband, the pain in her heart eased just a little bit.

When Sandie added her own prayer to the end of Kate's, the comfort of their Heavenly Father permeated Kate's mind and body, bringing with it a rush of compassion and sorrow for Cody. It wasn't enough to make her want to restore their marriage, but it gave her hope the future might not be as bleak as it appeared now.

Chapter Sixteen

Kate wheeled her once piece of carry-on luggage behind her as she approached the front of the line to board the plane. She glanced at her ticket for the flight to New York. The words *First Class* once again snagged her attention. The pricey airfare had been something she'd tried to talk Grace out of, but the young woman insisted.

"Good morning," the airline employee smiled and held out his hand for her boarding pass.

"Good morning," she returned his smile. As the man tore off a portion of the ticket, Kate gushed, "It's my first time to New York. I'm meeting with a friend for the weekend."

Cody wouldn't have volunteered so much information, but then Cody wasn't forthcoming about much of anything in his life.

"My friend is taking me sightseeing," Kate added.

"You're in for quite the experience," he said. "If you're planning to see the Statue of Liberty, bundle up. February in California is nothing like February in New York City, where it's supposed to be in the 40s today."

"I packed for cooler temperatures." She'd checked the weather this morning before even getting out of bed.

"I'm sure you'll enjoy your stay in the Big Apple. Here you go," he said, handing back her ticket before turning his attention to the next person in line.

"Thank you. I'm sure I will." Kate followed the people ahead of her down the enclosed passenger bridge to the plane. A flight attendant, a woman, greeted her with a smile and directed Kate to the first-class section of the aircraft.

Kate stowed her carry-on bag in the spacious overhead bin with ease. The first-class accommodations were already proving to be a treat. She slipped into her window seat and eyed the activity on the ground before retrieving her cell phone from her purse to switch the setting to airplane mode.

She groaned. Cody had called at some point. It appeared he'd left a message. She reclined the seat and closed her eyes. Still gripping her cell phone, she debated on whether or not to delete the message. Most likely, he had called to wish her a happy Valentine's Day, but aside from this trip, there was nothing happy about the day.

Curiosity won out. Not wanting anyone to overhear Cody's recording, she held the phone to her ear. "Katelyn, I want to say again I'm sorry for how I've hurt you. I'm sorry for everything I've done over the years that has brought us to this point. I imagine my apologies don't mean much, if anything, to you, but I want you to know I'm deeply sorry. If there is a future for us, and I'm not saying there is—that's totally up to you. I want you to also know I promise to do better with God's help and—" Kate pressed pause.

Tears filled her eyes. She up-righted the seat and stared out the window, blinking away emotion that threatened to reduce her to a blubbering mess. A baggage handler parked his cart next to the plane, which drove her thoughts back to Cody. He must have left the message while she was being processed at the gate.

"Excuse me, Miss. May I get you anything to drink before takeoff?"

Kate gently cleared her throat then turned to the attendant. "Water, please."

"Would you like bottled or over ice?" The gold band on the woman's left ring finger knotted Kate's stomach.

"A bottle is fine. Thank you." Kate leaned across the empty seat. "Is anyone going to be sitting here?"

"Yes. The flight is fully booked, but I can provide you with a sleep mask if you'd like to circumvent any conversation." She handed Kate a chilled bottle of water from her pushcart.

"That won't be necessary but thank you for the water." Kate turned back to the window. She craned her neck to watch luggage being loaded onto the aircraft.

"Good morning, babe." As if she'd conjured him from thin air, Cody's voice grabbed her attention. Her body trembled as she turned and locked eyes with him. Her mind unable to fathom what he was doing on this flight. She simply stared.

"Welcome aboard, sir. Would you like to stow your bag?" The flight attendant pointed to Cody's laptop case.

Finally, Kate's tongue loosened enough to ask, "What are you doing here?"

"No, thank you," Cody said to the woman. "I'll be using it during the flight."Although his response may have sounded routine, the fullness of his meaning wasn't lost on Kate. He was up to something. For his sake, he'd better not be planning to clear his conscience by revealing his online escapades.

"This is a bad idea." Kate sat her purse in the empty seat. The only way he could know about the trip was from Sandie, but the two barely spoke to one another during better times, let alone now.

He faced the attendant. "Could you please give me and my wife a moment alone?"

###

Cody wedged himself into the space in front of his assigned seat, allowing the other passengers to get by him. He glanced at Kate's purse then back to her. "I'm blocking the aisle."

"I can see that." Kate's expression morphed from confusion to anger. "How do you know about my trip? Did Sandie tell you?"

"Yes. Be angry with me, not with her." Hopefully, after he'd shared why he wanted to join her on the flight, she would calm down.

Kate snatched her purse from the vacant seat. "You may as well sit." She tipped her chin up in the direction behind Cody. "You're creating a bottleneck."

He stowed his duffle bag under the seat, sat beside her, then placed the computer case on his lap. He'd envisioned boarding the plane before her with his Valentine's Day card and gift in hand, but haphazard planning resulted in leaving her card and gift at Ada's home.

Kate plunked her purse beside her feet. She folded her arms across her chest. "This is just great."

"I left you a message. Did you listen to it?" He hoped his tone conveyed how much the ball was really in her court, despite his clumsy attempt at a romantic ambush.

"Yes. I listened to your message. I didn't finish it." Kate uncapped the bottle of water and took a swallow. She blew out an exasperated breath. "What made you think this would be a good idea?"

"I'm desperate, and desperate people do desperate things." He leaned closer. "I love you. I don't want to lose you."

"I suppose you think showing up like this makes you some kind of knight in shining armor. Well, you're mistaken." She twisted the cap on the bottle of water back and forth. "If you didn't want to lose me, then you should have kept your pants zippered."

Cody stared straight ahead. The fasten seatbelts sign lit up. A chiming sound by way of the overhead speakers drew his attention to the flight attendant at the front of the plane.

"I'm sorry," he said under his breath while keeping his eyes forward. The thought crossed his mind to leave, but it was too late. The engines hummed while the attendant gave a spiel on how to respond during a mid-air emergency.

"You said that in your message," Kate hissed.

Cody closed his eyes. "Lord, it looks like I've blown it again. Now what?"

Chapter Seventeen

The minute the seat belt sign clicked off after departure, Kate turned to Cody. "This flight is about six hours, which means I can watch three two-hour movies—do you get my meaning?" She arched an eyebrow to punctuate her question.

Cody just stared at her and nodded.

While she longed to know why Sandie would share the New York trip information with him, Kate resisted the urge to ask. Instead, she looked out the window. Gradually her thoughts drifted from the residential neighborhoods they were flying over to her own house. Since Cody had moved most of his belongings out, it no longer felt like their home. She now viewed it as a place to sleep, eat, shower, and mostly cry over the awful choice he'd made. Reminders of their shared life cropped up everywhere. Last night, the toothbrush holder with only one toothbrush in it brought her to tears.

Kate closed her eyes as the plane slipped through a band of wispy clouds. At the gentle touch of Cody's hand on hers, she opened her eyes. Caught off guard and not wanting to draw attention by overreacting, she continued to look out the window. She expected him to say something, but the silence between them persisted. The warmth of his hand atop hers brought back a host of memories beginning with where they had met—at a neighborhood carwash. Her throat tightened with emotion over how he'd grinned when her face puckered after a first sip of the courtesy coffee. After she'd discarded the Styrofoam cup into the trash, he approached her. His brown eyes had danced under long lashes while making small talk. They chatted while her car was being washed and his truck was hand-dried. Even all these years later, she recalled the small details of their exchange and how she'd hoped the employee detailing Cody's truck would slow down so they'd have more time to get to know one another. Especially after she had found out they attended the same church.

"Babe," Cody said.

Kate snatched her hand out from under his and rested it in her lap. She was about to correct him on his repeated use of the endearment, but he spoke first.

"I don't want to make things worse," he continued. "I've been thinking about asking the flight attendant if I could swap seats with another passenger...but honestly, I prayed you'd ask me not to."

Kate turned to him with tears in her eyes. "What happened to us?" She firmed her lips. It hadn't been her intention to blurt the thought.

He sucked in a deep breath and let it out slowly. "My thinking has been wrong for years, but rather than ask God to help me with my thoughts, I assumed I'd blown it one too many times, and I didn't deserve His help."

The truthfulness and the sorrow in Cody's eyes stirred something in Kate she hadn't expected and didn't welcome.

Forgiveness. He had yet to explain his actions or express adequate remorse. If she were being truthful too, a part of her wanted him to work to redeem himself.

Kate blinked away more tears as she continued to look into his eyes. "I'm surprised to hear you taking responsibility for your role without blaming me or God for any of it."

"I'd say it's about time I stop being a hypocrite." His face remained solemn. "Would it be all right if I shared something regarding the old gentleman I bought the guns from?"

"I guess so," Kate shrugged. "But what does he have to do with us?"

"More than you can imagine." Cody's expression softened. "I believe God used Mr. Kennedy, that's his name, to open my eyes to how deceived I've been. I'd bought the lie I was shielding you from an ugly part of me when what I needed to do was be transparent about my weaknesses to God and to you."

"Weaknesses?" Kate's heart sped up. Was her hunch he'd been cheating on her since the beginning of their marriage right all along? "I'm not ready to hear how many times you've been unfaithful in our marriage."

The flight attendant stopped at their seats and smiled at Cody. "May I get either of you a glass of pink champagne to celebrate Valentine's Day?"

Cody regularly drew attention from the opposite sex, but right now, the last thing Kate wanted was a pretty attendant conversing with him. Resentment rose. This Valentine's Day, they had nothing to celebrate.

"No thanks," Kate answered on their behalf.

The clipped response didn't go unnoticed by Cody. He turned to her with a quizzical gaze before responding to the attendant. "We're fine, but thank you for checking."

"You're very welcome. We'll be serving lunch in about thirty minutes. Would either of you like to see a menu?"

Kate's stomach growled. She glanced at her watch—10:30. Hard to believe the flight took off over an hour ago. In a dash to get to the airport, she'd missed breakfast. Begrudgingly, she dropped her defenses. "Yes, please. I'd like to see a menu."

"And you, sir?"

"I'd like to see a menu as well. Thank you."

After the attendant moved on to the next passenger, Cody turned to Kate. "If you want me to change seats... I will."

"It's not possible," Kate answered without looking at him. "She already told me the plane is fully ticketed."

"Oh," he said under his breath. After several minutes passed, Cody broke the silence. "I was thinking about the first time we met." He faced her. "At Elite carwash—do you remember the terrible coffee?"

"I was thinking about the same thing. What are the odds? And to answer your question, yes, I remember the bad coffee. Unlike you, it was my first time at the carwash, and I made the mistake of adding one of those packaged dry creamers to my coffee."

He covered his mouth with his hand and stifled a chuckle, "I forgot."

She glared at him, but the response dissolved into a sheepish grin at the memory of spitting the coffee back into the Styrofoam cup before disposing of it.

"Babe," Cody began.

"Please stop calling me babe." In a flash, the lightheartedness of the moment was gone. She willed herself to ask about the gentleman who had sold his guns to Cody, despite what might be revealed. "I thought you were going to tell me about the seller you bought guns from Monday night."

###

Cody briefly closed his eyes to refocus from the mistake with Chelsea Monday night to earlier in the evening with Marty. "Mr. Kennedy helped me to see; people can and do change when they rely on God."

Kate's deeply furrowed brows revealed confusion.

"Let me explain how he shed light on a few things," Cody said. He turned in his seat to face Kate. Her eyes revealed lingering sadness, and while he wanted to address it, the best thing he could do would be to share what he'd learned from Marty. Then he could try to open up with Kate about the dark parts of his life and how God was undoing the lies he'd come to believe.

"For some reason," Kate said, "I expected the gun seller to be our age or younger." She shook her head. "I'm sorry, go ahead."

"Mr. Kennedy is in his eighties. He's a widower. His wife, Beatrice, died sixteen years ago, but to hear him talk about his love for her stirred emotions in me I didn't know existed. The interesting thing is while he misses his wife, *he truly believes he'll see her again in Heaven*."

Kate's brows rose. She'd obviously picked up on the unintentional inflection in his voice when he'd said "truly." Like his mother, Kate apparently sensed something amiss, but how long she'd known, he had no idea. While he'd read the Bible from cover to cover, prayed, tithed, and joined Kate at church when work didn't create a conflict, he hadn't known the peace of God. In fact, he'd only recently tasted it.

At his wife's continued look of bemusement, he decided to ask, rather than assume, what she was thinking. "Do you have a question? It looks as though you're surprised by what I said. Am I wrong?"

"No. You're not wrong. I have to say, you've surprised me again."

"How so?" Cody doubted she was aware of the faint smile that rested on her lips.

"You asked me what I'm thinking versus just assuming." She reached over and touched his bristled jawline. "You need a shave."

His face warmed at the unintentional intimacy of her gesture. "I need a lot of things."

She returned her hand to her lap. "Your tone a moment ago suggests you might not fully believe in Heaven, and if so, then how do you place your trust in God?"

"Halfheartedly," he stammered, blindsided by her touch more than the question. "But I'm learning it's not about God answering my prayers the way I believe they should be answered. That logic got me into trouble. I wound up feeling like God didn't love me."

For a split second, her mouth was agape. "I don't know what to say."

"What I saw in unanswered prayers did a number on me early in life. I prayed God would save my folks' marriage." Cody shrugged. "They got divorced anyway. I also prayed God would help me with a battle I've waged since my teen years, but—"

"What battle?" Kate leaned into him.

"Excuse me." The flight attendant handed them each a menu. "I'll return in a few moments to take your orders."

"Thank you," Cody said. A lot needed to be shared with Kate, and while only a short time had passed since the plane took off, he was mindful there would be too much time if things went badly.

As Kate looked over the menu, he wondered if she was also feeling anxious. He opened his mouth to ask, but she turned to him and spoke first. "My stomach is upset. Something light might help settle it." She handed her menu to him. "I am hungry, but maybe just crackers to see what happens."

He recalled the other night and didn't want her to have a repeat of what happened at the house. "I don't have much of an appetite, so I'll pass for now."

He'd been such a fool. The women online didn't hold a candle to Kate's beauty, but inattentiveness on his part had fed her insecurities. She tipped her chin toward the aisle signaling the flight attendant's return. He asked for plain crackers to calm Kate's stomach and two sparkling waters. Once the woman walked away, he let down the tray in front of him and placed his computer on it, then opened his laptop and powered it on.

"I want to show you something," he said. "Mr. Kennedy has a blog. I'd like you to read something he wrote."

"*Humph*. Good for him." The surprise in her voice amused him, in part because it had also been Cody's reaction.

"His grandson created the blog for him and maintains it. The content is Mr. Kennedy's."

He watched Kate from his peripheral vision as the homepage of his computer loaded. Hopefully, she'd be pleased the image of the woman holding a military-style rifle was gone. In its place was a photograph of Kate in her wedding dress. A few weeks ago, that image of his bride had haunted his thoughts and triggered shame over the despicable choices made throughout the marriage, but now it ushered in hope and thankfulness to God—even amidst the uncertainty of his future with her.

Kate's eyes glistened. The portrait of her on their wedding day had an impact on her.

Cody resisted asking her about it. He keyed in the URL and waited for the page to load. "I think you'll like Mr. Kennedy's perspective."

"You've piqued my curiosity." She rested her elbow on the armrest and inched closer to his seat.

While her action was probably only to get a better view of the computer screen, the nearness of her overwhelmed him, and the distraction wasn't what he needed right now. He needed every ounce of his faculties to get through the next few hours of conversation.

Chapter Eighteen

Kate silently read the words on Cody's computer screen. The gentleman who wrote the blog post understood the need for God in his life and in his marriage. Several times, she had to swallow hard to clear a lump in her throat. Even now, her vision blurred with tears. This man expressed beliefs she'd prayed Cody would one day grab hold of, yet she didn't want to get her hopes up.

She cleared her throat with a sip of sparkling water. She needed to eat the crackers, but talking with Cody about their marital problems had distracted her. As she read, her mind swirled with questions she wanted to ask Cody for the first time in their marriage; she sensed he was truly ready to answer.

Kate sat back in her seat. "The man you bought the guns from wrote this? How old did you say he was?"

"I believe he said eighty-seven." Cody pointed to the screen. "What do you think about what he said here?"

Kate reread the sentence in her head. "Insightful."

"I agree. Would you mind if I read it out loud?" Cody's passion was contradictory to his usual laidback demeanor, so she agreed.

He looked over at her, "Thank you."

"You're welcome." She held his gaze for a moment, but the intensity of his stare seemed to burrow into her thoughts, and she wasn't ready to be that vulnerable. "Please, read it."

Turning his attention back to the screen, he began. "Scripture teaches fear is mitigated by love. First John 4:18 tells us, 'There is no fear in love.'"

Cody shut down his laptop, returned it to the case then stowed it under his seat. "My counselor is debunking the lies that have created fear in my life. Fear my parents not only didn't love one another, but they didn't love Blake and me. As a teen, I'd lie in bed many a night and ask God why my folks ever got married. They argued with one another all the time. God didn't give me the answer."

"You sound resentful, but you've always praised your mother for raising you and Blake on her own."

He firmed the visible quiver of his bottom lip. "I'm not taking anything away from her, but I'm sure you'd agree my mom isn't the most affectionate person in the world. She's come a long way in that area, and I give her credit for the change."

His voice cracked. "Please don't hear this as me blaming my mom or even my dad for my choices as an adult, but like my counselor says, I do need to acknowledge what has shaped my perspective and contributed to landing me where I'm at in life. Am I making sense?"

"Yes." Cody's sullen expression didn't trouble her as it had in the past. He appeared to be taking a hard look at areas of his life he'd ignored or made excuses for, and she empathized. Over the past few days, she had also taken a hard look at the list of excuses made for not taking better care of her body.

"I thought about calling your mom and telling her how you'd betrayed me." Kate hung her head. "But I didn't want to hear her tell me to divorce you." Her heart pounded. She'd said more than she'd intended.

The silence that hung in the air between them seemed to last several minutes. Cody always had an answer for everything, but Kate imagined he didn't know how to respond any more than she did.

The flight attendant made her way down the aisle; not wanting another interruption before she could say what she wanted to say, Kate leaned into Cody. "I hate what you did," she said in a hushed voice.

"Katelyn, I don't want us to divorce. I love you."

"Please don't say that."

"I do love you, and that's what makes all of this so hard to understand. At first, I thought I must not love you if I was willing to make the choices I've made, but that's not true. It's going to take a while before I'm able to explain—"

"Why you did this to us?" Desperation rose in her like a drowning woman breaking the surface for a gulp of air. The sharpness of her question underscored she might never be able to look at Cody without wondering about the other woman.

The flight attendant stopped at their seats. "Would you like anything else?"

"No." Kate turned away to stare at the clouds. Tears burned her eyes, but she blinked them away while willing herself to toughen up. The flight wouldn't arrive in New York for another three hours—maybe four—she'd lost track of time. At the moment, all she wanted to do was shake Cody by the shoulders and demand to know why he hadn't put God first in his life because if he had—none of this would be happening.

"Thank you, but we're fine," he said to the attendant. After a moment, he tapped Kate on the forearm. She flinched at his touch but kept her back to him.

"She's gone," he said. "I won't say anything else. Not because I don't want to discuss what's happened, but because I don't want to hurt you more than I already have."

She responded without facing him, "Tell me about this battle you've been fighting since you were a teenager." Determined to hear it all—she might not have the resolve later on, and he might lose his nerve. "I also want to know why an old man selling guns has had such an impact on your thinking. Start talking."

###

Cody swallowed the lump of embarrassment in his throat. "It would be easier to say what I have to say if we were in different surroundings; then again, this is happening for a reason."

Kate squared her shoulders then turned to him. There were no tears in her eyes. He would have preferred tears over her soul-piercing gaze. "I'm waiting."

Looking into the face of so much hurt, he froze

"Are you going to tell me or not?"

"I need to pray." He bowed his head and closed his eyes. *Lord, I want to be truthful with my wife, but at the same time, I don't want to hurt her by sharing details she's not prepared to hear. Please give me the words. Amen.*

Cody swiveled his body toward Kate's. "I'll begin at the beginning." He took a cleansing breath. "Since I was about thirteen years old, I've been addicted to pornography."

He braced for a response, even a slight physical drawback, but there was none, so he pressed on. "I'm not talking about a typical reaction like most teenage boys, who get a thrill out of looking at porn. I mean a real, driving addiction."

She continued to look at him, but this time instead of cowering in the face of truth, he had peace that surpassed understanding. "I should have told you about my addiction when we began dating seriously. I was afraid. I didn't want you to think badly of me."

He dropped his gaze briefly, but it was as if an angel extended a hand from Heaven to lift his chin. "I wanted to tell you so many times before we married. I kept chickening out. Years later, after my mom told you about my dad's unfaithfulness and you said if it ever happened in our marriage, you'd divorce me—I panicked. On some level, I convinced myself I'd be able to abstain from the porn and for long stretches of time, I did, but the urges always came back and stronger."

He hoped what he'd said so far wasn't coming across as excuses or blaming her for his lack of honesty. "I've had many opportunities to come clean with you since then, but fear kept getting in the way. Fear of losing you. Fear of being looked at as a pervert. Fear of..." His voice trailed off, not sure he could voice the rest of his thought.

"Finish your sentence." Her gaze softened, "Please."

Cody took courage from the sympathy he perceived in her eyes. "My greatest fear has been I'm not truly a child of God. I'm not saved, and I've been deceived all these years."

His heart beat wildly, but he forged ahead. "A Bible verse in Matthew haunts me."

Kate's brows crinkled. "What's the verse?"

"Jesus warns not everyone who says, 'Lord, Lord,' will enter the kingdom of Heaven" (Matthew 7:21).

Kate placed her right hand against his heart. "Those who commit themselves to Christ, believe in Him, and depend on Him will spend eternity with Him. For the first time since I've known you, I believe that's what you're doing right now."

He hated he couldn't accept her loving response as the final truth. But he needed more. This was about being honest. He refused to hide his doubts. "How can I be sure?"

Her hand remained planted against his chest. "Were you sincere when you invited Jesus into your life as a teen?"

"Yes, but—"

"Hold on," she said tenderly. "Do you believe Jesus died on the cross for your sins and rose three days later? Did you repent for your sins and asked Him to be your Savior? Those are the foundational truths behind spending eternity with Him."

Kate removed her hand, but the truth she'd spoken with love remained and opened the door for more transparency.

"As best as I understood it at the time, yes to each of your questions." He wasn't trying to be difficult, but he longed to have the matter of his salvation resolved once and for all, and if it meant appearing argumentative or naïve, so be it. Tightness gripped his chest. He tried to ignore it, but when beads of perspiration dotted his forehead, he swiped them away with the back of his hand.

"I can't help but think, if I were truly saved, I wouldn't do the things I know to be wrong." The Bible passage Ada had shared about the apostle Paul wrestling with himself over the things he didn't want to do versus the things he wanted to do bubbled up in his thoughts.

Somehow, this conversation had gone from taking ownership of the wrong choices in his life to something much bigger. Every struggle he'd faced to this point, he'd done so apart from God. Going forward, he longed to know for certain God viewed him as His own, and his prayers were heard.

"I'm so confused," he muttered. The air in the plane became thick. He struggled to catch his breath without alarming Kate. Panic gripped his thoughts. He recited the breathing exercise in his head, but it didn't help.

Cody swiped his sweaty palms against his pant legs. The idea to excuse himself from the difficult topics being discussed and go to the bathroom to splash his face with cold water crossed his mind, but the cramped facilities might exacerbate the anxiety.

Overthinking was only making things worse. He closed his eyes and tried to pray, but the prayer was halted by the thoughts of others looking at him and whispering.

His eyes sprung open. He had to get off this plane.

Chapter Nineteen

"Are you all right?" Kate leaned across the seat to take a closer look at Cody. His shallow breathing warned of trouble. He appeared to be in the throes of a panic attack. "You're going to be okay."

Eyes closed, he shook his head. The color had all but drained from his face.

Kate pressed the call button for the flight attendant. "Cody, talk to me." She craned her neck to see if help was on the way. No one approached in reply to her summons.

"I feel like—" he gulped air, "I can't breathe."

"I need you to listen to me—this will pass."

He gripped the armrests. "I have to get off the plane."

"You're not making any sense." She placed her index and middle finger against his neck to check his pulse. Thank goodness she'd been through a few panic attacks with him before and had an inkling of what would help calm him down.

The flight attendant greeted Kate with a smile, but it quickly dissolved into concern. "Is there a medical problem?"

"He'll be fine," Kate said more for Cody's sake. "May I get a glass of water?" She kept her voice tranquil. "With ice, please?"

The flight attendant nodded then walked away. Whenever Cody experienced one of these attacks, helping to keep him calm worked wonders. Lightly touching his hand, she began to pray in a soft voice.

"Lord, thank you for always having our best interest in mind. Thank you for calming my husband's emotions. Thank you for the peace washing over him even as I pray this prayer. Father, I invite you to take this moment and use it for good. In Jesus' name. Amen."

While Cody's eyes remained closed, the crease in his brow softened, gradually his breathing slowed, and he unclenched his hands from their death grip on the armrests.

"Thank you, Jesus," she said.

The flight attendant reappeared with the glass of water, and Kate mouthed Cody would be fine.

"If you need anything else, please let me know." After studying him for a moment, the woman walked away.

"Cody," Kate managed to keep her voice soothing, "I want you to take a sip of water. Take some of the ice, too."

The distraction of chewing ice might help him to focus on something other than fear and could minimize the severity and the duration of the attack. Slowly, he opened his eyes and took a sip from the glass of water she placed to his lips. Kate encouraged him to take another. After the second sip, Cody took the cup from her hand and drank more.

"Have some ice, too," she reminded softly.

He followed her instruction and sat staring straight ahead while munching on a mouthful of the crushed ice. He kept his gaze on the seatback in front of him. "I'm embarrassed."

"No need to be embarrassed." She hoped the flight attendant hadn't told the captain what was going on, but if she had, at least he didn't feel it necessary to take the short walk back to first-class to see for himself.

Cody turned to her, a deep sadness in his eyes. "You're too good for me."

"Talk about irony. I used to think you were too good for me."

He snorted. "I certainly proved you wrong." He took another swallow of water.

"I should never have looked to you to be my knight in shining armor. You're just a man. And don't take that the wrong way."

"I don't. In fact, it's like a weight off of my shoulders." He paused. "Kate—"

"Cody, I—"

"Go ahead," she said.

"No. I'm sorry. You first." He polished off the remaining water then tapped the bottom of the glass to finish the ice.

"When you're feeling better, I want to know why you felt you couldn't come to me with your problem. I also want to know more about the old gentleman, who seems to have had such a profound effect on your thinking."

He let the tray in front of him down and set the empty glass on it. "I now see why God planted the idea of me joining you on this flight. God knew given a chance to chicken out on talking about things with you, and I mean everything—I'd probably take it."

He faced her. "So, here I am, thousands of feet in the air with no escape. I'm thankful He arranged it so I couldn't get away. God keeps showing me I need to depend on Him and not try to do things in my own strength. He underscored it for me a few moments ago with the panic attack."

###

In almost an hour of silence between them, Cody surmised Kate was waiting to see if he would resume the conversation and address her questions. "I feel much better," he said, breaking the quiet.

She turned in her seat and faced him. "Thank you for not making me fish for information."

He nodded. "You shouldn't have to." A tremor in his voice halted him from saying more.

Cody sensed she was weighing his sincerity. Although tempted to reassure Kate, he would instead trust God to reveal the changes in him.

He pointed to the two empty cracker wrappers beside his glass of water on the fold-down tray. "I'm glad you ate a little something. How does your stomach feel?"

"Better." She folded her arms across her chest.

Fair enough. Kate wanted to resume the conversation. He sent up a silent prayer for God to guide his words. "Before we get deeper into the talk we were having, I must say something about Sandie. I haven't supported your friendship with her, but I see things differently now. She's got your best interest in mind. Initially, I called her to plead my case. She quickly shut me down and suggested I own up to being a colossal jerk—her words. After we'd talked for about an hour, she revealed your plans. I believe God used Sandie to help me see joining you on this flight was needed."

Cody swallowed hard. Everything could go really well right now, or it could go terribly wrong. He forged ahead, hoping she wouldn't feel betrayed by Sandie or controlled by him. "I asked God to shut the door if my joining you wasn't what He wanted me to do. I half-expected to find there weren't any seats available on this flight."

His mind raced with a dozen different things to say about how the baby steps in trusting God had made a difference in his choices but battled back the urge to overload her.

"What did you say to make her hear you out?"

"I did as she said, I owned up for being a jerk—a colossal jerk. I also told her I love you, and I'd spend the rest of my life proving it if given the chance. I don't like acknowledging this, but she's a truer friend to you than I've been. In the end, Sandie confided she believes you still love me." He mustered the courage to ask—"Do you?"

Kate remained quiet. Her expression unreadable for the first time since the flight began.

Cody's shoulders buckled under the weight of her silence. He was about to withdraw the question when she spoke.

"You've hurt me deeply. One day, the fullness of it may hit you, and when it does, I'm not sure I want to be around."

He eyed her left hand in her lap and the wedding ring he'd placed there over a decade ago. "You're right. I don't know how badly I've hurt you." He sat tall in his seat. "I may never fully understand, but I'll do whatever it takes to save our marriage. We can go as slowly as you need to. I love you."

Kate drummed her fingers against her thigh. "You don't get it. I'm angry with you over what you've done to us. I want you to answer my questions. I don't care we're on a plane. Count yourself fortunate we're not flying coach where anyone and everyone could hear you spill your guts. I don't understand why you didn't come to me about this secret battle of yours. And stop saying fear. I'm your wife."

"Pride, too," Cody said barely above a whisper. "I mean, what type of man would do this to the woman he loves? I'll answer for you. A man who is selfish and wants what he wants."

"Go on." Kate's ferocious gaze locked on him.

"I'm ashamed to say I put my perverted desires before God and before you." He didn't take his eyes off her face, even though he wanted to hang his head in regret.

"I couldn't bring myself to tell you what was going on because of fear. I believed even if I told you everything and changed, somewhere down the road, you'd question if I was thinking of another woman. In my twisted logic, I believed I could handle it on my own, and I'd spare you a lot of heartaches. I know it's crazy, but that's what controlled my thoughts."

Kate faced him. "You're right. I don't want to know how often or where or when you've indulged in this sick pastime. The idea of you looking at that filth when I was in bed sick with a cold or exhausted after a long day at work would only add to the devastation. And the idea of you viewing images on special occasions, like my birthday or our anniversary, well, I couldn't bear it. So please, don't ever unburden your conscience at my expense."

Each word hit in the gut like a powerful blow, but he steadied himself to take it. He deserved this and more. He wanted to assure her he'd drawn some boundaries but thought better of it.

Her brows creased. "On some level, I get the whole 'men will be men' thing, but I also see it as a phase, not something that can't be controlled with God's help."

A conversation as private as this would be hard to have alone with Kate, but in a public place such as an airplane made it all the more intense. Who was he kidding? This discussion would be intense and difficult, no matter the location. Over the next six and a half hours, Cody laid open his innermost thoughts about the sexual temptations that had pursued him since youth. How time after time, he'd tried and failed in his own strength to distance himself from triggers that led to bad choices. How rather than feeling defeated when he failed to abstain, he would walk away telling himself next time would be different. Only it never was.

Prepping himself to talk about his encounter with Chelsea, he sent up a silent prayer God would give him the right words to say. Throughout his confession, Kate withdrew more and more into herself, asking only a few questions about Chelsea but otherwise not commenting. The lifelessness in Kate's eyes brought tears to his own. He had done this to her. He had taken a thing of beauty—their marriage—and turned it into ashes.

"Katelyn, I feel like I've been in survival mode since you found out."

She narrowed her eyes. "Survival mode, I don't understand. Explain."

"Survival mode meaning, I want our marriage to survive."

"I'm glad I asked." Her expression softened. "Go on."

Cody recognized many women would've immediately asked for a divorce. Instead, Kate sought answers, and for it, he thanked God. As unbelievably gracious as she'd been, he couldn't help but wonder if denial and an unwillingness to face the pain kept her from dropping the hammer.

"I feel more guilt than I ever felt over the pornography. At least with the porn, I could kind of justify it. Like you said, the 'men will be men,' perspective." His heart thudded so loudly he wouldn't be surprised if she commented. "Don't get me wrong. I'm not minimizing porn and the struggle with sexual integrity. It's just I had compartmentalized the degrees of infidelity."

He thought about checking in with Kate to see if she wanted him to continue speaking. The truth be told, a part of him didn't want to keep talking. "I have a confession."

She took a deep breath and let it out slowly. "Just tell me."

"I don't want you to hear this as an excuse—"

"Just say it." The irritation in her voice set off an alarm bell. The calm in the chaos might be shorter-lived than realized. Yes, she'd been angry and even tossed him out of the house, but there was a much bigger storm brewing on the horizon.

"Do you think I'm a monster—a pervert—a pitiful excuse for a husband? Because that's what I feel like, and it's hard to stay focused in this conversation wondering if you're thinking the same thing."

"Would it surprise you if I answered, yes?" She held up her hand. "Don't answer." Kate lowered her arm and discreetly pointed toward the aisle. "The flight attendant is coming our way."

Cody slumped. When the woman stopped at their seats, he looked up and volunteered he felt better.

"Good to hear." She smiled and gestured to the fold-down tray with water glass and cracker wrappers. "Would you like me to take that for you?"

Cody nodded, "Thank you."

Once the flight attendant continued her stroll down the aisle, he resumed. "Just because I didn't go to massage parlors, strip clubs, or hire prostitutes, doesn't mean what I did is any less devastating—to use your word."

"I'll give you credit for acknowledging unfaithfulness is unfaithfulness. I'm going to answer your question. Yes, at times, I think you're all the things you've said and more. I also think you may be better off alone."

Cody's stomach clenched. Her words had hit with the power of a heavyweight fighter. "Katelyn..." He wiped the tears from his eyes before facing her. He didn't want sympathy. This was about her. "As hard as it is to talk to you about all of this, it's likely even harder for you to hear about it. I'm committed to figuring why I did what I did."

"That's as important as I'm sorry." Kate turned to the window then back. "I'd like to stop talking for now."

Chapter Twenty

As the plane touched down on the runway, Kate glanced at her watch. Four—California time, she readjusted the time to seven. Staring out the window into the New York night, she made a decision. Grace hadn't mentioned plans for the first night in the city, and since Cody appeared willing to talk honestly, she'd let him know spending time together this evening to resume their conversation over dinner would be okay with her.

Kate turned to him. "Grace is having a driver pick me up. Because she's unaware that you joined me, I'll ask if it's okay to have the driver drop you at your hotel. I don't imagine it will be an issue. Once you've checked in—if you'd like to get together for dinner, we can resume where we left off in our conversation."

"I hope the driver knows of a place where we can have a quiet meal. Being Valentine's Day, it might be a challenge." Cody unfastened his seat belt once the plane taxied to a stop at the gate. He stood, retrieved his duffle bag beneath his seat, then Kate's carry-on from the overhead storage bin.

Her cheeks warmed. He'd obviously misunderstood the offer. "I hope you don't see this as a Valentine's Day type dinner."

"Not at all." He extended his hand to her, but instead, she gripped the back of the seat to steady herself.

Kate followed him down the aisle toward the exit. The flight attendant smiled as they neared her. "Enjoy your time in the Big Apple, and happy Valentine's Day."

"Thank you." Cody looked over his shoulder at Kate but turned back when she didn't smile. Once they exited the passenger bridge for the flight and entered the terminal, she walked alongside him as he navigated through the crowds.

"This place is busy," she said in a raised voice.

"It sure is, lady," a man responded from behind her. "Nature of the beast for JFK."

Kate didn't turn to respond for fear she'd take a misstep, stumble, and be trampled by the herd of travelers. Thankfully, Cody seemed undaunted by the throngs of people, many of whom talked on their phones and even managed to text as they hurried along.

An immense mural of a skyline along the wall to Kate's left captured her attention. The artistry was breathtaking. The drawing seemed to go on and on. While she would've liked to stop to take a photo, she'd forgo it in favor of forwarding momentum. Good thing she wore flats for the trip. Along with a new pair of jeans, a black sweater, and a cashmere scarf coiled around her neck, maybe others viewed her as fitting into the whole New Yorker scene.

"I think he's our guy." Cody paused as they neared the baggage carrousel.

"Where?" Standing beside Cody, she tippy-toed.

"Right there." Cody pointed to a slender young man wearing a white dress shirt and dark slacks. The driver held a sign with her name printed in block letters across it.

"He looks like he should be a model," Kate said to Cody under her breath. Once there was an opening in the crowd of people, she waved at the driver until she'd captured his attention. The young man waved back then began to make his way toward them.

"Cody, do you think I should call Grace now or wait until we're in the car?"

"I'd wait." He adjusted the laptop strap on his shoulder. "Once we're situated, you can speak to her without any distractions."

"Good idea." Hopefully Grace would be okay with the plans for this evening.

"Hello. Kate James?" The driver tucked the sign under his left arm and extended his right hand.

"Yes, and this is my husband, Cody." She shook hands with the driver, and Cody did the same. Except Cody leaned in while still holding the man's hand and said something into his ear, which prompted a smile from the driver.

"I can take you wherever you'd like to go." He released his grip on Cody's hand. "Do you have additional luggage?"

"No, just our carry-on bags," Cody said.

"It's nice to meet you, Mr. and Mrs. James." The driver's joint greeting anchored Kate in the reality of her troubles.

"Allow me to take those for you, Mr. James." The young man relieved Cody of his duffle bag, Kate's carry-on luggage, and also the laptop case.

"Thank you." Cody wrapped his arm around Kate's waist, and she flinched.

"Habit," he mouthed to her before removing his arm.

If she was honest with Cody, and she would be if the driver wasn't within earshot, she'd assumed the response hadn't been deliberate.

"Follow me." The man led them to a curbside Lincoln Town Car. He opened the rear passenger door of the vehicle with his free hand and then gestured Kate inside. Once Cody was seated, the driver returned his laptop case to him and closed the door.

In the instant before the driver got in the front seat, Cody burst out with an apology. "I'm sorry about what happened back there. I—"

"It's okay. Don't worry about it." His being considerate went a long way in opening her heart to hear the rest of what he had to share later tonight.

###

At the beginning of their relationship, Kate used to plan little getaways, but this wasn't something either of them had planned for, and so she didn't hesitate to press him. "Are you going to tell me what's at 623 East 68th Street in Manhattan and why you want the driver to take us there?"

"You'll see." He winked, a little unsettling, but she'd overlook it.

The man turned and faced them in the backseat. "Mr. James, the address you gave me in the terminal doesn't exist."

"Are you sure?" Cody's tone revealed disappointment, but rather than explain himself, he slumped in his seat.

"Positive. The address didn't register until I looked it up. Don't feel bad. You're not the first person to make a mistake. People tend to forget television and movie productions often use bogus addresses."

Kate angled her head toward Cody. "Television and movie productions, what's this all about?"

"I was going to take you by a place you've seen hundreds of times, just not in person." He cleared his throat. "I wanted to surprise you with a stop by the brownstone where Ricky and Lucy Ricardo lived, well, in television-land anyway."

"Mr. and Mrs. James, I'll proceed to the hotel." The driver flipped his left blinker before smoothly pulling away from the curb. Classical music filled the automobile, which allowed for some privacy.

"Thank you for wanting to surprise me." The gesture was sweet, but her head argued to keep quiet.

The classical music in the car washed over Kate, and little by little, the chamber piece captured her thoughts. "Wait." She pursued her lips. "Cody, do something. The driver thinks you and I are staying at the same hotel. You need to ask him for a recommendation of another hotel in the area. I need to call Grace."

He leaned in. "I was thinking I'd stay at the same hotel but get my own room. Isn't that enough distance between us? I also thought you might prefer we order room service for dinner."

His brows rose. "I just realized that sounds suggestive. It's not meant to be. I figured it's too late to reserve a table for dinner on Valentine's Day, so we'd share a meal together in one of our rooms."

Fatigue had set in. Suddenly the idea of him staying at the same hotel was no longer a big deal—as long as he had his own room. And right about now, a warm bath, pajamas, and a room service gourmet burger with French fries sounded like a slice of Heaven.

"I didn't hear it as suggestive. I actually like the idea of room service, but I want to bathe first." Maybe the hotel room has a Jacuzzi tub. She could hope. "I'd prefer to eat in your room after I've freshened up."

"Good. Then it's settled."

His tone carried a hint of optimism, but she didn't have the energy to stick a pin in his balloon right now. "I'm going to call Grace; explaining the recent turn of events should be interesting."

Chapter Twenty-One

Thankful for Kate's agreement about booking a separate room, even at the exorbitant cost, Cody was relieved not to have to stay at a different hotel. In his room, he dropped his duffle bag onto the queen-sized bed. The floor-to-ceiling window caught his attention. He crossed the thick carpet to pull back the curtains and stood looking out at the skyscrapers. Maybe Kate had the same spectacular view.

Cody tugged one sleeve of his T-shirt to his nose and breathed deeply. The fragrance Kate wore lingered on the cotton material. During the flight, he'd resisted asking if it was a perfume he'd given her. Now, alone in the room, he was certain of it.

The women online had distracted him from his true love, Kate, and he'd allowed it to happen. He rested his head against the cool glass. He tried to place the name of the man in the Bible who ran from a seductress.

His cell phone vibrated in the front pocket of his jeans; he placed his hand on the device but didn't retrieve it. His heart sped up as the vibrations continued. *Chelsea wouldn't call me again.* Not after the message he'd left telling her he loves his wife and he'd made a mistake. *Would she?*

"Relax," he said to calm his rising panic. Still, something warned him the call was going to be bad news. Slowly, he pulled the phone from his pocket. A deep sigh escaped his lips as he viewed the caller ID.

"Blake, this isn't a good time."

"Bro, what's going on? I have to find out you're in New York City from mom." He barely took a breath. "Good time or not, I'm calling to give you a heads up. Chelsea was in the shop this morning. She said, 'Tell your selfish brother he could've said he loved his wife before going to bed with me.' End quote. She asked where you and Kate live. Said something about wanting to let your wife know how much you enjoyed your time at her place. She is one scary woman."

Cody plunked onto a wingback chair beside the window. His mind raced. He knew nothing about Chelsea other than she'd hawked a DVD player for gas money to get back and forth to work. She sounded mentally unstable.

"Are you there?" Blake's panicked voice cut through his thoughts.

"Of course, I'm here." He hunched forward in the chair and hung his head.

"Bro, what are you going to do?"

"I have no idea. It's not like I've been through this before." He groaned, not caring how Blake might respond.

"Call her," Blake said. "She's probably mad because you left her a message instead of talking to her. Why didn't you answer your phone? I'd think as angry as she is, you would've picked up on the first ring."

"No lectures," Cody mumbled. "I can't call her now. I'm with Kate. Well, I'm not with her at the moment, but we are going to get together shortly. I imagine Mom told you about my plan to connect with Kate and hopefully talk."

"Yeah, she did, but I wouldn't call it a plan. What was Kate's reaction when you showed up on the flight?"

"At first, she wanted me off the plane, but then she—hold on a sec." Cody pulled the phone away from his ear to check the caller ID. "It's Kate. I'll call you back."

"You better," Blake said. "Bye."

"Hello, babe, I mean Kate. Is everything okay?"

"My suite is amazing," she said. "How do you like your room?"

Cody paced back and forth in front of the window. "It's very nice."

"Grace went all out," Kate excitedly announced. "I feel a little guilty at the expense, but she keeps telling me I'm worth it."

"You are worth it." Cody struggled to stay focused. "Did you talk to her again?"

"Yes. She is the sweetest woman and so understanding. Although she didn't say so directly, I got the feeling she's more than in favor of you and I talking this evening."

Kate softly cleared her throat. "Speaking of this evening, I've had a change of heart. I think we should have dinner in my suite. I ordered room service. I hope you don't mind. I took the liberty of looking over the menu and chose a pan-seared New York strip steak, along with a baked potato and a Cesar salad for you. I told them I'd call back to confirm what time I'd like it sent up."

"I guess so, but why the change in plans?" Cody gripped the sheers covering the window and gave them a hard tug. Part of him wanted to rip them off the rod and thrash the room. He was so close to having time alone with Kate and explaining his actions. He held out hope she'd find it in her heart to forgive him one day, and yet he couldn't shake the thought of being on the brink of losing everything—again.

"Good," she sighed. "I realized after a bubble bath I wouldn't feel like leaving my room. I'm preparing my bath as we speak."

He relaxed his clenched fist. As soon as she'd said so, he detected the sound of water running in the background. For all he knew, it could've been audible the whole time.

He pulled the phone from his ear to check the clock on his cell. Quarter to nine. "Maybe it's best we settle for breakfast tomorrow morning."

"What's going on?" The cooing of her voice had transformed into sharpness and reminded him of the night he'd been with Chelsea and Kate's reaction.

Cody sat on one corner of the bed. Hunkered over, he let the truth spill out. "Blake called. He said Chelsea was in the shop this morning looking for me. She's the woman I—"

"Please, I know who she is." The sound of the running water stopped abruptly. "Why is she looking for you?"

"I have no idea." The muscles in his neck and back were so taut he rolled his shoulders forward and backward. "That's not exactly right."

"What do you mean?" Her tone now razor-sharp, "What exactly is going on?"

###

"Hold on." Kate gripped the phone tighter. She thought they were moving in the right direction earlier, now this. "Before you say anything, I need to know if you've spoken to her. Have you?"

"No." He exhaled into the phone. "But I left her a message while staying at my mom's place. I told her I'd made a mistake, and I love you and want to work on my marriage."

Kate took a seat on the edge of the tub. "There's nothing ambiguous in what you said to her. So why is she calling you?"

"Honestly, I don't know. Maybe she's hurt and lashing out. Blake said she wanted to know our address because—"

"What?" Kate bolted upright. "Your brother didn't give her our address, did he?"

"Of course not."

"Did you tell him specifically not to?" Kate didn't allow her husband a chance to respond before plowing ahead. "This is just great." She stormed out of the bathroom and into the bedroom, where her opened suitcase still rested on a luggage rack. "I'm flying home tonight—coming to New York was a bad idea."

"Slow down!" Cody's raised voice halted her frantic movements.

"I'm sorry," he continued in a calmer tone, "but please listen to me."

"Fine, I'm listening, but make it quick." Kate grabbed a white blouse and black slacks she'd intended on wearing while sightseeing with Grace.

"I'll call Blake back and directly ask if he gave Chelsea our address. Then I'll get in touch with the police—"

"The police!" Kate placed a hand over her heart as her pulse hammered. "So, you do think she'll do something to our house?"

"I don't know, but Blake said she was screaming at him."

"How could you bring this woman into our lives?" Kate sank onto the bed. "No, don't answer. This doesn't seem like a reaction to a one-night stand." Her shoulders wilted. "You told me it was one encounter. Did you lie to me?"

"No, I didn't lie to you. It was one night." The firmness in his tone returned. "Let me handle this, Katelynn. I got us into this mess, and I will get us out of it. I promise."

She opened her mouth to remind him of how he'd already broken the most important promise they'd made to one another. Instead, she focused on what she needed from him—reassurance he would handle things. "You're right. I think it's best you head back to California to deal with this mess. Tonight."

Chapter Twenty-Two

The redeye flight had landed in California a little past four in the morning. Cody sent a text to Kate letting her know he was driving to the house and planned to catch a few hours of shuteye before contacting Chelsea as he'd been unable to sleep during the flight.

His bedside alarm sounded at nine, and with his eyes still closed, he fumbled to hit the snooze button. "God," he groaned as he fought off sleep. "Show me how to handle things today." He rolled onto his side and drew Kate's pillow close. The passage in the Bible about putting on the full armor of God came to mind.

Cody sat up in bed bare-chested. "I put on the helmet of salvation, the breast plate of righteousness, and..." His mind had drawn a blank as to the other pieces of armor. He closed his eyes tightly. "Truth," he muttered. "I put on the belt of truth. I shod my feet with the shoes of the good news of the gospel. I pick up the sword of the Word and the shield of faith. I pray this protection on in the name of Jesus Christ. Amen."

Cody's phone vibrated on the nightstand and his upper body tensed. He craned his neck to glance at the caller ID.

Kate.

His shoulders relaxed. He grabbed his phone, put the call on speaker, and then greeted her before she had a chance to say anything. "Good morning, beautiful." He meant it, and he hoped she wouldn't cut him off for telling her. "Did you see my text about being exhausted and wanting a clear head before talking to Chelsea?"

"Yes. I read it a few hours ago. I wanted to touch base with you before I leave."

"Leave?" Cody dialed down his surprise. "Where are you going?"

"I'm meeting Grace for lunch."

He palmed his head. "I should've said good afternoon. I forgot about the three-hour time difference."

"Grace is sending her driver. He'll be here shortly. He's chauffeuring me to a famous pizza place in Manhattan where I'll meet with her. I told her I didn't feel up to it but didn't go into why, so she insisted."

After a brief lull in the conversation, Kate cleared her throat. "Have you at least talked with Blake?"

"Yes. He repeated what he told me last night, which is Chelsea has threatened us. I'm going to meet him at the shop." Cody swung his legs out of bed and stood. "Kate, I want to tell you something."

"Yes?" Her voice sounded annoyed.

"I love you." The silence on the other end of the phone dragged on for what seemed like several minutes. He scrambled to think of something to say that would remove any pressure on Kate to respond in like manner, but she spoke first.

"I don't know how to reply, Cody. Healing isn't going to happen overnight. I think the best thing you can do is continue to see your counselor."

She paused, but he kept silent, sensing Kate had more to share.

"I can't make any promises about what the future holds for us," she added. "I am praying for God to show me His will in all of this, and He gives me the ability to embrace it."

He stared Heavenward, his spirit thanking God for the slight progress in their relationship despite the setback of Chelsea's visit to Blake. Still, best not to acknowledge to Kate the glimmer of hope she'd provided.

"Cody—"

"Yes?"

"Please be safe."

"I will. I promise." She ended the call before he could suggest a prayer. He shouldn't have been so disappointed. After all, they hadn't prayed together in years, but that was about to change. He pressed recent calls and selected Kate's number. She answered on the first ring.

"There's one other thing," he said. "I want to pray for us. I haven't been doing a good job at being the head of our home, but I want to do things differently. Can we pray together?"

Kate's sobs caught him off guard. All he seemed to do lately was make her cry. Cody plunked down on the bed. "I'm sorry. I shouldn't have called you back. I should've just prayed for us without expecting you to jump onboard."

"Hold on," she choked out.

The muffled sounds of her sobs tightened his chest. His mind raced through responses to comfort her, but the options rang sappy and contrived—even though heartfelt.

Finally, Kate drew in a ragged breath. "You have no idea how long I've waited for you to initiate prayer between us."

Her words, heavy with emotion, touched his heart. Cody turned up the volume as she continued to speak.

"I've asked God more times than I can count to help you be the man He's called you be. I'd all but lost hope, and then this affair happened. God may want me to forgive you, but I don't know if I can. I'll pray about it."

###

Cody nodded at Blake and a customer at the gun display as he made his way to his office. Any other time he would have stopped and introduced himself as the owner of the pawnshop, but right now, he had only one thing on his mind—talking with Chelsea and getting her out of his life for good. He took a seat behind his desk and locked eyes with the poster on the wall of the bikini-clad model holding the Springfield XDM pistol. The Bible passage about little foxes spoiling the vine came to mind. He crossed the room, snatched the poster off the wall, and crumpled it before disposing of it in the metal trash can beside his desk.

Seated at his desk again, he revisited the meeting with the gun seller, Marty, and how the older gentleman spoke so adoringly of his late wife, Beatrice. The note Beatrice tucked into her husband's gun case had been a complete surprise to

Marty. The older man had raced back to the pawnshop, excited to read it. As Marty silently read the words, he'd fought back the tears, losing the battle more than once.

When Marty had finished the note, he looked up and astounded Cody by handing him the obviously treasured missive. Even now, Cody's chest tightened with emotion. Beatrice's words about entrusting her second love, Marty, to her first love, Jesus Christ, resonated. While she had concerns for her husband's safety in owning firearms, Beatrice realized no amount of lecturing or pleading with him to see things her way would change his mind—so she prayerfully changed hers. By entrusting Marty to Jesus, she'd untangled herself from worry.

Cody sat forward and interlaced his fingers on his desk. "Why do you worry?" he said barely above a whisper. Jesus' question to His disciples remained a literal one, thousands of years later. No amount of apologizing to Kate, pledging his fidelity to her, and showing her a true willingness to make amends guaranteed she wouldn't ask for a divorce based on biblical grounds. He needed to acknowledge the possibility and be at peace with it.

"Father, please forgive me." He blew out a weary breath. "I committed the sin of adultery long before Chelsea." Emotions choked him, and he struggled to continue giving voice to his thoughts.

"I see now pornography violated my marriage vows way before the sex with Chelsea. I ask for your forgiveness. Cleanse me of these sins in every way. I repent. Please heal Kate of the pain I've caused her. Help Kate to forgive me. Bring restoration to our marriage. Help me to honor you from this day forward.

In Jesus' name, I pray. Amen. And Lord, please help Chelsea, too. What I did to her was wrong. Amen."

Cody pulled out his cell phone, checked his recent calls, and then pressed Chelsea's number. As the phone rang, he took a deep breath and let it out slowly. When the call went to voicemail, a sense of relief washed over him. He was about to hang up when he pictured Kate's face and his promise to talk with Chelsea today and to resolve things. Avoiding conflict was what he'd done for years, and this conflict needed a resolution—the sooner, the better.

"Chelsea, this is Cody. It's important we talk. I'm back in town. Give me a call when you receive this message. Thanks."

He'd barely ended the message when the office door opened, and Blake walked in. "Bro, you look terrible!" He plopped down in one of the two chairs opposite Cody's desk. "So, have you talked to your fatal attraction this morning?"

"First off, thanks for the kind observation." Cody reeled in his sarcastic response. "I need some coffee. Do you want a cup?" He stood.

"Yeah, but let me get it for us." Blake gestured for Cody to retake his seat. "Were you praying when I walked in?" He grabbed two K-Cup pods from an open box on the filing cabinet beside the coffee maker.

"It's okay if you were praying." Blake looked over his shoulder at Cody. "If I were in your shoes, I'd be praying, too."

"I prayed earlier. I was leaving a message for Chelsea." Cody sat forward. "Look, I get you're angry over what I've done to Kate, but I'd rather you just come out and say it than hint at it."

"Hint at it?" Blake glanced at Cody, smirked, then returned to brewing the coffee. "I was clear about how I felt when you showed up at my place. As I recall, we were seconds away from throwing blows."

Blake set a cup of steaming coffee before Cody. "What you did was wrong, but I've done a lot of stupid things in my life. Who am I to throw stones?"

"If you mean it, thanks." Cody blew into his cup then took a sip of his coffee.

"I mean it." Blake sat across from him. "So, how is it?"

"It's fine. Why do you ask?" Cody raised his free hand to silence his kid brother. "Never mind—this is about the other night."

Blake grinned, "Everyone's entitled to act stupid once in a while, but you're abusing the privilege."

"I'm not amused." Cody shook his head. "I thought you were serious, but I guess—"

"Bro, bottom line, we've always got each other's back." Blake set his cup on the desk and leaned forward. "Tell me what you need me to do, and I'll do it."

"You've already done it." Cody touched his hand to his heart. "You've been a friend to Kate at a time when I couldn't see past my own selfish desires. It seems everyone's been a friend to my wife, but me." He ran his hand across his bristled cheeks. "I'm going to spend the rest of my life correcting the mistake—if she'll let me."

"I don't know how good of a friend I've been, considering I was oblivious to the problems you two were having."

"Kate was just following my lead in keeping quiet about the troubles we were having."

Blake sat back and frowned. "Months ago, when I was talking to Kate on the phone one night you worked late, she confided she felt fat. Before I could say anything, she blurted out her seeing a model's photograph on your computer. I assumed she felt insecure because of the pic, so I told her photos like those are a dime a dozen and not to give it a second thought. I also told her she's beautiful and you love her."

Cody's shoulders wilted, "What did she say?"

"I think she was crying after I told her you love her. I asked if she was okay, but she said she had to take another call. We never talked about it again."

"I've been an idiot." Cody buried his hands in his face and openly wept, even with Blake seeing his vulnerability. Blake's conversation with Kate highlighted how much repair work was needed to help mend his wife's broken heart.

Chapter Twenty-Three

"Thank you for everything," Kate said as she leaned in and gave Grace a lingering hug.

"I wish you would change your mind about leaving." The younger woman persisted in voicing her thoughts amidst the friendly embrace. "I had so many fun things planned for us."

Kate patted her back before separating from the hug. "You've already done too much, the flight here and back, the gorgeous hotel, a driver to get around, an amazing lunch."

She glanced over Grace's shoulder at the pizzeria. "This place was great. I can hardly believe all the celebrities I spotted. When I tell my friend Sandie, she's going to be green with envy. Don't worry, the secret hotspot is safe with me, but I may have to bring her here one day. She'd love it. It would be like the time Lucy, Fred, and Ethel ate at the Brown Derby while ogling movie stars."

Grace's brows pinched together. "Lucy and Ethel?"

"Old friends," Kate chuckled. She turned to the chauffeur a few feet away. "I hope you like the pizza." She pointed to the carry-out box in his hands. "You've been such a help to me and my husband."

"It's been my pleasure, ma'am. And thank you." He looked down at the box then back up at Kate. "This was very thoughtful."

Grace leaned into Kate. "Speaking of your husband," she bunched the cobalt blue wool scarf she was wearing under her neck and held it in place while she spoke, "So let me get this straight, Cody's not expecting you tonight?"

"No. He's not, but my place is with my husband. I see that now. I'm not sure how to deal with all the emotions, but I know God will help us through it."

"I'll pray things go well. I'm sorry my husband wasn't able to be here this afternoon. He planned on joining us for dinner tonight. I wanted you to meet him."

"An apology isn't needed. Please thank him for sharing his lovely wife with me for the day." Kate turned the collar up on her leather jacket, but the cold air still sent a chill down her spine.

"I've learned a lot from you about forgiveness in a very short period of time. I see why my grandmother adored you. You're a very generous woman."

"You're pretty generous yourself. You have given so freely to a new friend."

"Kate, you're generous in love, which is far more meaningful."

"It's only because God is helping me. Always remember, you don't have to do things in your own strength."

"I'll try," Grace blinked back tears. After a moment of silence, she stepped closer to Kate. "I think you may have figured out my marriage isn't as good as it could be," she said in a hushed tone.

"I sensed something might be wrong," Kate said in an equally lowered voice, "but people generally don't like you to know things before they're ready to tell you. I've learned the hard way."

Grace pointed to the town car. "Could we talk for a few minutes?"

"Of course we can."

Seated in the backseat, Grace turned her face away from Kate. She spoke after several seconds. "I love my husband, and..."

"Take your time." Kate unzipped her leather jacket.

At Grace's request, the driver went inside the pizzeria to enjoy his pizza, but before doing, so he'd turned on the heater inside the vehicle.

"My flight isn't for several hours," Kate said. "I've got as much time as you need."

Grace's body stiffened, but she faced Kate with tears in her eyes. "I love my husband, and I believe he loves me, but I feel as though he's unwilling to make me a priority in his life, and it hurts. What makes things worse is I did the same thing to him after we were married. You would think I'd be more understanding, but his empty promises have built a wall of resentment I can't seem to tear down."

Kate nodded knowingly. She'd fought for Cody's attention for as long as she could remember. "Wanting to be desired by the person you love is not a bad thing, yet at the same time, the right desires for the wrong reasons can wreak havoc to our self-esteem and to our loved one."

"What are you saying?" Grace's tone sharpened. "Am I being selfish for wanting my husband to spend time with me?"

Kate cupped Grace's hands in her own. "Not at all, but our husbands can't meet all of our needs."

"True." Grace's brows rose. "But I'm only human."

"Yes, you are." Kate gave Grace's hands a gentle squeeze then released her grip. "And so is your husband. The Bible teaches us God's priorities, and when we put those first, He adds all the other things."

Her gaze locked on Kate. "What are God's priorities?"

"Jesus told us, He said to seek first the kingdom of God and His righteousness, and all these things shall be added to you—in this case, our spouses. Does that mean our spouse will suddenly begin to chase us around the bedroom twenty-four seven or become unable to spend time apart from us for longer than five minutes? Of course not, but who would really want that much attention—especially if it relegated God to second place?"

"The chasing around the bedroom part might not be so bad for a while," Grace chuckled.

Kate joined in her laughter.

"Being serious," Grace began, "I get what you're saying. Grandma was a living example of putting God first. I don't know if she shared with you how much physical pain she was in at times, but no matter how her day was going, she was intentional about seeking and praying for God's will in her circumstances."

"I imagine it wasn't always a cakewalk for your grandmother. You said something key—she intentionally sought and prayed for God's will." Kate rested her head against the back of the seat. "Praying Thy will be done can be a scary prayer if you don't know how much God loves you." She turned to Grace. "He loves us a lot, in fact, more than we can comprehend."

Kate extended her arm. The younger woman collapsed on her shoulder, sobbing. "Your grandmother was wise, but she didn't gain wisdom without many walks through many valleys with Jesus. I've come to a point in my life where I'm ready to take those walks with Him. I don't know what's ahead for me and Cody, but I will face whatever it is with Jesus. Going forward, I choose to make Jesus first in my life. How about you?"

###

Cody held the phone away from his ear, but Chelsea's voice still reverberated in the room. His stomach clenched as she yelled profanities about being left in the middle of the night. It had been hours since he'd left the voicemail message for her, so he'd assumed Blake had blown things out of proportion—it wouldn't have been a first. But her profane-laden rant underscored Blake's assessment of the situation.

"I need you to calm down." He kept his tone even despite her talking over him. Cody rose to shut the door to his office and locked it.

"I will not be brushed aside now that you've had your fun—"

"Hold on," he interjected in a firmer tone. "I called you at noon, and it's after five. Who's ignoring whom?" As soon as the words left his mouth, he wanted to pull them back. Pointing a finger at her actions would only stall their conversation.

"Some people have to actually work for a living. Not everyone is their own boss. This is the first chance I've had to call you back. Did your weirdo brother tell you I wanted your home address? I'd like to meet your wife. I think she'd be interested to know how you treat a woman who might be carrying your child."

"What did you say?" Cody's knees buckled. He braced himself against one of the gun safes nearest his desk.

"You heard me. Hold on a minute. I need to go someplace where I can talk privately."

His mind spun with the details of what led to that night. He had wanted to use protection and said he'd make a quick trip to the drugstore. She objected, saying it would ruin the moment. Cody palmed his forehead as he recalled the lack of common sense in the heat of the moment. Chelsea assured him she took birth control, and he needn't worry—foolishly, he'd believed her.

"Okay, I can talk now." Her tone of voice had softened. "We need to get together and discuss a few things. Are you free now?"

"No! I'm not free now. And get together to discuss exactly what?" He needed to control his emotions and to think clearly. Off-the-cuff responses wouldn't be effective in getting things resolved. He had to slow his thoughts down and speak reasonably. She was mad about how he'd treated her, and rightly so.

He took a seat at his desk. "Chelsea, I understand the way I treated you was wrong. I'm sorry for my choices and the hurt it's caused. If I could do things differently, I would, but I can't. However, what I can do is sincerely apologize. Please, hear me out—"

Cody pulled the phone from his ear and stared at the screen with his jaw slack. After a couple of seconds, the disbelief registered. She'd hung up. He dropped his cell phone onto his desk. *What am I going to do now?*

Chapter Twenty-Four

Seated in the backseat of the town car, Kate continued to quietly hold Grace as the young woman sobbed.

"I'm afraid he doesn't love me anymore," Grace murmured through her tears.

Kate righted the young woman and looked her in the eyes. "I can't recall the last time I wasn't second-guessing Cody's love and trying to fix our marriage. Truth is, I can't fix him or our marriage."

Grace blotted her tears with her fingertips. "I'm exhausted from trying to fix things."

The woman's transparency led Kate to share more about her own struggles. "I don't think Cody knows how deeply fear is rooted in me, too. It's prevented me from having children. "

"How so?" Grace grimaced. "I'm sorry, that's none of my business."

Kate smiled to dispel the awkwardness of the moment. "The night you scooped me up from the bathroom floor at Ling's, then drove me home is the night you earned the right to ask me anything. Besides, you've been open with me."

"Still, if you'd prefer not to answer, I understand."

"I'd like to try and explain." Kate sat back. "My husband's folks did the best they knew how given they didn't have positive role models for parents. Still, they failed him terribly."

Grace's eyes widened. "But weren't they Christians like you and your husband, and what about your parents?"

Kate took a moment to think through her response. It was one thing to judge a person's actions, but another to judge their salvation. "Cody's father didn't profess faith in Jesus Christ, so I'll leave it at that. Cody's mother is still alive. She identifies as a Christian, and I see Jesus in her life. As for my parents, we're estranged. They don't believe Jesus is the only way to Heaven. A couple of years ago, I got the courage to share a handful of Bible verses with them, and I asked a few questions. I thought I spoke respectfully and lovingly. They called me a fanatic. We haven't talked since—by their choice. I continue to pray for them."

"I'm so sorry," Grace said.

"In my mind, our parents taught us how to fail in relationships. I feared a broken or, at best, dysfunctional home for any children we might have together. Our strained relationship solidified the fear."

"I'm glad you're praying for your parents, but have you also prayed about having a child with Cody—I mean before all of this stuff with another woman happened?"

"More times than I can count. I've come to realize I left no room in my thinking for correction. My decision not to bring a child into this world excluded not only Cody from the process, but more importantly, God."

"It's not too late for you and Cody to have children," Grace chimed in, halting deeper thought on Kate's part.

"Prior to Cody and I even talking about a baby, we need to work on our relationship with God and with each other. I will say I feel hopeful about our future. Something I haven't felt in a long time."

Kate glanced at the time on the dashboard clock. An hour had passed since they climbed into the back of the town car. As insightful as it was to open up to Grace, Kate guided her back to the issues that had prompted a request to talk in the first place. "What are your thoughts about this conversation?"

"Honestly, I've allowed everyone and everything to come before God, so it's no wonder everyone and everything has disappointed me. Present company and my grandma excluded, of course." Grace smiled.

Kate leaned forward. "Everyone will disappoint us at one time or another." Her tone remained serious. "Don't put me or anyone else on the pedestal reserved for God."

"You're right." Grace looked over Kate's shoulder. "My driver is headed this way. Before he gets here, may I suggest something?"

"Sure." She imagined the young woman wanted to ride along to the airport to see her off.

Grace locked eyes with Kate. "It's about Cody."

"Not what I expected, but please go ahead."

"Thank you," Grace said. "Once you and Cody have worked through the hurts of the affair, and I believe you will, you should tell him what you've told me about having children."

###

Cody paced his small office while trying to process the news Chelsea might be pregnant, but instead, his thoughts ricocheted off one another. *This can't be happening.*

He kicked the metal trash can across the room and immediately regretted it. Emotions couldn't be allowed to rule—it would only make things worse—if that was even possible. He retook his seat and stared at the mound of paperwork on his desk. The large ammunition calendar grabbed his attention, and with one swipe, he cleared the stacks of papers and receipts which obscured the dates.

Leaned forward, he slowly ran his index finger along the previous week to double-check when Chelsea had returned to reclaim her merchandise, little over a week ago. It's too soon for her to be pregnant. This was obviously an irate woman lashing out. If only he'd called her after she left the first message, but fear had ruled the decision to make a clean break. All he'd thought about was Kate.

"Bro!" Blake pounded on the door. "You okay?"

Cody remained hunched over his desk. He shifted his gaze from the calendar to the doorknob but didn't have the physical or emotional energy to cross the room, unlock the door, and explain what just happened. "I'm okay. I'll be out in a few minutes."

"No way. Let me in now." Blake thumped the door again. "If you don't open this door, I'm going to kick it in."

Blake's threat was empty because they both knew the door was impenetrable, but his younger brother's concern propelled him out of the chair. He would reveal what just transpired with Chelsea, including her pregnancy scare tactic, and then he'd retell everything to Kate. This was something she had to hear from him.

As he crossed the room to open the door, the realization he hadn't suffered a panic attack dawned on him. If ever there was a moment to panic, it was during the exchange with Chelsea. Maybe, it was like Kate said, God was going to use this horrible experience for good.

Chapter Twenty-Five

"Chelsea says she's pregnant, and the baby is mine," Cody blurted to Blake, whose mouth fell open. "I don't buy it," Cody quickly added.

"What do you mean, you don't buy it?" Blake dropped into a chair opposite Cody's desk. "That she's pregnant or the baby is yours?"

"Pregnant." Cody sat at his desk. "Did the locksmith get out here and repair the buzzer for the front door?"

"Yes. We're all good. It was a simple wiring issue—hold on," Blake held up his hand, "Back to Chelsea. When did you talk to her?"

"A few minutes ago." Cody's chest heaved with a deep breath; he exhaled in one burst of air, "What am I going to do?"

"Bro, if you tell Kate what Chelsea said, she's going to go ballistic."

He clasped the back of his neck with both hands. "This is the biggest mistake of my life. I don't know how she can ever forgive me. Right now, I don't know if I even want her to forgive me."

"Wait..." Blake stood. "You didn't use a raincoat?"

"That's a disgusting phrase." Cody shook his head. "To answer your question, I don't use condoms with Kate, so why would I have any with me? It's not like I planned for this to happen."

Blake sat forward. "Is Chelsea angry?"

"Talk about an understatement. The only thing she wanted was for us to meet. When I said no to her scare tactic, she hung up."

"Scare tactic?" Blake sat back. He folded his arms across his chest. "You had sex with a woman you don't know; you didn't use a condom, she says she's pregnant with your kid, and you're telling me you don't buy the possibility she could be telling the truth?"

Cody rubbed his temples. "My mind is all over the place. One minute I'm thinking there is no way she's pregnant by me, and the next I'm thinking, what if she really is. I'm also thinking about Kate and the fact Chelsea has said more than once she wants to meet her."

Cody glanced over Blake's shoulder. "One of us needs to be out front for customers. Maybe I should just close up today."

"Bro, calm down; the front door is locked. No one is getting inside the shop without our knowledge. Your mind really is jumping around."

Blake walked around the desk and knelt beside Cody. "Here's what your little brother suggests. Call Chelsea back and agree to meet with her. Tell her to come here. I'll hang out in case things get squirrely."

"Squirrelly?" Cody shook his head. "I feel like I'm getting bad advice from dad. As for Chelsea meeting me here, no way—not happening. I'd rather call her back and talk this out over the phone. First I have to call Kate. No more secrets."

"Chelsea's already made it clear she wants to see you face-to-face. A phone conversation isn't going to fly with her."

"Maybe I could tell her I want to—"

"Stop." Blake tapped the arm of the chair and recaptured Cody's full attention. "I hate to be the bearer of bad news, but she could actually be pregnant, and the baby might be your kid. So she's calling the shots right now."

Cody clutched a handful of his hair. "She's lying. Those over-the-counter pregnancy tests don't confirm pregnancy this early. She can't be pregnant by me."

"You can keep saying that all you want, but I'm telling you there's a possibility. The kid I was babysitting the night you came over, well Stephanie, the mom, had a blood test done when she was only three days late."

Cody grabbed his phone from the center of the desk, where he'd tossed it after ending the call with Chelsea. He typed in the words "soonest you can a take pregnancy test," into the search bar. He slumped in his seat as he read the information. "This says a test can be taken as early as seven days post ovulation."

"I told you," Blake said.

Cody dropped his phone on his desk before covering his eyes with his hands. "I have to tell Kate and right now."

"Bad idea," Blake said calmly. "Meet with Chelsea here first. Listen to what she has to say and go from there. I don't see the point in freaking Kate out unless there's really a baby?"

Cody groaned. "A baby," he repeated the word under his breath several times. "My wife has a right to have a say in how I should handle it."

"Fine, there's no time like the present." Blake cleared his throat. Cody looked up to see Blake pointing at the cell phone on the desk. "That's her calling."

###

"Hello, Katelynn."

Kate swallowed back her disappointment at the dullness in Cody's tone. "Is everything okay?"

"Your timing couldn't be worse," he said.

She locked eyes with Grace, seated at the foot of the bed beside an opened suitcase. "Hold on a second, Cody."

Kate muted her phone. "Excuse me for a moment," she said to her friend before making her way to the bathroom. As she closed the bathroom door, Kate recalled the last time she had received life-changing news in similar surroundings. Grace's last-minute invitation to accompany her to the airport had probably been God intervening once again.

Unmuting her phone, Kate resumed the conversation with Cody. "What's going on?"

Although she didn't believe in déjà vu, staring at her reflection in the mirror above the sink, eyes brimming with tears, it was as if she'd been catapulted in time back to Ling's restaurant. She leaned back against the door and closed her eyes, bracing for whatever he might say.

"Hang on, babe." Cody hadn't muted the phone, so she listened intently. "Blake, I need to talk to my wife—alone, please." After a few seconds, Cody resumed speaking, "May I say a prayer for us, first?"

Kate took a deep breath then opened her eyes. His request grounded her at the moment. She needed to trust God. "Please do."

"Lord, I'm afraid right now, but then you already know this. You also know I want to heal my marriage." He cleared his throat. "Help, me. Help us. In Jesus' name. Amen."

"Thank you for praying." Her voice cracked. "I want to say something before you tell me whatever it is you're going tell me."

While eyeing her reflection in the mirror, Kate recalled the Bible verse she'd written out as encouragement at home. I can do all things through Christ who strengthens me.

She firmed her quivering lower lip. "I'm trying to focus on forgiveness because I know God wants me to, but truthfully, I'm not there yet. It's like I'm on constant alert something will go wrong. Do you understand?"

"More than you know. I'm discovering this isn't a sprint but a marathon. I'm in it for the long haul. I want to show you over time how much I love you, and like you, there's this looming sense something is going to prevent us from working things out."

The tension in her shoulders increased. "Blake didn't give her our address, did he?"

"No." Cody exhaled loudly. "But she wants to meet with me to talk."

"Talk with you about what?" Surely this woman didn't think Cody would be with her after he'd told her he loved his wife and wanted to work on the marriage. "You did make it clear being with her was a mistake, so what could she possibly want to talk to you about?"

"Chelsea says she's pregnant—"

"Pregnant!" Kate lowered her voice. She turned away from the mirror and gently thumped her head against the bathroom door. Top of her list to discuss with Cody had been whether or not he'd used a condom. She didn't want to worry about contracting a sexually transmitted disease.

"Katelyn, there's no way that could be possible—"

"But she's saying the child is yours. Please tell me you used protection."

"No." He mumbled something that ended with the word stupid, then groaned. "I'm not sure what she plans to gain from telling me she's pregnant, but there's a motive."

"How do you know she's not pregnant?" Kate's mind flooded with questions. "Have you seen a doctor to be tested for any STDs? How could you bring this misery into our lives?"

"I'm sorry," Cody wept as he spoke. "I know I keep saying I'm sorry, but it's true. This has been the biggest mistake I've ever made. I don't want to lose you over it. I want to be the man you hoped you'd married."

The temptation to ignore his emotional apology and end the call gnawed at her thoughts, while a memory of him standing at the altar and mouthing the words "I love you" even before the minister spoke softened her heart. If she didn't believe Cody truly loved her, forgiveness would be impossible. She didn't want to throw away the hope of a changed man, one who had learned his lesson and was better for it.

"I want you to be that man, too," she finally said.

"You do?" The optimism in his voice stretched cross the miles. "Really?"

"Yes, but more importantly, I want you to be the man God is calling you to be." She faced the mirror and squared her shoulders. "I also want to scream at you, shake you, and a part of me wants you to grovel for forgiveness."

"I'll grovel," he said. "I'll do whatever it takes to prove myself to you and earn your trust."

The thought of someone extorting money from her family ignited a fire in Kate's belly. "Do you think she wants cash to keep quiet?"

"She is struggling financially. She mentioned the pawnshop and my being a successful businessman more than once."

Kate walked over to the mirror and stared at her reflection. "Set a meeting. I want to be there. And Cody, don't let her know I'm going to be present."

"I don't like this. I could be placing you in harm's way. We don't know what she's capable of."

"Whatever it is she wants to say to you, she'll say to us. I need you to do two more things."

"Name it."

"Let's meet with your counselor as soon as possible."

"I'll call first thing in the morning and make an appointment. What's the other thing?"

"Get checked out thoroughly by a doctor."

"I'll make both appointments as soon we hang up. So you're coming back tonight?"

"Yes. My flight is at 7:40. I'll get in at 11:05. Can you pick me up at the airport?"

"Of course, text the flight information to me, and I'll be there. Is it okay if I stay at the house with you? I'll sleep in the guest room. I don't want you to be alone."

She looked at her left hand, and her throat tightened with emotion. The gold band on her ring finger once represented the beginning of a life with Cody quite different from the one being lived out now. "I'll think about it."

Chapter Twenty-Six

"Hello, Cody." Dr. Sam shook Cody's hand and then turned to his wife. "Good afternoon, Mrs. James." The counselor extended her hand to Kate. "I'm Dr. Samantha Novak. Please, make yourselves comfortable."

Cody ushered Kate to one of the two oversized sand-colored chairs opposite the doctor's desk. Based on Kate's composed expression, she didn't appear to be as uncomfortable as he'd been during the first session. But then, she wasn't the guilty party. He took a seat beside her and placed his hands in his lap, interlocking his fingers to better control his restlessness.

"Thank you for seeing us on such short notice, Dr. Sam." Cody turned to Kate. "She suggested I call her that."

Kate nodded her understanding, even though she hadn't asked for an explanation.

"Again, thank you for seeing us on such short notice," Cody said. "Who calls Monday morning and gets an appointment the same day." He tugged at the collar of his shirt. Hopefully, Dr. Sam would disprove Kate's idea to meet with Chelsea later today.

"I'd like to jump right in as to why my wife and I needed to see you so urgently. We want your professional advice."

"I'd like to hear what your wife thinks about being here. Is that okay with you, Mrs. James?"

"Thank you, Dr. Novak," Kate glanced around the room. "By the way, your office is lovely. The space is very tranquil."

"Thank you."

Cody sat forward. "I said the same thing my first visit."

"Actually," Dr. Sam smiled at Cody, "You said my office was 'peaceful,' but you've each expressed a similar point of view." She faced Kate. "Would you say you and your husband often have like thoughts?"

Kate's posture stiffened. "Sometimes."

"Your husband has made it clear he wants you to attend his sessions. How do you feel about that?"

Cody resisted the urge to look at Kate. He didn't want the doctor to think he was leading his wife to an answer. Lately, Kate had become quite vocal about what she did and did not want to do. He'd only recently come to realize she'd gone along with whatever whims he fancied at the cost of her own happiness.

Kate smoothed her skirt. "I don't think he fully understands how much damage has been done."

Cody sank a little in his seat. The blunt truth had pierced his heart. He pressed his lips together to sit quietly and listen even though he longed to say, again, how sorry he was for the choices he'd made.

"Before we delve into why you're here today, I'd like to pray. Is that okay with both of you?"

Cody nodded without hesitation.

"That's a good idea," Kate said. "I want what God wants, which is to forgive Cody, but I can't do that when every time I close my eyes, I see him in the arms of another woman."

He reached over to rest his hand on his wife's forearm, but she jerked away.

"See," Kate said sharply. "It's as if he expects everything to be better overnight."

"Hurt and anger are normal reactions to what's happened in your marriage," Dr. Sam glanced at Cody, then back to Kate. "Your trust has been betrayed. And it's been compromised by someone you've pledged your life to and believed they'd pledged the same."

Kate grabbed a handful of tissues from a box on the corner of the doctor's desk, wiping away tears as she spoke. "I don't know if our marriage can survive what's happened."

Panic hijacked his thoughts. "Hearing my wife say these things scares me, Dr. Sam. I'm willing to do whatever it takes to make things better. Tell me what I need to do, and I'll do it." He knelt beside Kate's chair, and although she didn't make eye contact with him, she didn't push him away.

He gripped the armrest. "Katelyn, we need God's help. We cannot do this in our own strength."

"Amen," the doctor said softly.

"Cody," Kate's voice cracked, "Did you tell the doctor how I learned of your cheating on me?"

He looked into her tear-filled eyes. "Yes, I told her." Many thoughts raced through his mind, but the one that captured his voice was the most humbling. She needed to hear him speak the truth without glossing over it. "Yes. I told Dr. Sam you overheard me and Chelsea on my cell phone because I inadvertently called you."

Kate shook her head, and tears spilled down her cheeks.

"Mrs. James, what your husband is talking about, whether he realizes it or not, is a form of redemptive love. Jesus exemplifies redemptive love. He died for us while we chose the wrong things in life. With God's help, there is hope for your marriage. You will each be called upon to not only entrust one another to God but, more importantly, yourselves during this messy process called healing. Would you like to hear more?"

"Yes." Kate nodded toward his empty chair, suggesting she needed space.

He cleared his throat of heartache and retook his seat.

"I'm going to share with you out of first Peter." She glanced at Cody, "This Scripture beautifully holds hands with what I had you read in Corinthians."After the doctor shared the verses about Christ's suffering and His example to follow, she looked up at Kate. "What do you think?"

"It's a lot to ask." Kate's chest expanded with a deep breath she let out in a rush. "Treating Cody with love and patience in hopes he will change and honor God is a daunting mission."

###

Kate's throat tightened as the counselor clasped her hands in the center of her desk. A loaded statement would likely follow, and Kate wasn't sure how much she wanted to say in front of Cody right now.

"Mrs. James, if you had the power to change your circumstances, would you?"

If the woman was joking, it wasn't funny. "That sounds like a rhetorical question." Kate reminded herself Pastor Jordan had recommended this counselor for a reason.

Dr. Novak turned to Cody. "In your previous session, you were clear about wanting to change your circumstances, but you also expressed not feeling as though you have the power to do so. Do you still feel that way?"

Cody nodded. "I'm a little more optimistic since Kate is here with me today."

"Mrs. James, what I'm getting from you is that you see only two options: live with the circumstances and move on from it, or walk away. You don't see any middle ground. Is my assessment accurate?"

Kate crossed her arms. "Pretty much."

The doctor rested one of her hands on the Bible she'd read from earlier. "The apostle Paul was familiar with tough times, yet he didn't allow the difficulties he faced to get the best of him. In Philippians, he talks about how his imprisonment was used for the advancement of the Gospel. When we look at our hardships through the lens of fulfilling God's purpose, we free ourselves from being enslaved to anger."

"I'm not following you," Cody said.

"Me either." Kate tapped her foot in place, her frustration rising from simmering to a full boil inside her gut. If the counselor had a remedy for overcoming the anger, then she had better spit it out—and soon, or Kate would explode from the pressure.

Dr. Novak reopened her Bible. "May I read the passage in Philippians I just mentioned?"

"We're here to be enlightened." Kate smiled in hopes of softening her sarcasm.

After the doctor finished reading about apostle Paul's imprisonment and perspective, she looked up. "Thoughts?"

"I still don't understand," Kate said.

"The solution is to focus on Christ, and not the circumstance," Dr. Novak said. "Paul, who was unjustly imprisoned, was no longer free to preach the Gospel, yet he rejoiced, and he encouraged others to rejoice in their circumstances. Paul chose to focus on Jesus instead of his confinement, and in doing so, Paul sought to discover what he could learn from his predicament."

Kate leaned forward, needing to understand. "Paul's situation was quite different than ours."

"His situation was far direr than anything most of us will ever face. He understood God uses all circumstances in the lives of His children for good."

Kate sat back. "I recently shared that verse about God using all things for good with Cody." She faced him. "I don't know if you remember, but that promise from God was part of my prayer for you when you had the panic attack on the flight to New York."

"I remember," his eyes welled.

Kate turned back to the doctor, "Go on."

"I'm not trying to excuse or minimize your husband's behavior. In no way do I want you to hear me as negating the pain you're experiencing. My hope is each of you will put God first along this path and trust through faith He will give you the healing you need."

Cody grabbed several tissues from the box on the doctor's desk and wiped his eyes. "You're saying it will take time to heal the hurts, but God's promise is to never leave us or forsake us."

"In part, yes, that's what I'm saying." She angled her head to one side and locked eyes with Kate. "What do you think I'm saying?"

"I believe you used the apostle Paul as an example to show a mere man—or a woman in my case—needs to choose to see beyond our feelings and our circumstances. My heartache isn't without a purpose. Right now, I can't say I see the purpose."

"You're correct in your belief, Kate. I'd also like to assure you; there is a purpose."

"Should Cody and I separate while we try to work through things? He's currently staying at his mother's home. I don't see that as being a long-term solution."

"Me either," Cody chimed in.

"Mrs. James, I counsel husbands and wives against making big decisions in a desperate pursuit to find peace and stability. Big decisions include everything from trial separations to divorce and all that lies between. There's a time for big decisions, it's part of the process, but there are no quick fixes."

"Are you saying Cody should be at home?" Part of her liked the idea of him being at home. She'd know what he was up to, but another part of her doubted she would ever be able to trust him again if suspicion was the foundation she was building on.

"If you two continue to see me, we can navigate decisions together prayerfully. The last thing either of you wants is kneejerk reactions. For now, where Cody is staying seems reasonable. This temporary arrangement will give each of you a chance to reflect and process things independently, which isn't bad, given the intensity of emotions."

"I'd like to see you again," Kate said.

"I'm pleased to hear that, and feel free to call me Dr. Sam."

"Okay, and you can call me Kate."

Cody let out a hefty sigh. "There's an old joke about marriage that goes, 'Marriage is about becoming one. The question is which one?'"

"Cute," the doctor smiled. "A little levity can make a difficult situation more bearable. Cody, we still have some time left. I'd like to hear the reason for needing to see me so urgently?"

Chapter Twenty-Seven

Cody pulled into traffic then glanced over at Kate, who remained quiet since they'd left Dr. Sam's office. "Would you like to talk?"

"About?" Kate's gaze remained fixed on the front windshield. Her body language and facial expression revealed the disappointment over Dr. Sam's advisement against the two of them meeting with Chelsea, but rather than say so, Kate went along with the recommendation. He couldn't help but think she felt he'd betrayed her again.

"I know you believe meeting with Chelsea could be beneficial. I wanted to think the same. But the doctor's right; Chelsea might have ulterior motives. It's not safe." He stole another glance as he slowed for a red light.

After several agonizing seconds of silence, he reached across the seat to tap her on the shoulder but drew back his hand. The last thing he wanted was to demand anything of her. "Please don't do this."

She sighed, "Do what?"

"This. Not telling me what you're feeling." His tone had been sharper than intended. He tightened his grip on the steering wheel. The light turned green. "I'm looking out for your safety.

Besides, we don't even know if Chelsea would agree to meet with me if you're present."

Kate turned to him. "You said she keeps mentioning me. I'm beginning to wonder if you don't want the two of us together because you're afraid she will tell me something you haven't already told me."

"Like?" Cody speared her with a look he instantly regretted. He needed help—fast. "I want to pray." He flipped on the right blinker to pull over to the curb. Once parked, he turned in his seat to face her. "I'd like God to guide me in this conversation. I tend to foul things up."

"True." Her agreement conveyed annoyance.

"Look, you're working yourself into a snit over nothing." Before he could backpedal his comment and remind her that he wanted to pray, she opened the door to the Jeep.

She arched her brows. "We're close enough to home. I'll walk the rest of the way."

He gently held onto her forearm to prevent her from exiting the vehicle. "Consider this, we're in counseling to help us get our marriage back on track, and what happens? We're doing what the doctor counseled against—we're focused on ourselves, rather than on God." He waited a moment for her reaction. At least she hadn't broken free from his grasp and stormed off.

"Katelynn, I think it's important we stay mindful the devil doesn't want healing for us. I believe God does, and with His help, day by day, we can come out on the other side of this."

Kate closed the door.

He released his hold on her. "I want our marriage to be better than it was before, and that means not clamming up when something is bothering us. We've both been guilty of this and for far too long. Let's do it differently."

He sat back in his seat and joined her in staring out the windshield. "I should have said what I really thought when you first suggested meeting with Chelsea. I didn't because I wanted you to be happy. I ended up going along with something I didn't feel right about in my gut."

"You may be right," Kate finally said. "But what if we meet with Chelsea in Dr. Sam's office? Clearly, she could benefit from some godly counseling."

"I don't know," he mumbled. If only she'd made this suggestion twenty minutes ago while in the doctor's office. Looking into Kate's beautiful green eyes weakened his revolve. His heart pounded. "I'll agree if the doctor is willing."

While he wasn't afraid of anything Chelsea could say to Kate, he couldn't shake the feeling this was still a bad idea.

###

"Hello, Chelsea. I hope you'll listen to this message." Cody looked at Kate, who sat across from him at the kitchen table. It was bad enough he was setting a meeting with Chelsea, but he was doing so with his wife's blessing and in their own kitchen.

"I hate this..." he mouthed to Kate. Regaining his focus, he continued with the voicemail message. "I'm sorry for just now following up with you. My wife and I wanted to discuss your request to meet. I'll agree to it on two conditions. One, my wife will be present, and two, we meet at my therapist's office."

Once Dr. Sam's questions about Chelsea's temperament and what he and Kate hoped to gain from meeting with Chelsea had been addressed, Dr. Sam consented. If Chelsea would agree to the meeting—and that was a big "if"—Dr. Sam would meet for a session this Friday.

"I'd like to apologize to you face-to-face for how things have turned out. We can also talk about what you mentioned, but only if you agree to the guidelines. My therapist has blocked out time for this Friday. The appointment is at 6:00 p.m. I scheduled it late because you're working. Please call me at your earliest convenience."

Cody ended the call. He swallowed hard. The thought of sitting in the same room with Chelsea tightened his chest.

"Do you think she will call back?" Kate's tone conveyed anticipation, yet he couldn't help but think of the old adage, "Be careful what you wish for; it might come true."

"There's no telling. She hung up on me the last time we talked." He glanced at the cuckoo clock above the kitchen door. "It's almost six now. If she's going to call, it would be anytime from now until—"

His phone vibrated in his hand, and he clenched it. "It looks like we have your answer."

Kate sat forward. "Put the call on speakerphone."

Cody looked at the screen on his phone and groaned. "It's only Blake."

"Oh," Kate slumped in her chair. "You still need to answer it."

He swiped the screen to respond without putting the call on speakerphone. "What's up, Blake?"

"Are you with Kate?"

"Yes. What's wrong?" The urgency in Blake's voice unsettled Cody, and he stood. "You sound weird."

Kate looked up at him. "Is everything okay?"

"I don't know," Cody mouthed.

"Bro, Chelsea was just here with some dude who looked like he belongs in a UFC ring. She demanded your address. I didn't give it to her. Lucky for me, a couple was looking at the jewelry case because if I'd been alone in the shop, I think the guy with Chelsea would've tried to persuade me—if you know what I mean."

"Don't say anything more. I need to think." Cody paced in front of the table.

"The dude looked like he could snap me like a toothpick. You need to get a restraining order against this chick until you can figure out what's what with the whole pregnancy thing."

"Blake! I said, give me a minute." He lowered his voice. "Sorry."

Kate stood. "What's going on?" Her brows furrowed. "You're scaring me. Is Blake all right? What's happening?"

"It's Chelsea," Cody told her. "This is exactly what I feared would happen. Blake says she was at the shop a few minutes ago with a big guy to try to get our home address again."

Belatedly, Cody remembered Blake still on the phone. "I've got to go. Kate and I need to talk."

"Sure. But do what I said and get a restraining order."

"She hasn't done anything—yet, so it's not an option. Thanks for the heads up. To be safe, close the shop."

"Sounds good to me. I don't like the idea of Chelsea coming back with that dude and offing me because I wouldn't give her your address."

"Not funny," Cody said sternly. "Go home. Call me when you get there."

Kate took a seat and crossed her arms. "I feel like you're not telling me everything. What else did Blake say?"

"The guy who accompanied Chelsea didn't outright threaten him, but the 'big dude' as Blake said, was definitely with her for intimidation."

"Intimidation?" Her eyes widened. "Is Blake okay?"

"Yes, but I think it's time I involve the police."

"I can't believe this is happening." Her posture stiffened. "I agree about calling the police."

"Another thing," Cody said. "I'm sleeping here tonight. I'll bunk in the guest bedroom again. We're also getting an alarm installed. I'm not taking any more chances when it comes to Chelsea."

He thought of the gun safe in the master bedroom. Kate had been against having what she called an arsenal at home yet agreed to two firearms for home security. "I've done a poor job of fulfilling the head of house role in our marriage, but that's over."

Chapter Twenty-Eight

Kate rolled over in bed. She stared at the illuminated digital clock on Cody's nightstand set to go off in ten minutes. Her stomach churned as the time changed from five twenty to five twenty-one. If she called in sick this morning, it wouldn't be a total lie.

A few bars of The Eagle's song "Peaceful, Easy Feeling" played on her phone, signaling an incoming call from Cody. She fumbled to reach her cell phone on the nightstand then swiped the screen to answer the call.

"Good morning," he said softly.

"Good morning." Kate refused to smile at the sound of his voice, even though he wouldn't have been the wiser since he was in another room of the house. "How did you sleep?"

"Not great, and you?"

"Same for me." Kate tugged the covers over her shoulders. She would call in sick today—definitely not ready to get out of bed, much less head to her office. "Are you going to the shop this morning?"

"No. I'll give Blake a callback and ask him to hold the fort down. He left two voice messages for me during the night. I'll find out what that's about in a few minutes. I also plan to call the company I use at the shop and get someone out here to install an alarm on the house."

She sat up in bed. "So you haven't heard from Chelsea about meeting at Dr. Sam's office?"

"No," he exhaled loudly. "How about we finish this conversation in the kitchen? It feels a little silly to be talking to you on the phone when you're just down the hall from me."

"Okay. Give me a few minutes." Kate reluctantly tossed back the covers. "I'll make coffee for us—"

"You don't have to." His tone brightened. "I already brewed coffee and made bacon and eggs."

Seated on the edge of the mattress, her body slumped. "I thought I wanted this kind of attention from you, but it feels insincere. It's as though you're only doing it because—"

"I'm doing it because I love you," Cody cut her off.

She hadn't noticed the aroma of food wafting from the kitchen to the bedroom until now. Her tummy rumbled. "I want to believe you, but I am struggling with it."

"I understand," Cody's voice remained light. "I'm trusting God to heal our marriage in His time. So on to practical matters—are you hungry?"

A smile curled the corners of her mouth. "As a matter of fact, yes, I am."

The doorbell rang. Kate stiffened. No one should be coming to their house this early in the morning.

"Hey, hold on a minute. Someone's at the front door."

"I heard the bell." Kate stood. "Who is it?"

"I don't know yet."

She swallowed her fear and asked what had to be the obvious question—"Is it Chelsea?"

"It better not be," Cody sounded grim and determined.

Kate pressed the phone to her ear but could only make out the faint sound of Cody walking from the kitchen to the front door. "I'll get dressed and be right out."

"Get dressed, but I want you to stay put."

His hushed but firm response triggered a multitude of frightening scenarios. Her breath hitched. "Can you see who it is yet?"

Cody exhaled noisily, "It's Blake." He opened the front door then greeted his brother with a playful jab to the ribs. "Babe, everything's fine."

"Everything's not fine!" Blake spoke loudly enough for Kate to hear over her husband's phone.

"What are you talking about?" Cody said sharply.

"I heard Blake. What's wrong?" Kate switched the call to speaker, then grabbed a pair of jeans and a sweatshirt from the closet.

"Katelyn, I can't talk to you and him at the same time." He ended the call.

She stared at the phone for a second while longing to believe Blake's early morning visit, and the frantic remark had nothing to do with Chelsea. Dressed, Kate entered the living room to find the two men standing side by side.

"Sorry to come here so early," Blake said to Kate. He took a seat in the armchair by the window but promptly stood. "Has Chelsea been here?" His gaze darted from Cody over to her, then back to Cody.

Kate gasped. "She knows where we live?"

"I didn't tell her. I promise," Blake said.

Cody guided Blake back into the chair with a hand on his shoulder. "Talk to me."

Thankful for Cody taking control, Kate dialed down her panic in hopes of deescalating Blake's agitation.

"Chelsea came by the shop last night." Blake wrung his hands as he spoke. "When I told her you weren't in, she said she'd see you tomorrow morning at your house, not at a doctor's office. What is she even talking about?"

"Why didn't you warn us before now?" Kate's tone sounded harsher than intended in her own ears.

"I did," Blake looked over at her. "I called Cody. I kept getting his voicemail. I checked with my mom a few minutes ago to see if she knew where he was at but didn't let on as to why I wanted to reach him. Mom said he was here."

Cody groaned, "I put my phone on sleep mode last night. I was exhausted."

"I don't understand how she got our home address," Kate said. "We're not listed in the white pages. Cody made sure of it because of the pawnshop business."

She turned to Cody. "Do you think she followed you home one night?"

"Not likely. I'm intentional about keeping an eye on my surroundings and even more so when I leave the shop."

"I don't get it," Kate stammered. "If she didn't follow you and our address isn't listed—"

Cody held up one hand. "I took precautions, but the information is in cyberspace, and it is retrievable. People circumvent safeguards all the time. It's not as difficult as you might think to obtain a home address on just about anyone."

Kate's mouth fell open for a split second. "What do we do now?" She sounded as terrified as she felt. "Let's call the police."

"And say what?" Cody's sucked in a deep breath and exhaled it in a rush. "She hasn't done anything."

"Yet..." Kate said. "At least we could have it on record she's an unwanted visitor."

Blake stood and pulled out his cell phone. "I'm calling."

"Wait." Cody clamped his hand over Blake's. "If anyone's going to call the police, it will be me."

Blake shrugged, and Cody released his grip. "Then make the call."

"I will." Cody turned to Kate. "Why don't you get our coffee? It's getting cold."

Her eyes widened. "I don't care about coffee. Call the police right this minute."

"All right, but let's take this down a couple of notches."

The doorbell rang.

###

"It might not be her," Cody said over his shoulder as he walked toward the front door. He glanced back at Kate, who stood wide-eyed next to Blake. His heart ached at the panic in her eyes. "Everything's going to be okay. God is in control."

Kate nodded, but her expression remained unchanged.

He looked through the peephole. It was Chelsea, and she hadn't come alone. The man standing beside her had at least three inches on his own five-foot-ten-inch frame. The massive size of the guy's biceps quickened Cody's pulse.

"Is it her?" Kate's voice cracked.

"Yes. And she's not alone."

"I'm calling the police," Blake said.

Cody shook his head. "Not yet. We don't want to escalate things. A call to the police might trigger a more aggressive response."

"I don't want to wait." Kate snatched the phone still in Blake's hand.

"Kate's right," Blake chimed in. "Chelsea bringing her goon with her spells trouble with a capital T."

The doorbell sounded again as Kate called 911 on Blake's phone.

Cody clasped the back of his neck as he weighed, opening the door or waiting until law enforcement arrived. Sweat broke out on his forehead. "I'll find out what she wants and put an end to this insanity."

His hand lingered on the doorknob as Kate spoke to a police dispatcher. He took a deep breath he released slowly before opening the door, and prayed for the Lord to protect them all.

"Hello, Chelsea," he said in an even tone. The woman shot him a look of simmering anger. Cody shifted his focus to her burly sidekick. "I'm not looking for any trouble."

"It's a little late for that, buddy," the man took a step forward.

Chelsea gripped his forearm. "We don't want any trouble either, Damien, right?" Chelsea's directness and physical interaction with someone twice her size conveyed she knew him well.

The hulking man glared at Cody. "Depends on what this character does in the next few minutes, sis." Her brother looked as though he would gladly body-slam a man onto the pavement for even the smallest infraction.

"The police are on their way," Kate called out from behind Cody.

"Police?" Chelsea planted her hands on her hips as Damien cracked his knuckles. "Why would you call the police?"

Kate opened the door wider and sidled alongside Cody. "He didn't call the police. I did."

"You must be the betrayed little wife." Chelsea grinned while extending her hand. "It's nice to finally meet you."

"Are you kidding me?" Kate ignored Chelsea's hand. "If you know what's good for you, you'll leave right now."

Blake inched into the doorway. "You two should take off before the cops get here."

Chelsea pointed her finger in Blake's direction. "Butt out. This isn't any of your business."

"Hey," Cody said, "How about we all calm down?" He locked eyes with Chelsea's sibling. "We're open to hear what Chelsea has to say, but I don't know why you're here, Damien."

"She's my little sister. I want to make sure some loser isn't taking advantage of her." He pointed at Kate. "Did your husband tell you he got Chelsea pregnant?"

"Yes, I mean, no." Kate stammered. Cody's heart ached afresh for what he'd put her through.

"My husband told me that she says she's pregnant. However, it's unlikely she's pregnant with his child."

Damien narrowed his eyes, "Are you calling my sister a liar?"

"Dude," Blake spoke, "No one is calling your sister a liar."

"Don't call me dude." Damien snarled like a junkyard dog. "And if you keep running your mouth where it doesn't belong, I'm going to shut it for you. Understood?"

Cody turned to Blake and addressed him in a hushed voice. "Go back inside. Now, please."

"Whatever," Blake muttered.

Cody waited until Blake had walked away, then he turned to Kate. "Are you okay?"

"Yes." She cut her eyes toward the unwelcomed visitors. "I want them to leave."

The behemoth chuckled. "Lady, people in hell want ice water, too. Doesn't mean they're gonna get it."

Chelsea snickered, "Too funny." She looked up at her brother. "Did I tell you they're Christians?"

"You told me," he snorted. "People like these two give religion a bad name. They preach one thing and do another."

"Hold on a minute," Cody said; their insinuation stirred him to explain. "Yes, I've made mistakes, and I'll make more, but I—"

"You hear him?" The man looked over at Kate. "He just admitted he's going to cheat on you again."

"That's not what he's saying," Kate firmed her lips. "I have something I want to say."

Cody looked over at Kate and shook his head. "I did this to us. It's my place to try and correct things." He turned to Chelsea and Damien. "Would you two like to talk inside?"

Although fear momentarily hijacked what Cody believed to be God's leading on inviting the pair into his home, he refused to be ruled by his emotions. When they didn't respond, Cody repeated the question.

Chapter Twenty-Nine

"Have a seat," Cody said to Chelsea and Damien in the living room. He led Kate to the sofa, where Blake joined them. In a quiet voice, he asked Kate not to say anything—at least not yet. She nodded.

Chelsea sat in one of two matching wingback chairs near a window facing the street, while Damien remained standing beside her. "Like I said," Chelsea began, "We don't want any trouble. I came here because I don't want to talk over the phone."

The tension in Cody's shoulders diminished.

"Bro, this is crazy," Blake said loud enough for all to hear. Thankfully, Kate didn't lend verbal support to Blake's statement despite she probably longed to given her heavily furrowed brow.

"Chelsea, I want to apologize for what's happened." Cody turned to Kate. "I not only betrayed my wife, but I also betrayed God." He turned back to Chelsea, who sat with a pinched expression and her arms crossed over her chest.

"I'm deeply sorry for the hurt I've caused everyone." Cody leaned forward. "My hope and prayer are for healing—for everyone."

"Sis," Damien bent at the waist, whispered something into Chelsea's ear, then righted himself.

"My brother's correct," she said coolly. "I don't need an apology. What I need is for you to take responsibility. I'm pregnant with your child."

Cody drew a deep breath to keep his emotions in check then exhaled slowly.

"I'm praying." Kate's voice was low and for his ears only. The tears brimming in her eyes revealed not only the extravagant grace and mercy she'd bestowed him since finding out about the infidelity and decades-long battle with pornography but also a glimpse of the pain and devastation she was experiencing.

"How do you know you're pregnant?" Blake burst out. "Let alone with my brother's kid?"

Chelsea remained stony-faced.

"Have you had a blood test?" Blake stood. "An over-the-counter pregnancy test isn't going to show positive after only a week."

Damien walked over to Blake, then jabbed him in the chest, so forcefully Blake stumbled backward against the sofa. "I warned you to stop running your mouth, or I'd shut it for you."

"That's enough," Cody said, rising to his feet. "If we can't have a civil conversation, then it's best you two leave."

"Who's gonna make us leave?" After a couple of tense seconds, Damien grinned at Cody. "I'm just having a little fun with you." He turned to Blake and playfully patted his shoulder, but Blake shrugged his hand off.

Cody pointed to the matching wingback chair alongside Chelsea's. "Can we all have a seat and try this again?"

"Damien," Chelsea said sternly, "Sit with me. I'm not leaving without what I came for." The hulking man plodded over to the empty chair and took a seat with a thud.

Cody reclaimed his place on the sofa beside Kate. He prayed he hadn't misheard God on inviting these two inside.

Blake let out a disgusted breath but retook his seat opposite Kate. "I still say this is crazy."

"What's happened has happened." Chelsea's icy tone contradicted her smile. "Let's handle this as adults and move on."

Kate flinched, "Exactly what do you mean?" The dread in his wife's voice was a red flag—at least to Cody.

"Don't play dumb," Chelsea said. "I'm not ready to be a mother. I'm also not in a financial position to make the problem go away on my own."

"A baby is not a problem," Kate's voice rose. "You're unbelievable." She stood. "I want both of you out of our home."

Chelsea glared at Cody. "You would think she'd be happy—"

"Stop, you've already said too much." Righteous anger rose in Cody over Chelsea's indirect suggestion of ending a baby's life; whether she was truly pregnant or not, the idea was reprehensible.

"I don't feel well," Kate said. The color drained from her face as she eased onto the sofa. "I think I'm going to be sick."

Blake walked to the front door. "Enough is enough. It's time you two hit the road." He grabbed the knob but turned back before opening the door. "And for the record, I overheard you mocking my brother's faith, but you don't know my brother. Is he perfect? No. Does he love Jesus? Yes. Does he stumble in his walk, you bet, but my brother—"

"Blake," Cody said as he remained by Kate's side, "Please have a seat. You don't have to defend my faith. I understand how they've drawn their conclusions about me. The choices I've made do not reflect God to them."

Kate looked over at Cody, her eyes brimming with tears. On the one hand, sharing these truths with her was a blessing, but doing so in the presence of others was humbling, yet humility appeared to be a part of God's redemptive plan.

"Babe," Cody sat beside her and tried to tune out the others in the room. "Shame has been a vortex that sucked me into silence for years, but not any longer. I've discovered comfort, hope, and deliverance in being truthful, no matter what."

"Are you finished?" Chelsea blasted.

Cody turned to respond, but before he could say anything to her, Blake quipped, "Put a cork in it."

"I'll put a cork in you," Damien said, scowling at Blake.

"Go ahead and try it, tough guy."

Cody eyed Blake's fisted hands at his brother's sides. He needed to do something before a fight erupted. Cody took a vocal stance that surprised even him—"Lord, help."

"Amen," Kate's agreement encouraged a fuller petition, so he continued.

"Father, I believe you are healing me from the inside out. We both know I have been preoccupied with how things look versus how they really are, but you're changing me. Thank you."

Cody's shoulders relaxed, and the tension drained from his body. "I can hardly believe I'm praying this prayer in front of others, so I know you are working through me. Give us ears to hear and the willingness to follow your plan—"

"Stop with all the God stuff," Chelsea raised her voice. "I can't take another second of your rambling. Here's what I want—five thousand dollars, and I'll be out of your life—forever."

###

The second Chelsea mentioned money, it became clear to Kate the woman was not pregnant. Chelsea had seen Cody as a blank check and penciled in an amount she figured an adulterer would pay to keep his secret. What Chelsea hadn't counted on was Kate discovering the truth about the affair on her own.

"There's no way my wife and I are going to give you money to kill a child," Cody said.

Kate took Cody's hand in her own and gave it a light squeeze. "She's not pregnant."

"Excuse me!" Chelsea stood, hands on her hips. "You don't know what you're talking about, lady."

At that moment, God impressed upon Kate forgiveness is a promise, which Jesus Christ modeled on the cross. She settled into the unfolding revelation of God's love for hurting people, which included her own hurts. Forgiveness wasn't something you had to feel before it could be extended. Determined not to quench what the Holy Spirit was showing her and comforted by the knowledge God was in control, Kate smiled at the other woman. Amazingly, Chelsea returned her smile then retook her seat beside Damien, who appeared transfixed by the exchange.

Cody reached behind Kate and poked at Blake, who promptly crossed the room and opened the front door. The police had arrived. As Blake spoke to officers, the immeasurable love of God and His forgiveness washed over Kate, once again.

"Bro," Blake called out from the front door, "The officer wants to talk to you and Kate." It was then Kate realized Cody had been in prayer as he said, "In Jesus' name. Amen."

Cody stood and outstretched his hand to Kate. As they walked past Chelsea and Damien toward the front door, Chelsea averted her eyes. The Bible verse written on the bathroom mirror came to mind. God had something much bigger in mind for that verse than the well-being of her physical body. He was focused on spiritual health.

"Good morning, sir," Cody said to the lone officer on the doorstep. Kate echoed the greeting as she stood beside him. He wrapped his arm around her waist. Astonishingly, the same gesture, which caused Kate to flinch at the airport a few days ago, was now comforting.

"Mornin' folks." The officer's eyes traveled from Cody to Kate, then briefly over their shoulders to Blake. "Is everything okay?"

"Yes," Cody said. "My wife made a 911 call because she was airing on the side of safety, but things have calmed down, and we should be fine."

"I presume this your wife?" He locked eyes with Kate.

"Yes, I'm Mrs. James. We were having a conversation with guests in our home, and the exchange got a little heated, but as my husband said, we've all calmed down." She resisted the urge to over-explain.

"My dispatcher logged the call as trespassers?" He peered over their shoulders for the second time. "The gentleman standing behind you says he's your brother-in-law. Is that true?"

Kate nodded.

"He's my brother," Cody volunteered.

"I got that much from him. I wanted to confirm it with you two. Where are your other guests? Have they left?"

"No," Kate looked over her shoulder at Chelsea. "They're going to stay for coffee."

"Thank you," Damien said. His sudden cordiality seemed to hide something. As much as Kate wanted to believe prayer had stirred his heart, she suspected he would do anything to avoid talking with law enforcement.

"Mr. James, would it be possible to speak with your guests?"

Kate turned back to face the officer. "Is it necessary?"

"I think it is, Mrs. James." He stepped back from the door. "Would you please ask them to step outside? I have a few questions I'd like to ask them."

Chapter Thirty

Cody and Kate stepped aside, clearing the way for Chelsea and Damien to acknowledge the police officer's request. A part of Cody hoped the two connivers would voluntarily leave after answering the officer's questions, yet Kate's statement about inviting them for coffee intrigued him on a spiritual level. Maybe God had spoken something to Kate. He tried to gain her attention with eye contact, but she remained focused on Chelsea and Damien, who now stood on the porch talking with the policeman.

"What's going on, folks?" The officer didn't appear to be daunted by Damien's stature and even extended his hand to the man.

"Just a misunderstanding between friends," Damien replied as he shook the policeman's hand.

"I'm glad things have been resolved." The officer smiled for the first time since his arrival. "Generally speaking, getting us involved in friendly disputes can often escalate things. People tend to take offense when police are called and become defensive, which can turn to anger. Before you know it, the situation is out of control."

"We're all good," Chelsea piped up.

"The young lady is right," Cody said, even though it had yet to be revealed if she was sincere.

"If you folks are sure everything's fine," the office said, "then I'll take off."

Cody stepped onto the porch. "We're sure. Thank you for being understanding." After the officer walked away, Kate joined Cody on the porch and winked at him, which conveyed she had something up her spiritual sleeve. His hope of getting rid of the two scammers dissolved in light of her presumed leading from God.

"Chelsea, Damien," Kate began, "Will you join us for coffee?"

Damien stepped down from the porch. "No thanks."

"It's just coffee," Kate persisted with a smile.

Again, Chelsea reciprocated with a smile.

The non-verbal interaction unfolding between two women who should be adversaries was beyond Cody's comprehension. He looked over his shoulder for Blake to gauge if he might have a problem with Damien staying for coffee, but Blake had disappeared from the living room.

"I'd like to," Chelsea said, drawing Cody's attention back to the conversation.

Cody was taken aback by the tears in Chelsea's eyes. Whatever her motivation had been in trying to extort money with a false pregnancy, the tears were evidence God was softening her heart to His voice. Witnessing even a subtle change in the young woman stirred thankfulness in Cody he hadn't intended to verbalize.

Chelsea groaned, "Did you just say 'thank you, Lord?'"

Warmth blanketed his face. He opened his mouth to explain, but Blake reappeared.

"Bro, what's going on? I had to go to the bathroom." He craned his neck between the two of them. "Where did the cop go? And what are they still doing here?"

"I dunno know about this, sis." Damien's objection let slip his guardedness was real, and maybe he wasn't looking for trouble—at least not anymore. "You know I can't risk—"

"Okay," Chelsea shrugged. "We can go."

"Good idea," Blake said.

Kate gently elbowed Cody. "Chelsea, Damien, I'd like to talk to my husband privately for a moment. Will you two promise not to leave?"

Chelsea looked at Damien for a long moment. He nodded, albeit with furrowed brows. "Sure," Chelsea said. "I want to talk privately with my brother, so this works for us, too."

Again, Cody had been caught off guard by Kate's friendliness, but again, he acquiesced when she gave his hand a gentle tug and led him to the living room. Blake, who remained in the doorway, leaned against the doorjamb.

"I don't understand," Cody began. "Is this something God is prompting you to do?"

"Yes, but I can't explain it other than to say, I believe God wants us to extend forgiveness to Chelsea and Damien."

Cody's mind spun with questions. If she was willing to forgive them, did it also mean she was willing to forgive him? Before he could question her, she raised her hand, silencing him.

"At first, I wanted to lash out at them for trying to swindle us by using the pretense of a baby to extort money; then God revealed how broken they are to attempt something this tragic. It's changed my outlook."

Cody glanced over his shoulder at the front door, then back to Kate. "I was tempted to have the police cart them off for an attempted shakedown, but it would be our word against theirs. What I can't figure out is why she thought making a demand for money is something we would agree to, given you know about her."

"God may reveal her motivation. I sense it will not be to satisfy our curiosity but instead to address the bigger picture."

Cody nodded understanding. Kate's nature was to go after the lost. She'd been chasing Blake for over a year. "I love you heart for others, perhaps—"

"I said a moment ago this was something God was prompting me to do. Will you support me?"

"Of course, but what if they don't accept your invitation?"

"Let's find out?" She pointed to the front door.

###

"I'm not sure I understand your question about what happens now," Cody said to Chelsea, who sat rigidly beside her brother at the kitchen table, both of whom looked as though they might bolt any second. He hoped she would elaborate.

Chelsea glanced at Kate seated next to him and smiled. The two women had some kind of mind-boggling connection.

Chelsea opened her mouth, but before she said anything, Damien tapped her on the shoulder, shook his head then stood.

"I'll spell it out for my sister," Damien said with sharpness. Kate gripped Cody's hand under the table. "Sis, they want proof you're pregnant. Next, they'll ask for a paternity test."

"Asking for proof is a reasonable request," Kate said. "However, it isn't why we invited you to join us for coffee."

"Bro, why are they even here?" Seated on the other side of Kate, Blake was beyond Cody's reach, or he would've nudged him for interrupting, which was a step down from his initial thought—a smack to the back of his head.

"I only agreed to coffee," Chelsea said, her focus now on Kate, "because I can't figure out why you're being so—"

"Forgiving?" Kate chimed in.

"I guess that could be a word for it." Chelsea moved her coffee cup aside. "Woman to woman, I—"

"Sis, you need to stop talking." Cody and Kate flinched when Damien kicked a leg of the table. The situation could explode if Cody didn't say something to extinguish the fuse.

"Damien, I get you want to protect your sister from saying anything incriminating, but if we wanted to involve the police, we could've done that when the officer was here. This is about getting to the truth."

"Whose truth are we talking about?" Damien pulled Chelsea up by her forearm. "It's time to go."

Cody clenched his jaw. "Get your hands off her," he said through gritted teeth.

"Mind your own business." Damien's dark eyebrows formed one grizzled line. He turned to Chelsea. "C'mon. We're getting out of here."

Chelsea jerked away, "I'm not ready to leave." The quiver in her voice betrayed her outward confidence.

Adrenaline pumping, Cody stormed to the other side of the table, ignoring Kate's plea to calm down. He wouldn't allow Damien to man-handle Chelsea or any other woman.

Cody wedged himself between the siblings. "Your sister said she's not ready to leave."

Blake joined Cody on the opposite of the table. "If you want to go, go, but Chelsea has a right to make her own choices."

"I told you before," Damien snarled at Blake. "If you know what's good for you, you'll get out of my face."

"Damien, please don't do this," Chelsea said. "We almost got busted last time. I don't want to do this anymore."

"Shut your mouth!" Damien's complexion turned the color of a ripe tomato. "Don't say another word."

The mention of "last time" went off like a flare inside Cody's head. He suspected Kate had caught Chelsea's unintentional reference to this being a scam. Out of his peripheral vision, he glimpsed Kate pick up her coffee cup. Something warned she might lob it at Damien's head. Cody turned to her, but instead of Kate targeting the Goliath across from her, she hurled the cup across the room. Mouth agape, he followed the trajectory with his eyes. The cup hit the cuckoo clock above the kitchen door explosively then crashed to the floor, leaving behind a trail of coffee on the wall. Kate's action revealed pent-up frustration ran much deeper than what was happening at the moment.

"That's it. Get out!" Blake pointed toward the front door.

Cody rejoined Kate. He wrapped his arms around her trembling body then looked over his shoulder at Damien. "You need to leave."

"Not without my sister," Damien exhaled through his mouth, breath ragged.

"Will you please go?" Chelsea spoke softly. After several seconds of silence, she took a step toward him. "Now?"

Chapter Thirty-One

Kate ushered Chelsea away from the front door where Cody and Blake stood talking with the police officer from earlier. Thankfully, Damien heeded Chelsea's advice to leave. Seated on the sofa beside Chelsea, the young woman faced her. "My brother is so angry."

"How long have you two been running this scam?"

"About a year." Chelsea shook her head. "That's a lie."

"Longer?" Kate tried to fathom the emotional wreckage inflicted by Chelsea and Damien. It was hard enough to persevere in the face of infidelity as a Christian, but if a couple didn't have God to turn to for healing and hope, well, Kate shuddered to think of it.

"Yes, longer." Chelsea swiped tears from her cheeks. "We were only supposed to do it one time. The guy deserved it."

"Deserved it?" Kate angled her head to see Chelsea's eyes, but Chelsea turned away, positioning her back to Kate. "What do you mean?"

"He led me to believe he was single, and he wanted to marry me." Her posture stiffened. "Men can't be trusted. They're all dogs."

Kate tapped her on the shoulder, and Chelsea faced her. "Cheating isn't limited to men. Women cheat too."

Cody crossed the room and joined Kate on the sofa while Blake settled in one of the armchairs. Kate turned to him. "What did the officer say we should do if Damien returns?"

"If he comes back, which I don't believe he will, we're to call the police."

"That's it?" Kate said. "For all we know, he's down the street watching the house. Once he sees the officer has left, he could come back and demand Chelsea go with him."

"That's not happening," Blake said.

"How can you be sure?" Kate directed the question at her brother-in-law.

Blake pointed to Chelsea, "Ask her."

Chelsea mumbled something.

Kate sat forward. "I didn't catch that, Chelsea. What did you say?"

"I said Damien won't be back. My brother has warrants. He won't risk getting busted."

"Busted?" Cody's voice sharpened.

Kate patted Cody's thigh to calm him down. The only way to get to the bottom of things was to have Chelsea share what she knew. Surely he'd caught when Chelsea let slip this wasn't the first time they'd done something like this to a married couple.

"Before you joined us," Kate said, "Chelsea was beginning to tell me about what she and Damien have been involved in."

"I knew something was up," Blake said. "Damien said he would make Cody pay big-time. But why target my brother instead of someone with big bucks?"

Chelsea knitted her hands together in her lap. "Damien has a motto; he says, 'More money means more risk.'"

Cody groaned.

"I know Damien seems like a bad guy." Chelsea's shoulders drooped. "But he's really not a bad guy he—"

"Yeah, sure," Blake said. "He just bullies people and destroys lives."

Kate turned to Blake. "Getting heated isn't going to accomplish anything positive."

Cody cleared his throat. "If I had handled things more calmly in the kitchen, maybe Kate wouldn't have thrown her coffee cup out of frustration."

Blake chuckled. "It sure got everyone's attention." He sank in his seat when Cody shot him a glare.

"I take responsibility for my outburst," Kate said, drawing a look from Cody. "I should've asked for God's help. He is the only reason I've been able to deal with what's going on and not lose my mind in the process."

"Katelyn," Cody's voice cracked with emotion. "I'm sorry for creating all of this hurt and confusion." There was no external hint of anything but humility in his words. As she looked into his eyes, a mental picture of the two of them seated on a beach, toes buried in the warm sand, captured her thoughts. The horizon stretched out before them on the beach, glistening with the hope of a fresh start. In the vision, a gentle sea breeze rippled their clothes and rustled their hair. Kate breathed deeply, a gentle sigh escaping her lips. As if being awakened from sweet slumber, his tender voice called to her.

"Babe, did you hear anything I said?"

Kate's surroundings poured into her consciousness, and the moment faded. She looked over at Chelsea. "Do you believe in God?"

Chelsea's eyes widened. "I don't do the whole church thing, but yeah, I talk to God sometimes."

The response rang hollow in Kate's ears. She wanted Chelsea to be honest with her, so she needed to be truthful with Chelsea. "At first, you lied about how long you've been extorting money from people, but then you told the truth. I'm going to be honest with you now."

Chapter Thirty-Two

"Chelsea, I think I know where my wife is going with this conversation." Cody hunched forward on the sofa. He rested his forearms on his thighs and clasped his hands. The temptation to hang his head in the face of Kate's boldness was great, but he resisted. In the uneasy silence, he was reminded of the awkward few moments with Chelsea before leaving her apartment, and like then—her eyes were darkened with emotion he couldn't label.

"I think I do, too," Blake said. "And I'd bet the few dollars in my bank account she's not interested. Am I wrong, Chelsea?"

"Well—" she shrugged. "This is starting to feel weird. Maybe I should go."

Kate sighed. "It's your choice."

"What?" Cody's voice sharpened. "I feel like I'm in the Twilight Zone. You brought God up, and now you're just going to drop it." He shot Blake a disgusted look for stirring the pot.

"Easy," Kate said under her breath while continuing to look straight ahead. "Stop trying to make things happen in your own strength."

"Bro," Blake grabbed Cody's attention. "No matter what I say or do, I always make things worse in your eyes. It's been that way since I was a kid. Who knows, if it hadn't been for me coming along when I did—maybe Mom and Dad would've stayed together, and you wouldn't have been saddled with raising your annoying kid brother."

"There you go, making this about you." All at once, the truth hit Cody like a tsunami. Drowning in thoughts of how poorly he'd treated Blake over the years, his chest tightened. Blake had spoken the truth. Not the best time to address childhood issues, but God seemed to have other plans.

Tears blurred Cody's vision as he studied Blake, whose lean frame and choppy haircut weren't so different from the young boy who had sought approval from his big brother all those years ago. Truth be told, he'd resented stepping into a fatherly role with Blake. Sacrificing his own youth for a kid who rebelled at every turn had been tiring. At this moment, Blake's rebellion mirrored his own rebellious approach toward God.

Cody did the things expected of a "good" Christian, except embrace God's unconditional love. He'd missed to whom the Scriptures pointed. For the first time, his folly in trying to force Blake to do better instead of inspiring him through his own actions became crystal clear. He had been a stumbling block to his brother—while engineering his own downfall.

"Pride comes before the fall," Cody whispered.

"What did you say?" Blake crossed his arms over his chest.

Cody cleared his throat of emotion. "I said, pride comes before the fall."

"You've lost me," Blake said.

Cody eased forward. "I owe you an apology." Out of the corner of his eye, he observed Kate bowing her head and closing her eyes, likely praying for a talk that was long overdue. If he had done more praying than browbeating, Blake might not have walked away from his faith.

"Think about King Saul..." Cody noticed Chelsea's puzzled expression. "King Saul is from the Bible. I'll be brief, but it's important I share this with my brother. Is that okay?"

"I guess so." She studied her fingernails, yet it was encouraging enough for Cody to continue.

"King Saul couldn't stand the people praising David more highly than himself. Jealousy ruled him. The King's mind became so warped about David he ultimately orchestrated David's death."

"I know the story." Impatience laced Blake's words.

"I have a confession, Blake." The lure to be less than truthful tugged at Cody's emotions, but he persevered. "I've been jealous of you for a long time."

Surrender to the truth hadn't come easily for Cody, and he doubted it would come easy for Blake, but it appeared God sparked this conversation, so he would trust Him with the outcome.

Blake's eyes glistened. "Make your point."

In spite of Blake's defensiveness, he resumed. "Jealousy is poison. It creates a breeding ground for other sins. Because I haven't acknowledged the hurt I felt over our past I've made a lot of bad choices in the present."

"Hurt?" Blake's brows pulled together, but his voice revealed more curiosity than irritation.

"Excuse me," Chelsea said, "but can you two have this brother-fest another time? "Blake, would you mind dropping me off at a friend's house?"

"Chelsea," Kate said sweetly. "Before you leave, could we talk in the kitchen for a moment?"

"I guess a minute won't hurt. Sure." Chelsea stood. "Cody, this may not sound sincere, but I hope you and Blake work things out. I'm going to try to do the same with Damien. Family is important. My brother may seem like a bad guy, but he's really not any different than you when it comes to hurting."

###

"Can I get you anything?" Kate asked Chelsea as the woman took a seat at the kitchen table.

"No, thank you."

Kate followed Chelsea's line of vision toward the coffee stain on the wall and the broken glass scattered across the floor. She walked over to the broken cup and gingerly picked up the larger pieces that landed near the baseboard. "I'm sorry about my reaction earlier."

"It's okay." Chelsea joined her but remained quiet while helping with the cleanup. Each piece the younger woman retrieved with her slender fingers reminded Kate those hands had been all over Cody's body.

"Really, you don't need to help me." Kate locked eyes with Chelsea, and more unwelcomed thoughts flooded her mind. This woman chose to cross the line with a married man—it didn't just happen.

"I don't mind helping." A faint smile curled the corners of Chelsea's mouth but quickly vanished. "My brother says I'm a people-pleaser. I imagine the people-pleasing part of me has something to do with being abandoned as a kid. Damien pretty much raised me."

Kate looked up at her, struck by her transparency.

"I watch a lot of talk shows," Chelsea resumed, "I agree with the doctors who say your childhood plays a part in the decisions you make as an adult. How can it not? Right?"

Kate nodded agreement before picking up the last shard of the coffee cup. "I'm going to put this in the trash. "So you had a difficult childhood, too?"

"You don't want to know." Chelsea followed Kate to the trash and disposed of the ceramic pieces she'd been holding. "This is going to sound crazy, but I like talking with you."

"Thank you. Let's rinse our hands." Kate led the way to the sink. The cool tap water rushed over her hands, removing any slivers of glass that might have remained.

"Your turn." Kate stepped aside to dry her hands with a dishtowel on the counter while Chelsea concentrated on rinsing her hands.

"It's okay if you want to talk to me about God." Chelsea turned the water off, and Kate handed her the dishtowel. "I have a friend who's a Christian. We've known each other since we were teenagers. She hasn't always been a Christian."

After Chelsea dried her hands, she returned the towel to the counter. Leaned back against the kitchen sink, Chelsea grinned. "I thought about dropping her as a friend when she announced, 'I found Jesus.' What does that mean? Was God lost?"

Kate smiled. Admittedly, she'd been known to speak Christianese from time to time. "What made you decide not to end the friendship?"

Chelsea shrugged, "She's got a big heart."

"She sounds like a lovely woman." Gripped with unexpected emotion, Kate blinked several times to clear her vision of tears. What she wanted most in life was to reflect God's love to others. Maybe here, alone, Chelsea would drop her guard and any preconceived ideas about Jesus, as well as any negative encounters with Christians. "Let's sit at the table."

Chelsea sat beside her instead of across from her. Silence claimed the room. Finally, Kate mustered the courage to speak more truth. "You have to know when I learned you'd been with my husband I wanted to—"

"Pull my hair out," Chelsea finished the sentence.

"No," Kate averted her eyes, "my husband's."

Chelsea couldn't be more than twenty-five, yet in her short span of life, she had also experienced crushing disappointment. "Why did your parents abandon you and your brother?"

"Do you want the long or short version?"

"Whatever you're comfortable with." Kate hoped the conversation between Cody and Blake in the living room was going as well as this one. Blake's playful attitude during serious talks more often than not provoked Cody while underscoring Blake's need to grow up.

Chelsea blew out a noisy breath. "I'll give you the less dramatic version. My dad was a drug user, and my mom was an alcoholic. Together, they were quite the chaos cocktail. One day, they decided they weren't up to facing the challenges of getting clean to raise Damien and me, so they split town together."

"That must have been devastating. How old were you?"

"Seven. Damien had just turned eighteen. I tell myself at least they hung around long enough to celebrate his eighteenth birthday. Truth is, they were probably celebrating Damien being of legal age so he could become my guardian."

The parallels between Cody and Chelsea's lives were astonishing. "What happened after they left?"

"Things got harder. How can an eighteen-year-old boy be expected to raise a seven-year-old girl? Not to mention providing food and shelter. I can talk matter-of-factly now, but at the time, I was angry at everyone—especially God."

Kate couldn't help but feel her pain. How heartbreaking, lonely, and hurt seven-year-old Chelsea must have been.

"Damien tried to help with my anger issues by making as normal a life as possible. He encouraged me to invite my friends over, but that only made matters worse. It was awkward for them when I answered questions about where my mom and dad were, but it was also tough on me coming up with lies."

Chelsea picked at chipped, red fingernail polish on her index finger as she spoke. "Each time a friend asked about my parents, I was reminded I didn't have a father who gave bear-hugs, and I didn't have a mother who fixed my school lunches. I remember one time Damien sent me to school with a package of Ramen noodles—of course, I had no way to cook them and an apple in a brown bag. That was it."

Kate cringed, and it didn't go unnoticed.

"He did the best he could. I'm grateful." Chelsea hung her head. "I am sorry about what happened between your husband and me. You're a nice lady, and—well, I wasn't thinking about anything other than doing what Damien asked of me."

"Wait," Kate said. "So your own brother—"

"Like I was saying earlier," Chelsea interjected, "Damien isn't a bad guy. I was the one who suggested pawning my DVD player." She looked up. "Talking about this probably isn't the smartest choice."

Chelsea stood, but Kate reached over and clasped one of her hands. "You're right. It's not easy to talk about what happened between you and my husband, but bringing everything out into the open is going to help each of us. Please don't leave."

Kate took a deep breath and exhaled slowly. She would trust the Lord to direct this conversation. At this moment, the talk seemed, at least on the surface, to have unraveled, but God could weave the loose ends together, and she trusted His handiwork would be revealed.

Chelsea reseated herself, "Can I ask you something?" She shook her head then tucked a strand of hair behind her ear. "Never mind, it's none of my business, I—"

"If I don't want to answer your question, then I'll tell you," Kate said.

"I'd..." Chelsea pursed her lips.

"Please, just ask." Kate persisted.

"Okay, I'd like to know how you can forgive someone who's hurt you so deeply."

Kate folded her hands in her lap. Not the question she'd expected, but if God wanted this conversation to go in another direction, then so be it.

"Are you referring to my forgiving you?"

Chelsea shook her head. Her gaze traveled toward the living room then back to Kate. "I'm talking about your husband."

Kate hadn't forgiven Cody, but maybe Chelsea saw something in her that she didn't see in herself. Chelsea labeled her friend as having a big heart; maybe Chelsea saw her in a similar light. She could hope. Still, Kate wrestled with genuinely forgiving Cody's actions.

"I haven't forgiven my husband—at least not fully."

Chelsea's face flushed red. "I shouldn't have asked. It's none of my business."

"I'd like to explain," Kate resumed. "A part of me wants to put Cody's lack of sexual integrity behind us and move on, while another part of me knows all I'm doing is burying it alive. Forgiveness is a journey. I'm still finding my way on that road."

"You don't have to say anymore."

Kate rested her hand on the young woman's forearm. This much transparency with a stranger wasn't easy. "People who have been hurt are often afraid of being fully known. I've come to see it in myself and in others."

Tears fell from Chelsea's eyes onto her pant legs. She repositioned her hands and covered the damp spots. "I don't know why I'm crying."

Kate gentled her voice. "As you said a few minutes ago, childhood wounds that haven't healed impact us now. How can they not?"

Chelsea's shoulders quivered as sobs poured out of her. Caught in the emotional moment, Kate recalled herself slumped and sobbing against the bathroom wall in Ling's restaurant. The strangely full-circle moment led Kate to console Chelsea by patting her back.

"Jesus. Jesus. Jesus," Kate spoke softly.

Chelsea looked up, tears brimming. "Why do you keep saying the name of Jesus?"

"There's power in the name of Jesus," Kate answered.

Chapter Thirty-Three

"I want to tell you why I feel jealous of you," Cody said. "Will you hear me out?"

"Go for it." Blake snorted. "I find it hard to believe you're jealous of me. What have I got?"

"It's not about material possessions."

"You not only have material possessions, but you also have a great wife. I've got zero." He held up his hand. "Before you say anything, I know you think meeting women in bars is a waste of time, but that's not the only way I try to meet them. I've posted on a few dating websites with no luck."

Cody had a hard time picturing Blake as coming across on a dating site as anything other than looking for a hookup. Then again, Blake's quirkiness might appeal to some women. "Did you include a nice pic on any of these dating sites and create a non-goofy profile?"

When Blake grinned, then scratched his head, the response took Cody back to their youth. "I would've helped if you asked."

"Bro, you've had a lot on your plate."

His perspective intrigued Cody. Granted, opening the pawnshop had been stressful, and while he still struggled to build a firearm inventory, the shop was making money now.

Maybe Blake was referring to juggling a startup business with home life. Cody's thoughts traveled back to Dr. Novak's office when he'd been asked about his fidelity. Again, the story from the Gospels about the invalid beside the pool flashed in his mind. He identified with the cripple even more as Blake's obvious meaning came to light.

"I would've never imagined looking at women in a magazine as a teenager could take me down the road I'm on."

"Boys will be boys—"

"No," Cody lowered his voice. "Boys shouldn't be ogling naked women in magazines. I'm not blaming Dad for where I am today, but he wasn't active in raising us. I should've been having father-son talks that steered me away from that sort of thing."

He shook his head then continued. "Dad didn't even know my dream as a kid was to play professional baseball because he wasn't around. You know who tried to teach me to pitch when I was twelve? Mom. She taught me with a neon orange Nerf ball and plastic bat in the front yard. In her defense, I think she wanted the neighbors to see she was doing fine raising us on her own. Every day after school, I'd pitch to her for a while then practice my batting. I remember on one occasion, she wore a dress and high heels to our daily practice. Talk about embarrassment. I wanted to crawl under the house."

Blake covered his mouth and partly stifled a chuckle. "Sorry, but the image is pathetic and funny at the same time."

"Yeah, well, my buddies thought it was pretty funny, too. I didn't have the heart to tell her I no longer wanted her help. Once I made the summer baseball league, the practices stopped."

Cody sat forward and pointed at Blake. "Don't tell mom, but Coach Murray is the one who helped me to hone my skills and make the summer league—not her. He overheard the boys on the playground calling me 'Wilhelmina Mays' after Willie Mayes, the major league player."

"I knew who you were referring to," Blake said. "Gimme some credit."

"Mom was proud when I made the league. She took me to celebrate at an ice-cream parlor. I can see her now, seated across from me. She was beaming from ear to ear. It made up for all humiliation in the front yard."

"Bro, there's so much about you that I don't know. I wish you would've shared this story with me years ago." Blake sat back. "You said you feel jealous of me, so are you going to tell me or keep me in suspense?"

###

Kate re-entered the living room with Chelsea at her side. "May we join you?"

"Fine by me." Cody turned to Blake. "Is it okay with you?"

"This is your ballgame," He grinned.

Kate followed Chelsea's line of vision to Blake. The young woman crossed the room to the chair beside him and took a seat. "Are you a Christian, too?"

"Uh..." Blake's eyes widened.

"You don't have to answer my question if you don't want to."

Cody gained Kate's attention by patting the sofa cushion. Once seated beside him, he enveloped her hand in his own.

God appeared to be using everyone's past pain, as different as it was, to heal hearts individually.

Blake shrugged. "I'm not a Christian anymore."

"What does that mean?" Cody said in a gentle way.

"I'm not sure." Blake's somber tone had to touch Cody's heart—it did hers.

The brothers hadn't spoken this way to one another in years. A tear trickled to the corner of Kate's lips, and she discreetly licked it away. "Blake, please come and sit with us."

When he didn't budge, Kate repeated the request. Blake moved slowly but joined them on the sofa. He sat silent between them for several seconds. "I'm not sure I want to talk about this right now."

Cody turned to him. "I'll respect your choice and not push. I've caused a lot of pain. If I could undo what I've done—I would, but I can't. What I can do is trust God's timing."

"Amen." Kate sat back on the sofa. While she longed to have Cody express more truths, she would wait until they were alone. God had arranged everything so far, and she would stand in agreement with Cody on God's timing.

Cody walked over to Kate and knelt in front of her. She resisted the urge to reach for him. "Katelyn, when we exchanged wedding vows, my past became your present. What I'm saying is I brought my baggage with me to the altar. I realize now I didn't blow our marriage up with one bad decision—it's been a bomb I've tinkered with for decades."

"Are you sure you want to say this in front of—"

"It doesn't matter who hears me. I believe this is more of God humbling me." He looked deeply into her eyes; Kate sensed he hoped she would feel his love—and she did.

Kate sat forward. "Will you do me a favor?"

"Anything," he said.

"We've all made mistakes, Cody—" The devil sought to be victorious in this conversation, but she recalled a Bible verse that fell from Heaven like manna and strengthened her resolve. Greater is He who is me than he who is in this world (1 John 4:4).

She resumed, "I believe your apology to be sincere. I forgive you. I want you to accept it, and we will take the rest one step at a time."

"You guys are all blowing my mind," Blake said. "I can't get my head around the fact you're in the same room with Chelsea, let alone forgiving him."

"Thank you, Katelyn." Cody turned to Blake. "Trust me— I'm blown away too."

"Bro, I've never heard you talk this way. I don't see ego. I see humility."

"The choice to do it differently has always been mine. Today, I'm choosing to do it differently."

"I can tell." Blake leaned back. "I'm sorry for interrupting. Go ahead. Finish talking with your wife."

"Babe, I don't deserve your forgiveness, but—" Cody blinked several times, clearing tears from his eyes, "my hope is one day I'll be able to fully accept it."

Kate could hardly believe the meekness she'd witnessed in Cody—saying everything he'd said in front of Blake and

Chelsea—this from a man who worked hard to keep his life private.

Her body stiffened over what needed to be said next, but unlike Jonah, who fought with God and ended up in the belly of a great fish, Kate would choose obedience, even as her knees knocked. The Gospel had always come easy to her, but with Blake's pessimistic view of God, she hoped he would keep quiet for the next few minutes. Her heart thumped wildly.

Cody sat on the corner of the coffee table nearest Kate. He swiveled and faced Chelsea. "Making amends isn't easy. I'd like to apologize to you as well. I'm sorry. I mean it with every fiber of my being. What I did to you is unconscionable."

"Thank you." Chelsea scrunched her nose and mouth together, making her appear even younger than her age—whatever it was.

"One more thing," Cody resumed. "The message of the gospel is about more than morality. That's important, but of first importance is Jesus coming to save sinners and the Ten Commandments show us our need for a Savior."

"I've already broken the Commandments." Her face flushed red. "Wait. Not every one of them," she groaned.

"We're all sinners," Kate said. "I don't need to convince you or anyone else of that truth. Jesus dying on the cross is witness there's sin in the world."

"The friend I told you about has shared some of what you're saying."

Kate turned to Cody. "Chelsea has a Christian friend."

"She wasn't a Christian when I met her," Chelsea added.

"Your friend sounds like someone pretty special," Cody said.

"I once asked her why God allowed suffering, and she said God's thoughts are higher than our thoughts. Made sense to me. Why would anyone follow a god who could be figured out? Might as well be god yourself."

"That's deep." Blake folded his hands in his lap. "I'll keep my mouth zipped." Blake unfolded his hands and sat forward. "One question, how long has your friend been a Christian?"

"A few years, but we've known each other since we were teenagers. Why do you ask?"

"No reason," Blake frowned. "Since we're all being honest, I'll be honest, too."

Chapter Thirty-Four

"Blake, I want to remind you of something," Kate said with as much love as she could invoke. "Do you recall our conversation about Cody working long hours and how I felt about it?"

"I do." His brows creased.

"Your astonishment isn't lost on me," Kate said. "If someone had told me this time last year, I'd be seated in the same room with the woman my husband had a one-night stand with, and he and I would be more interested in her salvation than our feelings, I'd have said they were crazy."

Cody nodded vigorously.

"I need you to listen carefully," Kate said firmly. "There is no part of me spiritual enough to do what we're doing right now. This is all God. It's hard to believe I'm saying and doing the things I'm doing."

"Excuse me, everyone." Chelsea pulled her phone from her purse and placed it to her ear. "Damien, stop." The one-sided call continued. "There's an outstanding warrant for you," her voice rose. "If you come back here, you could get arrested."

Cody crossed the room. He held out his hand to Chelsea for the phone. "Let me talk with him."

Eyes wide, Chelsea shook her head.

"He better not come back here," Blake said in a raised voice. Cody waved forcefully over his shoulder, silencing Blake.

"Yes, I hear you." Chelsea's gaze plummeted to her lap. "I understand. Yes. I'll be out front waiting for you."

Cody extended his hand further toward Chelsea. "Please, give me the phone."

After several tense seconds of silence, Chelsea mumbled something into the mouthpiece then covered the speaker with her thumb. "Don't say anything to make him madder."

"I won't." Cody's hand remained outstretched. "At least I'll try not to."

Chelsea swallowed visibly, then handed him the phone. She turned to Kate. "He said he wants me to ask you for five-thousand dollars, or he's going to have me tell the police I was—"

"He wants you to say you were—" Kate choked on the rest of the sentence.

"Raped," Chelsea finished in a hushed voice.

"Damien, this is Cody James." He walked toward the front door. "We got off on the wrong footing earlier. Can we start over?"

Kate locked eyes with Chelsea. "You wouldn't do it—would you?"

"My brother says we are not leaving empty-handed."

Kate gripped Blake's forearm. "Call the police."

"Cody is still talking to him." Blake scratched his head. "I'm not sure what to do."

"Blake, I want you to call the police." Kate stole a peek at Cody, who now stood with his back to them, looking out the window. Typically when Cody was agitated, he'd pace back and forth. Kate gave Blake's arm a squeeze. "We'll give him a couple of minutes. If he doesn't let us know everything is okay, then I'll call the police."

###

Cody stood beside the coffee table as Kate prayed with Blake and Chelsea. Once she'd finished, he addressed Chelsea. "He's on his way. Get your purse, Katelyn. We need to take off. Blake, you drive Chelsea to her friend's place."

Kate's eyes widened. "Are we leaving because of something Damien said?"

"Bro, what's going on?" Blake opened his mouth, but Cody held up his hand to silence him.

Cody wrapped his arms around Kate's waist and looked into her eyes. "I don't know what this guy is capable of, and I don't want to put us in a bad situation."

Blake bolted from his seat on the sofa. "I'm sick of this dude. I say we stay put and call the cops. It's not like you don't have the ability to protect yourself—and the rest of us." Blake crossed his arms over his chest. "I, for one, am not budging."

"Protect yourself?" Chelsea's voice cracked. "Is your brother talking about a gun?" Her gaze fixed on Cody.

"It's not going to come to that," Cody glared at Blake. He'd already called the police but didn't see the point in sharing information with the others. Blake would likely stand his ground all the more.

"I agree with Cody." Kate crossed the room and extended a hand to Chelsea, who sat motionless. "Let's get out of here.

There's no telling how long it will be before Damien's at our front door again, and I don't want to be here."

"I'm scared," Chelsea spoke in a monotone.

Cody gave Blake a shove. "Get her into your car and get out of here. Understand?"

"Fine, but I don't think this is the best decision—"

"No buts, get moving." Cody joined Kate and leaned in to keep what he was about to say private. "I want to make sure the gun case is secured."

"Cody..." Kate's eyes narrowed.

Her silence spoke volumes. She wanted an answer to her unspoken question, and there was no point in denying his plan to retrieve a firearm. He leaned in again and whispered into her ear. "I'm getting one of my guns. Please don't say anything."

"Okay," she said before retreating down the hallway for her purse.

Cody followed. He closed the bedroom door behind them. "I know how you feel about guns, but this is serious. The man threatened me. I've already called the police."

Kate grabbed her purse from the chaise lounge; she sat on the bed with it clutched to her stomach. While rocking back and forth in place, she looked up at him. "Damien threatened you?" Her voice spiked, "What exactly did he say?"

Cody joined her on the bed. As much as he longed to take her in his arms and comfort her, time was ticking. Damien could be five minutes or an hour away. "He said he'd snap my neck if I didn't give him ten-grand."

"Ten-grand?" Kate gasped. "Chelsea said he wanted five."

"It doesn't matter." Cody tried to be patient, but the ongoing conversation made him edgy. He needed to get Kate and the others out of the house. "We have to go. Let's not waste precious time talking about how much this man wants to extort from us."

Kate began to sob. "I don't understand how all of this happened." The rocking in place resumed as she continued, "One day, we're a regular married couple with relationship issues, and the next day our lives mimic something out of a twisted movie with a bad guy in pursuit of us."

"This is surreal to me too, but the best thing we can do right now is to take action and get out of here." Cody stood then guided Kate upright.

"Okay," she whimpered. "Do what you need to do. I'll be in the living room waiting."

"Thank you for supporting my decision about leaving and the firearm. I didn't make the choices lightly." Cody gently placed his fingertips under Kate's chin and lifted her downturned face. He kissed her forehead. "I love you. I will love you forever. Nothing is going to happen to you or to me. Okay?"

Kate nodded. Tears fell from her eyes and rolled down her cheeks. "I'll make sure Blake and Chelsea leave if they haven't already."

"That's my girl." Cody pressed his lips to Kate's. The saltiness of the kiss wrenched his heart. He'd been the bad guy, and Kate had either been too kind or too naïve to see it. "Go on. I'll be just a few seconds."

Chapter Thirty-Five

Kate's eyes darted from the knock on the front door to Blake and Chelsea. Given Chelsea had her sunglasses on and Blake held his keys in his hand, the two had probably been seconds away from leaving. If Damien was here, maybe he'd go away if no one answered. Kate pressed a finger to her lips as she made her way to the window and parted the slats of the blinds enough to peek out.

She turned back and whispered to Blake and Chelsea, "It's Damien, and he has a woman with him."

A glance down the hallway confirmed Cody hadn't heard the knock at the door. If Cody came barreling down the hall and demanded everyone leave, Damien might hear, and it could mean trouble, especially with Cody armed. She needed to warn him. Still, once he became aware of Damien's return, a clash between the two men would be inevitable.

"A woman is with him?" Chelsea tippy-toed across the room. She sidled alongside Kate and angled her head to look through the blinds. "Oh no, Kelly's with him. She's my brother's girlfriend. She'll do anything for a fix."

Kate motioned to Blake then pointed toward the hallway, hoping he'd understand her silent command to warn Cody.

"We know you're in there." The woman's singsong voice grated on Kate's already frazzled nerves, heightening the desperate emotions that swirled inside of her.

"Call the police," Chelsea said barely above a whisper.

"My husband has already called them." Kate's breathlessness intensified, and her pounding heart made her head ache. "We must be quiet."

Cody followed Blake back into the room. He immediately crossed to Kate then gently moved the two women away from the window. He peeked through the blinds. "Who's the woman with him?"

"I'm calling the cops." Blake's statement in a normal speaking voice drew Kate's attention, and she shushed him by waving her hand through the air.

"I already did," Cody said over his shoulder.

Kate eyed the gun holstered in the back waistband of Cody's pants. Both the magnitude of the crisis and the answer arrived in the same thought—prayer. "God," she whispered, "You say when we're weak, you are strong," Kate grew bolder but kept her voice low, "You say we can do nothing apart from you. You've shown me again you are faithful to your Word. We need you to intervene. In Jesus' name, amen."

"Amen," Cody said. Even Blake and Chelsea echoed the closing word.

A thunderous knock punctuated the silence. "Open the door," Damien shouted.

This time the command didn't unnerve Kate but instead emboldened her. "He has no right to make any demands." She took a step toward the door, but Cody quickly extended his arm, preventing her from reaching the handle.

"What are you doing?" Cody's eyes widened. "Let's wait until the police arrive," he added in a calmer tone.

The controlled anger in his voice balanced with reason reminded her of the many prayers she'd prayed, asking God to make Cody a leader in their home and to infuse that leadership with godly wisdom. She wouldn't challenge the calm resolve in Cody and what God appeared to be doing through him.

Kate stepped back. "What you're saying makes sense. We will wait for the police."

"Look who just arrived," Chelsea said, directing Kate's attention to the blinds the other woman had retracted to give a clear view outside. "My brother's at the curb. He's talking with the police."

Cody and Blake turned back to the window. "Katelyn, you and Chelsea wait here. Blake and I will talk with the officers."

"Put your gun away first," Kate said. "Please," she added. The request had been out of concern for his safety, and yet a part of her considered he might hear it as controlling.

Cody nodded. He left the room and returned within a few minutes. "I changed my mind. We should talk to the police together as husband and wife."

He extended his hand, and Kate responded by slipping hers into his firm grip.

"I'm still coming," Blake said.

Chelsea looked at each of them as if waiting for direction. Cody spoke first. "Why don't you stay here? Your brother could see your presence as traitorous, which might incite him and escalate things."

"Okay." Chelsea nibbled her bottom lip. "Will you tell him something for me?"

Cody cocked his head to one side. "Depends—what do you want me to say?"

Her eyes welled with tears. "Tell him I love him."

"That I can do." He gave Kate's hand a light squeeze. "C'mon."

"Wait." Kate turned to Chelsea. "Everything's going to be okay."

Blake stepped in and draped his arm over Chelsea's shoulder. "Strange as it may sound, I think so, too." When the young woman leaned into the embrace, Blake smiled.

This was the Blake she recognized from years ago, one who would set aside self-serving motives in favor of being the hands and feet of Jesus.

"Babe, c'mon," Cody said.

Kate walked alongside Cody to where two police cruisers parked facing one another. While there hadn't been any sirens, overheard lights flashed red and blue on each vehicle.

"What have I done?" Damien kept his hands on his head as he shouted at the officer in front of him. "Why am I being arrested?"

"You are not under arrest. You're being detained while we run your identification." The officer unhooked handcuffs from his utility belt. The woman who accompanied Damien sat on the curb, jabbering to two police officers, who stood on either side of her. One officer took notes. The other communicated on the radio affixed to the left shoulder of his uniform.

"I came to get my sister!" Damien's expression twisted with anger. "I'm not breaking any laws." He took a step forward.

"Stop right there!"

"I'm stopping already." Damien looked over his shoulder and locked eyes with Kate. "Lady, will you tell them I'm here to pick up my sister?"

"This man threatened to harm me," Cody said before Kate could respond. "He's trying to extort ten thousand dollars from us."

Damien turned and lunged in their direction. Cody jerked Kate close to his body while the arresting officer tackled Damien to the ground. The other two officers joined the first and wrestled Damien into submission, snapping handcuffs on his wrists.

Snarling like a rabid dog, Damien twisted his head and stilled Kate with a defiant stare. "This ain't over."

"Don't threaten my wife." Cody tucked Kate underneath his arm. "You chose this path. It didn't have to turn out this way."

Like a bad dream deserts a dreamer when awakened, the nightmare had come to an end. It had taken every bit of faith she could muster to hold on to God's promise He would not leave them or forsake them. Given Damien's warrants, he would be taken to jail, removing them and Chelsea from an attack.

"Mustard seed faith," Kate repeated under her breath as the officers hauled Damien to a cruiser, his legs and arms secured together behind his back and a mesh hood covering his face.

"Why is something over my brother's head?" Chelsea sounded on the verge of tears.

"He spat at the officer, who handcuffed him," Cody said. "It's a spit-guard." He frowned at Blake. "I don't think she should be out here."

"I tried to talk her out of it," Blake shrugged. "Short of physically forcing the woman to stay put, what could I do?"

"Is he..." Chelsea's voice cracked, "under arrest?"

"He tried to attack us in front of the officer." Kate rested one of her hands on Chelsea's trembling shoulder. "I presume his warrants have sealed his fate. Do you remember what I told you inside—everything's going to be okay. Hopefully, this is a wake-up call for Damien. Maybe—"

"You don't understand," she sobbed. "He's going to be so angry with me. Maybe Kelly can reason with him."

"I don't think it's a good idea," Kate said. "She hasn't budged from the spot on the curb, and she's jabbering to herself."

"I have to try." Chelsea walked away.

Damien had blamed everyone other than himself for the outcome, and his cohort would likely hold the same view.

Kate turned to Cody. "What can we do?"

"Try reasoning with her again," Cody said. "I'm going to talk with the arresting officer. I need to know how long they can hold Damien in jail. Since he's threatened us, I want to know if we can get a restraining order."

"I'll come with you," Blake said. He turned to Kate. "If anyone can reach Chelsea, it's probably going to be you."

Chapter Thirty-Six

"Chelsea, wait." It made little sense to Kate the woman would hear what she had to say, but her concern for someone who brought so much heartache into their lives made even less sense.

"Wait for what?" Chelsea spun around. Anger lurked in her voice despite her tear-filled eyes. The woundedness in the young woman had once again bubbled to the surface. "You don't understand what it's like to—"

"To what?" Kate's voice rose, "To feel betrayed by someone you love."

Chelsea's hardened expression softened, and she dipped her chin.

"I want you to understand something," Kate caught up to her and lowered her voice. "I could choose to hate you, but God has helped me see you and your brother the way He sees you—with love."

Chelsea blotted her cheeks with the back of her hands, then glanced over her shoulder at Kelly. "Does God love her, too?"

"Yes." Kate took a step toward Chelsea. "If you're determined to talk with her, how about we do it together?"

Chelsea shook her head. The tears had been replaced with an unspoken desperation Kate related to from years of wanting change in her own life.

"She might not even talk to me," Chelsea said. "I know she won't talk to you. It's better if I do this alone."

"I have a better suggestion." Kate locked eyes with Chelsea. "Let's ask for God's help."

Chelsea averted her eyes. "It's easy for you to trust God, but He has never been there for me."

"I haven't always trusted God. In fact, more times than I'm proud to admit, I've doubted God. I've even tried to figure things out apart from Him, which has never turned out well."

"Really?" Chelsea held Kate's gaze. "You seem so—"

"Strong in my faith?" Kate said.

"Actually, I was going to say saintly." Chelsea cracked a smile, but it quickly vanished. "I mean in a good way."

"Thank you." Kate pointed to over Chelsea's shoulder. "It looks as though the officers are letting your brother's friend go. If we're going to talk to her, it needs to happen soon."

Chelsea turned hastily toward Kelly then turned back to Kate. "You really think God will help?"

"Yes," Kate said a prayer enlisting God's help as she walked alongside Chelsea.

Kelly's skeletal physique startled Kate. She hadn't noticed in all the commotion. Kelly's jeans hung loosely on her narrow hips, and holes in the knees of the pants looked to be more for wear than for style. An oversized hoodie with food stains did little to mask her fragile stature. Unexpected sadness gripped Kate. The thought resonated she was someone's daughter.

"I hope you're happy," the woman said to Chelsea. The salty greeting confirmed Chelsea had been right to assume a conversation might not be a possibility.

"Your brother will never forgive you for getting him busted." She turned to the officer on her right. "Am I free to go now or what?"

"You're free to go." The officer held up his hand. "But I strongly suggest you not come back here. If we have to make another trip to this residence because of you, you'll be sitting in a cell, too. Got it?"

"Yes, Mr. Policeman." The smirk on Kelly's face wiped away when the officer narrowed his eyes at her.

Kate extended her hand to the officer. "Thank you for your help."

"You're welcome." He shot a glance at Kelly. "If you folks have any problems, give us a call."

"We will. Thank you again." Once the officer walked away, Kate addressed Kelly. "I'd like to introduce myself. I'm—"

"I don't care who you are." Kelly wagged a bony finger in the air. "You and little miss snitch got my man arrested. You'll be sorry, wait and see."

"Snitch?" Chelsea's tone held more surprise than disdain. "He did this to himself. I was going to ask you to talk to him for me, but I can see that's pointless."

Kelly eyeballed Kate, "If I was you, lady, I'd think twice about protecting a snitch."

Chelsea stepped back, "I'm done. Go ahead, leave." She turned to Kate. "You're wrong about what you said. She's a horrible person. No one could love her."

Kate rested a hand on Chelsea's shoulder. "You don't mean—"

"Yes, I do!" Tears welled in Chelsea's eyes. "I've tried to help her in the past, and she's stabbed me in the back for it. I'm done!"

"What's going on?" Cody eased up alongside Kate.

"This isn't going very well," Kate said. She looked over at Blake, "I tried."

"Try again," Blake said to her surprise. He gave her a gentle nudge, "You tell me not to give up."

The look of astonishment must've been apparent on Kate's face. Blake quickly added, "What I mean is, you always encourage me to persevere because you say God doesn't give up on us, so we shouldn't give up on ourselves or others."

Once again, Kate had been reminded the fullness of this moment wasn't about her. As justified as it might seem to walk away, Blake, of all people, had spoken truth wrapped in love for others.

"Can I have a glass of water?" Kelly said, drawing everyone's attention from Blake.

"I'll get it," Cody said. "Blake, you stay here."

Kelly sat on the curb with her spindly legs outstretched and crossed at the ankles. "Lady, all I want is a drink of water—then I'll be gone." Seated, with her shoulders hunched and her head hung, Kelly resembled an elderly woman instead of someone Kate suspected might be in her early thirties. The woman's bleach-blonde hair was in need of a good washing and a root job.

Cody reappeared with a glass of water, and his Bible tucked under his arm. Kate pointed to his Bible and shook her head, but he missed the warning or chose to follow a leading she was unaware of, either way, it was too late to conceal it.

Kelly stood, took the glass of water, and gulped it. She handed the empty glass back and narrowed her eyes. "I see what you have under your arm. I don't want to hear it."

"Bro, how about you offer her something to eat? She looks like she could use it."

Kelly's eyes brightened for the first time since they had been talking.

"Are you hungry?" Kate recognized the eagerness in her voice and hoped it wouldn't result in the woman declining the offer for fear of ulterior motives.

"Are you kidding?" Chelsea said. "She basically threatened us, and you're going to have her in for bacon and eggs? Is there anything that can't be forgiven?"

###

Cody opened his mouth to respond to Chelsea's question about forgiveness then it hit him. Kate could best answer about forgiveness. He looked over at her. She nodded as if reading his mind.

Blake nudged Cody. "What's the answer? I think I already know, but I could be wrong."

Kate craned her neck around Cody and smiled at Blake. "You're probably right." She turned back to Chelsea and Kelly at her side. "There's one thing God says is an unforgivable sin."

"I knew it, "Blake said before he clasped his hand over his mouth."

Chelsea's eyes narrowed. "What's the one thing?"

Cody's phone buzzed in his shirt pocket, and he jumped. He tried to remove it casually, but the action halted the conversation, "Excuse me." A quick glance at the screen revealed it was Mr. Kennedy, the elderly man who had sold him two pistols. At a loss as to why the gentleman might call, Cody thought better of responding at this moment. Whatever Mr. Kennedy wanted could be discovered later.

"I'm sorry," Cody said to Kate. "Please go ahead."

"I'm leaving." Kelly's voice held a quiver, but her sight on Kate was firm. As expected, Kelly's eyes were dilated. The conversation about God at the curb had fizzled.

Cody's phone buzzed in his shirt pocket again, and this time he made no effort to be indifferent. He glanced at the screen, another call from Mr. Kennedy. "Forgive me, but I need to take this call. Please don't leave, Kelly. I'll be right back."

Chapter Thirty-Seven

"Mr. Kennedy, how are you?" Cody tried to mask his surprise in greeting the other man's phone call. He walked a few feet away from Kate and the others to talk privately.

"No need for false pretenses," the man chuckled. "You're as surprised to hear from me as I am to be making this call."

Cody's face warmed. Mr. Kennedy had been a straight shooter from their first meeting, but he had no idea why the man would be calling after the sale. He stole a peek over his shoulder at Kate, who was talking with Kelly while Chelsea and Blake flanked her in silence. The troubled expression on Blake's face distracted Cody to the point of missing what Mr. Kennedy said. It took the older man clearing his throat to recapture his attention.

"I'm sorry, Mr. Kennedy. I didn't catch what you said." Cody's face grew hot for a second time. Thankfully, the gentleman was none the wiser. "I'd like to give you my undivided attention, but this isn't a good time to talk."

"I appreciate your being forthright," the man paused. "It confirms something for me."

"Yeah, what's that?" Cody turned around to focus on the conversation. The quicker he dealt with Mr. Kennedy, the quicker he'd be back at Kate's side.

Mr. Kennedy exhaled loudly. "Allow me to back up. I resisted calling earlier because I thought it might be this old mind of mine playing an evil trick on me."

"Evil trick? I don't understand." The impulse to sneak another peek won out, and he sent another glance in Kate's direction. Kelly was now pacing at the curb with her head hung. The disheveled woman concealed her hands under the hem of the oversized sweatshirt she wore, which spiked concern.

"Is your wife with you?" Something in the older man's tone set off alarm bells. Cody headed toward the group.

"As a matter of fact, she is—why do you ask?"

"This may sound odd," the elderly man said with a degree of urgency that caused Cody to quicken his steps.

"Mr. James, I was in prayer earlier, and I got a sense of trouble surrounding you and your wife.

Cody's pulse sped up. "Hold on." Cody muted his phone then slid it into his shirt pocket. By the time he reached Kate and the others, dread hijacked his thoughts. Maybe Kelly had a gun in the waistband of her pants. Maybe she would use it in retaliation for Damien being hauled off to jail.

"What's going on?" Cody looked at Blake first, but when his brother's eyes narrowed, Cody followed Blake's line of vision to Kelly. The woman crossed her arms tightly around her waist as if trying to still her twitching body.

"Are you okay?" Cody eased in between Kate and the woman.

"I'm fine." Kelly stepped off the curb into the gutter. "I don't need to hear any more from your wife about God." The waiflike woman drummed her fingers against her lean biceps as she spoke. "You and your wife are getting on my nerves."

Cody's protection antenna rose. "You're free to leave anytime." He reached behind him and extended his hand to Kate. Out of his peripheral vision, Blake scooted back with Chelsea following his lead.

"How about I head back inside with my wife and the others to have breakfast, and we leave you alone." He cracked a smile to deescalate the exchange. "I don't know about anybody else, but I'm staved."

Cody turned to look at Kate. "Babe, aren't you hungry?"

"Bro!" Blake's tone mentally hurled Cody back to the incident on the freeway when he'd almost been taken out by a semi-truck. Without hesitation, he broke his grip on Kate's hand and spun around to face Kelly. Brandishing a firearm not much bigger than the palm of her hand, she glared at him.

Kate inched close to Cody. "Jesus, help us."

"Listen up!" Kelly's eyes darted from Cody to Kate, then back to him. "You don't tell me what to do! People like you two, living a cushy life, always think they know everything. Well, you don't!"

"Okay, calm down." Cody kept his voice steady even though his heart raced. "It's not our place to tell you what to do. I was only suggesting—"

"Shut up!" Kelly pointed the pistol at Cody. "You talk too much." She turned the barrel on Kate. "And so does your wife."

Cody raised his left hand in the air to convey submission while discreetly extending his other hand to Kate. The feel of Kate's hand in his own would have been a comfort any other time, but now all he wanted to do was get her and the others as far away from Kelly as possible.

Blake stepped forward without Chelsea. "Look, my brother didn't mean to sound like he was telling you what to do. He just has a bossy tone." He playfully elbowed Cody, then lunged at Kelly.

A pop-pop-pop sound rent the air, triggering screams from Kate and Chelsea.

Blake crumpled against Kelly, and she stumbled backward. The two crashed onto the asphalt with Blake on top.

"Get him off me!" Kelly shrieked repeatedly while squirming under his weight. Blake tried to rise up on his elbows but collapsed onto her. Blood pooled in the street around Kelly's waist.

"Kate, call 911!" Cody knelt beside his brother. "Blake!" Not waiting for a response, he carefully lifted Blake off Kelly and rested him on his back. Blake's T-shirt, saturated with blood, ratcheted Cody's anxiety up another notch. "Blake, talk to me."

"She shot me," he winced. "Bro—I don't want to die." The glazed-over look in Blake's eyes intensified.

Cody dialed down his emotions. "You're not going to die." He looked down at his brother's blood-soaked T-shirt, unable to determine where he'd been shot or how many times. He gingerly lifted the garment that clung to Blake's abdomen—two entry wounds, both gushed blood, while the third wound appeared to be a surface strike.

"Chelsea," Cody said firmly. "I need something to slow the bleeding." The red bandana around her neck caught his attention. "Give me your scarf."

She quickly untied it. "Kelly, I can't believe you pointed a loaded gun at them," Chelsea screeched.

Cody snatched the bandana from her hands before balling and pressing it against the entry wounds on Blake's abdomen with both hands. Blake groaned.

"It's not my fault," Kelly stood sobbing. "He came at me. I didn't want to shoot him. The gun just went off."

"Where is the gun now," Cody said with intentional calmness.

"I have it," Kelly yelled. "I'm not going to hurt anybody. This was an accident."

"Kelly," Cody said. "I need you to set the gun on the curb. Can you do that for me?" He looked at Blake, whose eyes were still open but distant.

"You're crazy!" Chelsea sank beside Blake and cradled his head in her lap. "I tried to warn all of you." Chelsea began to sob. "I tried to tell you, but you wouldn't listen."

"I'm not crazy!" Kelly stomped her foot. "Don't say it again."

"Bro, it burns," Blake mumbled something else, but Cody turned his attention back to Kelly. The last thing needed was her lashing out while still in possession of a firearm.

"Kelly," Cody summoned her more forcefully. "Set the gun down. Now, please." His focus unwavering on the young woman, he repeated the command when she failed to respond.

Tears streaming down Kelly's face, she took a step toward them, the gun dangling at her side. "I'm not crazy. I'm not. Say you're sorry, Chelsea."

Without taking his eyes off the distressed woman, Cody asked Chelsea to apologize.

"You're right." Chelsea cowered near Blake. "You're not crazy. I don't know what I was saying. I'm sorry. We're sorry. Just put the gun down."

Kelly's countenance morphed from distraught to a satisfied smile, and with it, the tension in Cody's shoulders lessened. She stooped and set the pocket pistol on the curb, but before he could say another word, she turned and bolted down the street.

###

"The ambulance is on its way." Kate rested her free hand on Cody's back while holding her cell phone in the other hand. He kept his focus on applying pressure to the wound and didn't bring up the fact his brother's eyes were glassy.

"Lord," Kate spoke softly, "Help Blake. Please, get the ambulance here and fast."

"The dispatcher just said it won't be long," Kate looked down the street, willing help to get here quickly. She wanted to reassure Cody everything would be fine, but the blood pooled on the asphalt around Blake's midsection warned of a different outcome.

Kate turned her attention to Chelsea. "The dispatcher wants to know which direction Kelly went. I didn't see her takeoff. Did you?"

"I don't remember," Chelsea sobbed, and her body shook. "He doesn't deserve to die. It should be Kelly. She's evil." Chelsea bent forward and mumbled something through her tears to Blake, but he remained oblivious.

"Katelyn," Cody said over his shoulder. "Kelly headed north, then she hooked a left on Bradshaw. How much longer until the ambulance arrives?"

"I dunno. I'll ask the dispatcher." She gripped the phone. "Miss, I'm trying to remain calm, but my brother-in-law..." She couldn't bring herself to say Blake might not make it. His skin held a bluish tint around his lips, and his eyelids fluttered.

Kate looked in both directions of the street. "Please, tell them to hurry."

"You're doing a good job keeping calm," the dispatcher said evenly. "They should be there any minute. Is your bother-in-law still conscious?"

"Yes. I mean, let me check." Kate looked down at Blake, whose eyes were now closed. "God, no...." Her voice caught in her throat.

"What's happening?" The dispatcher said.

"His eyes are closed." Kate stared Heavenward. "Please, Jesus..." Tears streamed down her cheeks as she steeled her emotions. "Lord, don't let Blake die. Not now. Not like this—"

"Mrs. James, the ambulance should be there any moment."

The sound of sirens confirmed the dispatcher's statement, and Kate hastily ended the prayer with a thank you. Two police cars followed by an ambulance parked curbside to Cody, Blake, and Chelsea. A male paramedic rushed to Blake and knelt beside him. The other medic unloaded a gurney from the back of the ambulance. Kate tried to move out of the way, but her feet were planted. The adrenaline surge bottomed out in a whoosh, leaving her hearing jumbled conversations as though everyone's words were played in slow motion.

A police officer approached and said something her mind couldn't register. The man, twice her size, wrapped one arm around her waist and guided her to take a seat on the curb. "Are you injured?"

"No. I'm not injured." Kate sat trembling. She attempted to still her legs by drawing them to her chest and enveloping them in a bear hug, but the trembling persisted. "Is...is my brother-in-law—"

"Let's focus on you." The officer's tone was forceful but oddly reassuring. Maybe Blake wasn't dead. Surely, he would have used a gentler tone had Blake—she couldn't bring herself to finish the thought.

"Babe, are you okay?" Cody sat at arm's length, no doubt because of the blood on his shirt and jeans.

"I'll be fine," Kate said. "It's an adrenaline rush, but it's wearing off. This all seems like a bad dream. I can hardly believe Blake was shot."

"Me neither." Cody stared at his hands covered in Blake's blood. "The paramedics say it's lucky we were with him to call for help. I think he's going to be okay."

"How do you know?" She hoped Cody hadn't heard the disbelief in her voice. Blake's blood all over him eerily contradicted what he said.

"My brother still has a pulse." Silence hung heavy in the air for what seemed like several seconds. "Are you up to going to the hospital with me?"

"Yes, of course." She stood, relived the jittery feelings had passed. "Do you want to see if you can ride with Blake in the ambulance?"

Cody stood, his eyes welling with tears. "I can ask, but only if you're all right to drive. Are you okay?"

"Yes, I can drive myself to the hospital. You should be with Blake."

"Thank you." He looked as though he wanted to give her a hug but thought better of it.

The officer who had remained quiet at Kate's side raised his hand. "Mrs. James, I'll follow you to the hospital—just to be on the safe side. I need to get each of your statements about what happened. I can do that there just as well as here."

"Thank you, sir." Cody glanced over his shoulder then back to Kate. "I'd give you a hug goodbye, but—"

"I know," emotion caught in her throat. "It looks as though the paramedics are about to load Blake into the ambulance. You better go ask about riding with them."

"Okay, I'll see you there."

Chapter Thirty-Eight

After ensuring his brother had been handed off to a surgical team in the emergency department, Cody paused in the entryway to look for a seat in the small waiting area. In contrast to his depleted state, the room bustled with activity.

A group of people took up a bank of chairs near the back wall, talking quietly. A few members wiped tears as a toddler sitting on the floor nearby tore pages from a magazine. The little girl locked eyes on Cody as he moved into the room. Spotting an empty chair not far from the toddler, he hurried over to take the seat. As the child continued to stare, he followed her line of vision to his blood-splattered boots. He must look like he stepped out of a horror movie.

To redirect the child's gaze, Cody smiled and wriggled his fingers at her, but she burst into tears. An older woman with silver hair scooped the little girl into her arms and retook her place with the group. He surveyed the others in the waiting room for their reaction to the exchange. With the exception of a teenage girl in a superman tank top and jean cutoffs gawking at him, no one seemed to notice him at all.

Kate hadn't arrived yet, but then she didn't make the drive with lights and sirens clearing her path. On the ambulance ride over, Blake opened his eyes once and tried to speak, but the medic shushed him. With an oxygen mask covering Blake's nose and mouth, Cody probably wouldn't have been able to understand much of what his brother wanted to say anyhow. Still, now he pondered what Blake had tried to communicate.

Memories of Blake flooded his thoughts—so many moments—little things undeserving of fanfare now sparkled like stars in a night's sky. Blake's pirate voicemail greeting triggered a soft chuckle. He noticed the clock on the back wall. Thirty minutes had passed since he'd been separated from Blake.

Hard to believe an hour ago, he'd been on the phone with Mr. Kennedy, who warned of trouble. During the fifteen-minutes drive to the hospital, Cody reconnected with the man to briefly update him on what happened and why he hadn't returned to the call.

Thinking of that call reminded him to try his mom again. He'd left a message asking her to call him ASAP, but she hadn't yet. He pulled his phone from his shirt pocket then retrieved Ada's contact information. A shadow fell over the screen, and he looked up to see Kate standing there.

"I'm sorry it took me so long to get here. Every light caught me. How long have you been here? How's Blake? Have you heard anything?"

Cody stood and nodded toward the doorway. "Let's step into the hall." Kate frowned but followed his lead. Even if the hall was crowded, he wanted a change of scenery.

"I've been here for about an hour. Blake was conscious on the ride over—well, for a minute or so."

"That's good news." The frown tugging at Kate's brows relaxed.

Hope in her eyes stabbed him in the heart. To tell her about Blake's loss of consciousness and his blood pressure dropping to ninety over forty would panic her. He'd keep it to himself the paramedics nearly lost Blake right before their arrival at the hospital.

Kate waved her hand before Cody's face, capturing his attention.

"I'm sorry," he said. "What did you say?"

"Something isn't right," Kate's frown returned. "You're not telling me everything."

Maybe changing the subject would distract her. "Where's the police officer who followed you here?"

"Chelsea rode with him. He's taking a statement from her in the parking lot then he will meet with us. She insisted on coming, but she's so upset I didn't want her to ride with me."

A woman wearing a white hospital jacket and a stethoscope draped around her neck approached them. His heart beat wildly. "Are you a doctor?"

"Yes. I'm—" The physician must have picked up on his being distracted because she suggested they talk somewhere quieter. The woman led the way through the double doors. Kate clutched him down a painfully long hallway then into an empty exam room.

He hadn't noticed Kate's whitewashed complexion until she teetered in place. After the doctor closed the door behind them, Cody helped Kate to the lone chair.

"I'm Dr. Truss," she said to Cody, who identified himself as Blake's older brother.

His mind whirred with questions. He ran his sweaty palms down the sides of his pants, and his voice cracked as he asked for details on Blake's condition. Even with Kate looking up at him—he couldn't keep fear at bay.

"I'm sorry to inform you that your brother's injuries are significant," Dr. Truss continued. "I understand you rode in the ambulance with him, so you know he arrived in an arrested state."

"Yes, I am." Cody cleared his throat. "Doctor, exactly what are his injuries?" Placing one hand on Kate's shoulder, he closed his eyes, bracing for what he might be told.

"Mr. James," the doctor's sterile tone catapulted him back to the present. "He's suffered hypovolemic shock, and though your brother's extreme drop in blood pressure could account for a loss of consciousness, that doesn't appear to be the case. The intra-abdominal injuries are what I suspect caused your brother's heart to stop. If—"

"I don't understand. Are you saying my brother had a heart attack in addition to being shot?" Shrouded in numbness, Cody squatted next to the chair. He grasped Kate's hands in need of the same support and comfort he hoped to provide her. He cleared his throat. "How does someone his age have a heart attack? I don't understand."

"Mr. James, the three bullets that struck your brother damaged not only his stomach but also his colon and his liver. He lost a lot of blood, which sent his body into shock. As a result, his heart was severely damaged."

Cody took a deep breath and exhaled slowly. “Blake’s young. He’ll recover, right?”

“The body can respond to severe trauma in a variety of ways, Mr. James.”

Kate squeezed Cody’s hand tighter. “Is she saying Blake is going to die?”

“Mr. James, I can’t answer your question. I will say, given the severity of your brother’s injuries, it would be prudent to hope for the best yet prepare for the worst.”

Chapter Thirty-Nine

Cody's phone rang, halting his conservation with the doctor. "It's my mother. I need to take this call."

"Of course. I'll be in the hallway." Doctor Truss pointed to the door. "We can finish talking after you're done."

"Thank you," Cody said. Once the door closed, he spoke. "Mom, where are you right now?"

"I just got home from the grocery store. I was going to make pancakes for breakfast and discovered I was out of baking powder. And please don't lecture me about remembering to put my phone in my purse when I leave the house."

"I won't lecture you, but I—"

"Hold on. I want to sit. I haven't even put my groceries away yet. I saw two missed calls from you, so I thought I better call you."

She exhaled heavily into the phone. "I hate going to the store for one thing, so I also got stuff for dinner—your favorite—meatloaf. I want you and your brother to come over tonight. Tell Blake I'll make garlic mashed potatoes to go with the—"

"Mom!" Cody tightened his grip on the phone. "Listen to me." He nodded at Kate, who now stood in front of him, whispering he calm down. "Mom," he needed to lower his voice, "are you sitting?"

"Yes. What's going on? You're beginning to scare me."

"Mom..." He swallowed hard. "Blake's been shot."

"Shot? What are you talking about? Was there a robbery at the pawnshop? Is he okay?"

"Kate and I are at the hospital. We were talking with one of the doctors when you called. You need to come to the hospital. It doesn't look good." He closed his eyes tightly at the sound of his mother's sobs.

Cody's chest expanded with a deep breath he let out slowly. "Mom," he opened his eyes. "Do you have someone who can drive you to the hospital—a friend—a neighbor?"

"Drive me? I..." Her voice trailed off into more sobbing.

"Never mind," Cody said. "I'm going to have someone come by to get you." He pointed to Kate's purse, sitting in the chair and mouthed, "Call Sandie."

Kate nodded. She moved swiftly and retrieved her purse.

His shoulders wilted, and he hung his head as his mother pleaded with God to spare her son's life. At that moment, Blake's prognosis hit home.

Doctor Truss opened the door. "Forgive me for interrupting, Mr. James, but you and your wife need to come with me."

"Mom, the doctor says—"

"Talk to me, son." Her measured tone alarmed Cody. It was as if she knew something about her child yet to be discovered. He clasped the back of his neck with his free hand, the muscles taut under his fingertips. "Doctor Truss, is my brother okay?"

"We'll talk on the way to ICU." She pushed the door open wider. "Let's go, now."

Cody stared at the doctor. He wanted to ask the obvious question, but the words were caught in his throat. "Mom I..."

Kate sidled alongside Cody. "Doctor, just one moment, please." She eased the phone from Cody's hand. "Ada, this is Kate. I am sorry you're hearing about Blake over the phone. The doctor has asked Cody and me to go with her to see Blake in ICU. I've contacted a friend. She'll be at your place within twenty minutes. Her name is Sandie. She will drive you to the hospital. Once you're here, text me. I'll meet you in the lobby of the emergency room."

Hospital—the word echoed in Cody's mind, like a call into the dark with no response. He glanced at Kate then back to the opened door. The image of Blake on the gurney, unconscious, pale, his oversized T-shirt soaked with blood and his hands resting beside his hips, dried blood encrusted around his cuticles, staggered Cody. He palmed the wall and hung his head. "God, please help my brother fight this fight."

Kate rested her hand in the center of Cody's back. "Ada, we're praying. I know you're praying too—keep praying."

###

Kate held Cody's left hand tightly while he spoke to his brother, who lay unconscious. Thoughts of Blake earlier this morning, cracking jokes to ease the tension between Chelsea and her brother, replayed in her mind. Blake always delivered comedic relief. His unorthodox faith in God and love for others trumped all of his poor choices, as well as his impetuous decision to walk away from God. The Bible verse about God never leaving or forsaking His children came to her mind then—and now.

Tears fell as the beeping monitor at Blake's bedside caught her attention. She curled her tongue and swiped at a teardrop resting on the corner of her lip. Blake had not forsaken God—he'd forsaken himself because he didn't feel he could measure up. Her throat tightened.

Forsaking all others ran much deeper than marriage. Several Scriptures flitted through her mind about the gift of salvation not being dependent on worthiness but instead on faith in Jesus' righteousness. The fullness of that promise had escaped her, but now, seeing Blake motionless, there was no doubt if God called him home, he would be with His Savior. Blake loved God.

Blake's struggle was in loving himself.

How poignant he would point this out to others yet fail to see it for himself.

"Bro, I'm sorry for giving you a hard time," Cody continued to speak, now through his sobs. Kate could barely understand his words.

"I'm like the Pharisee in the Bible. You're like the tax collector. You recognize your need for God's mercy, and I—" his voice hitched.

When Cody didn't resume, Kate squeezed his hand. "Let's pray."

Cody turned to her, grief and sorrow stark on his face. "Can you do it, please?"

She nodded, then rested her head against his chest. Wrapping her arms around his waist, she summoned God for the words.

"Lord, we come to you as imperfect people, yet we are your people—the three of us, my husband, myself, and Blake. We trust you have our best interests at heart, even though we don't understand why this has happened. We want an outcome extending Blake's life this side of Heaven, but as Jesus prayed, so I pray." She drew in a breath and exhaled the words from her heart. "Lord, if there be any other way, please take this cup, but if not..." Kate tightened her grip on Cody's waist. "Thy will be done. In Jesus' name, I pray. Amen."

Cody buried his face in the nape of Kate's neck, and his body heaved with sobs. "Amen," he finally choked out.

"Mr. James," Dr. Truss' voice held a tender note, "Mrs. James."

Kate didn't have to look over at the doctor who had stood silently in the room until this moment. In fact, she'd been oblivious to the woman's presence until she'd spoken. The air thickened, and Kate fought to catch her breath as the truth slammed into her. Blake was gone.

Cody slowly raised his head but avoided Kate's eyes. Instead, he looked Heavenward, his cheeks wet with tears.

Peacefully, quietly, Blake's body had surrendered to God's call to come home. For that, Kate would be forever thankful, but now wasn't the time to talk to Cody about gratitude. She gently placed her hand in the center of Cody's chest. Beneath her palm, his heart hammered and spoke volumes of anguish, even though he remained silent.

"God," Cody's voice cracked. "I need you." His jaw clenched along with his fists at his sides. Gradually, he faced the hospital bed. "I remember the time Blake lost a Matchbox car in the sandbox at a park near our home. He must've been about four."

Cody squared his shoulders. "As his big brother, I told him not to cry because I'd find it. I looked for that car for an hour. Never found it."

Tears welled in Cody's eyes, but he continued. "Blake was the one who stopped the search. He patted my back with his grubby little fingers, smiled, and said, 'It's okay. At least you tried.'"

The doctor tapped Kate on the shoulder. "I'm going to leave you two alone. Take as long as you need."

"Thank you." Kate's focus returned to Cody

"I failed you, bro." He gripped the hospital bedrail, hung his head, and wept.

"Sweetheart, no, you didn't—you tried." She joined him bedside. When Cody looked at her, she enveloped him in her arms. "You always tried, and Blake knew it then just like he knew it today."

"But I needed more time with him. I wasted so many years trying to fix my brother instead of trusting God to work on each of us. I could have just loved him. I want to make the road trip we talked about to the Carolinas. I want him to tell me a joke or talk in that crazy pirate lingo. I want to tell him I love him."

She pulled back from the embrace. "Do you know what the three most powerful words are, sweetheart?" His eyes met hers with a blank stare. For a split second, she wondered if he'd heard the question.

"I love you," Cody answered with a croaky voice.

"Yes," she sighed with relief. "Do you know what the second two most powerful words are?"

His brow furrowed. Finally, he shook his head. The response made her think of how he must have looked in the sandbox as a young boy.

"The second two most powerful words are—I know. Blake knew you loved him."

Chapter Forty

Cody tried to get comfortable on the chair in Dr. Samantha Novak's office.

"Your brother passed a little over a month ago." The doctor allowed the silence to build after her statement, but when Cody didn't reply, she continued, "How are you doing?"

"To be honest, I don't know how I feel." The tears had stopped a few days after Blake's burial. Cody glanced down at his clasped hands. Though Kate had been tremendously supportive following Blake's death, she'd drawn a few boundaries, one of which being they do not rush back into living together as husband and wife.

He blew out a breath in an attempt to relax. Thankfully, Kate had stressed divorce wasn't her end goal. But the truth was, they both needed time alone to resolve the issues that had driven them apart. For his part, restarting his sessions with Dr. Sam would put him on the right path to become spiritually and emotionally stronger.

"Cody, you're in an emotionally raw place. I'd like you to share how you're feeling." Her voice firmed, leaving him without wiggle room to avoid the answer.

He quashed the impulse to take issue with her tone. Up to this point in life, no one had challenged him to be forthright when it came to his emotions. Over the years, even Kate had learned to back off when he refused to talk about sensitive topics. If he truly wanted to repair his relationship with his wife, he needed to answer tough questions.

"I didn't know your brother, but based on the few things you've told me, he sounds like he was a pretty special young man."

A lump formed in Cody's throat. He didn't recall sharing much if anything about Blake, let alone anything positive. Maybe what Kate said at the hospital on the day Blake died had been true. Maybe Blake knew how much his big bother loved him. After all, the Bible teaches what is in the heart comes out of the mouth.

Dr. Sam's expression tensed. She leaned forward in her chair. "What are you feeling right now?"

Cody shrugged, but his eyes burned with tears that spilled onto his cheeks. Brusquely, he wiped his face with the backs of his hands and sat taller in the chair. "I..."

"Take your time," she said.

He took a few minutes to regain his composure enough to speak. "I miss him." The truth caused his body to wilt. He rested his head against the back of the chair then covered his face with both palms. Though he fought hard to stay in control, tears fell. Soon he was sobbing then wailing all the emotions he had kept bottled up long before Blake's death.

"It should have been me," he finally choked out. Physically and emotionally drained, he uncovered his eyes and met her unwavering gaze. "I brought ungodliness into everyone's life, yet Blake paid the ultimate price for my disobedience to God." There, he'd said what he hadn't told a soul, even himself. He waited for the condemnation that was sure to fall from the doctor's lips.

"I need you to hear me," Dr. Sam said. "Are you listening?"

With what little energy Cody had, he replied instead, "Do you remember my telling you that I didn't want this to happen?"

She clasped her hands on her desk. "What are you referring to, specifically?"

"I didn't want to break down because if I did—"

"Ah, yes," she interrupted. "You told me that you feared if you ever started crying, you might never stop."

Her point registered. He'd just cried like never before. He hadn't even cried like this at Blake's bedside. At the funeral, he'd shed tears, but again, not like this—not to the point of feeling weak. Yet here he sat, able to not only reason but to speak coherently.

"Cody, what you're experiencing is survivor's guilt."

"Wait." He blinked several times in rapid succession. "Isn't that for people who have survived a plane crash or mass shooting? It doesn't apply to me."

"Why doesn't it?"

He drew his head back in disbelief. "I just told you. I did this to my family. Me."

Dr. Sam angled her head to one side.

"What? Say something." Cody's demand pierced the silence with sharpness. "I'm sorry. I know your job is to make me feel better, but it's not working."

"Actually, Cody, my job isn't to make you feel better." She held up her hand, and his objection died before he voiced it. "My job is to get you to look at truth and process it."

"Fair enough, I stand corrected." He studied her expression but couldn't determine her mood, let alone what she might be thinking. Perhaps she viewed Blake's death as his fault but wouldn't admit it

"You are no more responsible for Kelly fatally shooting your brother than you are responsible for your father cheating on your mother or your mother making the choice to divorce him."

Cody's gaze tumbled to his lap. "That's different."

"How so?"

"I feel like—" He looked up but stared out the window, thankful the blinds were open. It had begun to rain, and droplets speckled the glass.

"Please continue," she said.

He changed what he had been about to say. "I shouldn't let myself off the hook for my terrible choice. My actions put the wheels in motion for all of this to happen." The words hung in the air, so heavy, Cody could all but visualize them thudding onto the carpet with the weight of guilt they carried.

"You mentioned a desire to share the gospel with Chelsea after what transpired between you. In part, it's what motivated you to meet with her again with Kate by your side, correct?"

"Well, yes, and Kate seeking closure."

"You and Kate both wanted closure."

Cody nodded. The rain intensified, lashing the glass with a hard patter.

"If you could choose for others, you would have chosen for Chelsea to have a relationship with Jesus."

Cody turned to the doctor. "Absolutely. The thought of anyone spending eternity apart from Jesus is heart-wrenching. God knows I've made my share of bad choices in life, but I've never given up hope for others to make right choices."

"But it's not yours to make." Dr. Sam leaned forward, her eyes intent on his. "You can't decide how someone will or will not act."

The puzzle pieces were snapping into place. "And...."

"Cody, guilt is a common reaction to a traumatic event," she said. "You've been reacting out of guilt since you were a young boy. You needed to be loved and nurtured by your parents, but when they divorced, Blake became your responsibility, and you wouldn't allow yourself to receive love—at least not without strings attached."

"You mean like unworthiness?" He sat immobile, his body absorbing the truth much like the dry ground outside the office window drinking in the water.

"Cody, God calls us to love others as we love ourselves. Most of your choices have been rooted in not loving yourself. You sacrificed God's truths for the devil's lies. Little compromises often have big consequences. Can you see how not loving yourself manifests into a failure to love others?"

For several minutes, he let the words replay in his mind. Something loosened in his chest as if a burden he had carried for far too long had been lifted. Peace replaced it, allowing him to breathe more easily than he had done in years.

"I don't know what to say," he firmed his lips. "Yes, I do."

He straightened his slumped position in the chair. "I'm doing the exact thing you're talking about—I'm setting aside truth for lies, and I'm failing to honor—to even acknowledge—my own needs."

"As I said, little compromises often have big consequences. Cody, you got into a bad habit of choosing ungodly things. Instead of honoring who you are in Christ, the devil deceived you and had you believe the lie you're unworthy of God's love and care. But now you know this, you get to choose differently. You get to be parented by the Creator of the universe. How wonderful is that?"

She stood. "Please stand."

Cody obliged, not sure if she was ending the session but sensing she had something more to say.

"I have a spiritual exercise for you." She quirked one eyebrow. "Are you game?"

"Sure."

"Close your eyes and extend your arms out to your sides."

He shut his eyes and stretched out his arms. "Okay, now what?"

"Repeat after me," she said softly. "All who are heavy laden come unto Me."

Cody Shuddered. He opened his eyes wide and dropped his arms to his sides. "I can't do it—I'm not Jesus.

"Precisely, Cody—you're not Jesus."

Tears fell again, this time cleansing decades of lies. Joy coursed through his body. After several seconds of basking in the freedom that poured over him, Cody walked to the window and looked Heavenward. The rain had stopped. On the horizon, a rainbow appeared. "Who the Father sets free, is free indeed."

While God hadn't gifted him with a restored marriage yet, the rainbow inspired Cody to believe restoration could be on the horizon so long as he continued to place God first in his life. The rainbow underscored God's faithfulness and His caring not only about the future but also the journey of getting there.

The End